THE

SECOND

CHRISTMAS

MARTA PERRY

BERKLEY ROMANCE
New York

BERKLEY ROMANCE
Published by Berkley
An imprint of Penguin Random House LLC
penguinrandomhouse.com

Copyright © 2022 by Martha Johnson
Excerpt from *A Christmas Home* by Marta Perry copyright © 2019 by Martha Johnson
Penguin Random House supports copyright. Copyright fuels creativity, encourages
diverse voices, promotes free speech, and creates a vibrant culture. Thank you for buying
an authorized edition of this book and for complying with copyright laws by not
reproducing, scanning, or distributing any part of it in any form without permission.
You are supporting writers and allowing Penguin Random House to continue to
publish books for every reader.

BERKLEY is a registered trademark and Berkley Romance with B colophon
is a trademark of Penguin Random House LLC.

ISBN: 9780593337929

First Edition: September 2022

Printed in the United States of America
1   3   5   7   9   10   8   6   4   2

Book design by George Towne

This is a work of fiction. Names, characters, places, and incidents either are the product
of the author's imagination or are used fictitiously, and any resemblance to actual persons,
living or dead, business establishments, events, or locales is entirely coincidental.

PUBLISHER'S NOTE: The recipes contained in this book are to be followed
exactly as written. The publisher is not responsible for your specific health or allergy
needs that may require medical supervision. The publisher is not responsible for any
adverse reactions to the recipes contained in this book.

This book is dedicated to my family, in appreciation for many wonderful Christmas holidays.

CHAPTER ONE

❧

"THE COTTAGE NEEDS SOME WORK, BUT YOUR MAMM and I think it will be perfect for you."

Her father's comment brought a rueful smile to Leah Stoltz's face. Daad didn't mean that *she* needed work, but that was true, too. At least she was home in Promise Glen, and she couldn't think of a better place for getting herself back to normal again after the trials of the past year.

"I know it will take time and effort to turn it into the herbal business I want," she said, trying to reassure him. "But I have all winter before the spring growing season."

The small cottage sat on a wedge of land between Daad's farm and the next one, and it had been a thorn in her father's side for years. It had been owned by someone who lived halfway across the country and seemed happy to let it deteriorate, and the condition had upset Daad's ideas of what an Amish-owned property should look like. Her mother said that for the past year, he'd go out of his way to avoid passing it.

Finally the owner consented to sell, and Daad had snapped

it up. Then he'd turned around and given it to his eldest daughter, Leah. At least, he was trying to give it to her. They were still arguing about that point.

Leah wrapped her jacket more closely against the chill December breeze. "I still say you must let me buy the property from you. After all, I have money from my year of working with Aunt Miriam's business."

Leah forced herself to sound pleasant about that fact, but it still rankled. The truth was that her aunt had sold the business out from under her, and even the money Aunt Miriam had forced on her hadn't eased her intense disappointment about losing the business she'd thought would be hers. Or her sorrow that a person who meant so much to her didn't trust her any longer.

"Ach, don't be ferhoodled." Daad grasped her arm in his as they walked through the crisp frosty grass toward the cottage door. "What else do your mamm and I work for but to help our kinder? Your bruder Micah will want the farm, that's certain sure. He's a born farmer. As for James . . ." He shook his head, frowning a bit when he thought about her eighteen-year-old brother, who seemed in no hurry to finish his running-around time and settle into having a real job and, of course, a wife.

"He'll settle down when the time is right, Daad. You'll see."

James was just slow to accept the next step in growing up. He always had been, crawling long after he'd learned to toddle and letting Micah or Leah talk for him instead of trying it himself. According to Leah's grandmother, that was just the way he was made.

Leah's parents had always assumed that all six of their children would marry an Amish partner and have babies, the more the better as far as Mammi was concerned. Actually, they hadn't started urging the three youngest girls yet, and as for Leah herself . . . well, her one serious relationship had come to nothing but disappointment. It might be best if they gave up on her.

Marriage wasn't part of her plans, not after that unhappy romance. Her mind skittered briefly to Josiah Burkhalter, next-door neighbor, childhood friend, rumspringa romance, and very nearly husband until someone else caught his wandering eye. The Burkhalters had been a part of their lives forever, and she felt sure everyone had been thrilled at the thought of Leah and Josiah marrying. Except, apparently, Josiah.

Daad had accepted her jaundiced view of marriage, she thought, and so he was determined to see her set up with the work she wanted, although he'd think a business a poor exchange for a husband and family.

They'd reached the front of the cottage, which had a small front porch that would be ideal for displays once she'd opened. The step creaked and wobbled under her foot, and she made a mental note of repair needed. And the front door didn't respond to the key until Daad gave it a shove with his shoulder. Her list of repairs would grow quickly at this rate.

"The place is small, but it's not as if you'll be living here."

Daad planted himself in the middle of the front room and looked around. Windows on the sides and in front gave plenty of light, and she knew there was a kitchen and another room in back, along with two small rooms upstairs.

Leaving aside the question of where she might be living, Leah looked around the large room, picturing it with shelves for herbal teas and mixtures, tables holding plants for sale, and small bins for dried herbs. With this amount of space, she could devote a corner to crafts like the scented herbal pillows she'd been making.

"I think it will be just right once it's ready. Aunt Miriam gave me a lot of ideas for marketing, besides getting me started on herbs to begin with." She tried not to let her feelings color her voice when she spoke of her aunt.

Aunt Miriam had interested her small niece in making an herb garden on a visit when Leah was ten. She'd continued to encourage her, talking about the day when they'd have a business together. And at a time when Leah's romantic dreams had been shattered, Aunt Miriam had invited Leah to move across the state to live with her and learn the business.

Because Aunt Miriam had no children of her own, she'd made it clear that she wanted Leah to take over eventually. That had made it all the harder when Aunt Miriam decided to sell out to a stranger. Leah had been ashamed . . . knowing she'd failed and struggling to find out why or how.

"Miriam certain sure knew her business." Daad frowned a little, shaking his head slightly. "It's a shame, her being so far from your mother. They were always close when they were young."

Leah roused herself from unhappy thoughts to respond. "I remember hearing them sitting up late and giggling together like teenagers when she did come to visit, even if it wasn't very often."

Daad chuckled. "Yah, they did. But Miriam was caught up in her business, and your mother was busy with you young ones. Maybe now that Miriam is retiring, we'll see more of her."

Their lives had gone in different directions, and Leah wondered if they had regretted that. Had they been happy with their choices? Had they sometimes thought yearningly of each other's lives?

Decisions made early dictated the rest of your life, it seemed, and some decisions were pushed on you. Like her decision to leave Promise Glen, and now the decision to come back.

She reminded herself there was no use going over something that she couldn't change. The past just had to be lived with, she guessed.

"About the carpentry work that's needed . . ." Daad paused as if to be sure she was listening.

She looked at him. Was it her imagination, or did he seem ill at ease?

"Don't worry," she said quickly. "I know you and the boys don't have time to do it all. I can afford to hire someone, and that's what I plan to do."

"We'll want to help all we can," Daad said quickly, "but we can't do it all. Seems like you need a craftsman who knows cabinetmaking for a lot of the work."

"Yah, for sure. Who do you think would be best?" There were several possibilities within the church district. She didn't doubt Daad would know.

"As a matter of fact, someone was just talking to me about it a few days ago."

It wasn't her imagination. Daad definitely looked uncomfortable, and she couldn't imagine why.

He cleared his throat, glancing at the door as if considering an escape. "He's interested in doing the work, and there's no doubt in my mind he'd do it well."

"Gut," she said, trying to sound as brisk and confident as Aunt Miriam would. "Who is it?"

"I mentioned we'd probably be taking a look around this afternoon." Now Daad was looking out the back window. "I thought he might stop by to talk about it. And there he is."

Leah followed the direction of her father's gaze, and her heart seemed to stop beating. The person approaching the back door was hardly someone she'd consider reliable enough to do the job. Or to do anything else, for that matter. It was Josiah Burkhalter.

RIDICULOUS TO BE SO NERVOUS ABOUT TALKING TO people he'd known all his life. Josiah took a deep, calming breath, determined not to oversell this. Leah might hold the key to what he wanted most right now, but he'd best keep still about that. After all, they hadn't parted on the best of terms.

He spotted Leah and Isaiah looking at him from the window, and his stomach cramped. He could only hope Isaiah had explained why he was there.

Nothing ventured, nothing gained, as Josiah's daad was fond of saying. He stepped firmly onto the back stoop, trying to look assured. With a loud crack the board broke beneath his foot and his leg plunged down, leaving him trapped.

It took him a moment to realize what had happened and try to pull his foot clear, and by then both Isaiah and Leah had rushed out the door.

"Careful." He threw up his hand in a gesture. "We don't want anyone else stuck in here."

"Ach, I should have checked this back stoop out before I told you to meet us here. We came in the front." Isaiah stepped out, careful about where he put his foot.

"No problem," Josiah said lightly, trying to hide his embarrassment. Here he was, coming to repair the place, and the first thing he did was make it worse. And it struck him that Leah was enjoying his discomfort.

"Just hang on to my arm while you pull your leg out." Isaiah gripped him firmly, taking his weight so that he could regain his balance.

Josiah turned his attention to the one who stood watching. "Seems to me you need a carpenter, Leah," he said lightly.

He couldn't quite read her expression at his words. Funny, because he'd always been able to tell what Leah was feeling. Maybe he'd lost the gift after a year apart.

"Yah, we were just talking about that." Isaiah filled up the momentary silence. Gripping Josiah's arm with one hand, he helped pull his leg free of the jagged board. "I told Leah I'd found a carpenter for her already."

Something negative showed in the tightening of Leah's lips. "We haven't actually discussed it yet."

"Well, let's get inside and do that," Isaiah said briskly.

He took a long stride over the hole, and the others followed, stepping into the old kitchen with its worn cabinets and worn-out stove.

Too bad Josiah couldn't read Leah's expression. Maybe she was thinking that turning him down completely was an appropriate return for what he'd done to her.

The inside of the cottage was chilly, but not quite as cold as it was outside. Josiah rubbed his hands briskly and tried to think of something that would get them back on the old familiar footing.

"Leah, Mamm wants to know why you haven't been to see her yet. She's plenty eager to hear about your time out at your aunt's place."

Leah's face warmed at the mention of his mother, her cheeks regaining the peachy glow he remembered. "You tell her I'll stop by tomorrow afternoon. I made some of that herbal tea she likes, and I'll bring it over."

For that moment, at least, Leah looked like her old self. He hoped it would last. It would sure make things easier.

"Mammi will be pleased. Are you thinking you'll sell teas as well as plants once you get going?"

She nodded, glancing around as if picturing what her shop would look like when it was finally ready. "Yah. And maybe some crafts made with herbals, too. I'll want a corner with shelves for those things. That's what my aunt did in her shop."

The mention of her aunt seemed to produce a little wariness in Leah's expression, and her lips tightened.

"My wife's sister, Miriam," Isaiah added. "You'll remember her. She made a fine business out of herbs over the past twenty years or so."

Something his mother had said slipped through Josiah's thoughts. Wasn't it rumored that the aunt was going to leave her business to Leah? If so, why was Leah back home?

He certain sure couldn't ask, but if he'd be working for Leah, it would probably come out sometime. *If*, he reminded himself. It wasn't a deal yet.

He cleared his throat, thinking the silence had gone on too long. "How about showing me what you want done? Then I'll have an idea of how involved the job is and whether I can do it or not. No sense in talking until we know that, ain't so?"

Leah looked relieved. Maybe she figured that could give her an out if she wanted one. "Yah, sounds gut." She gestured around the kitchen.

"This will be a workroom for creating the teas and working on the crafts, and I'll want a couple of long tables for that, along with cabinets on one wall with a countertop and sink for some of the cutting and repotting. A lot of that will be done in the greenhouse, of course." She looked out the window as if she pictured a greenhouse instead of brush and a few trees.

Josiah took out his tape measure along with a notebook and pen. "Let's see what we've got, then. If you have the sink where the old one is, we won't have to move the pipes. How about if I take the measurements, make notes of what you want and the supplies needed? Then I can work up an estimate of time and cost."

"That seems reasonable." Isaiah sounded as if the barbed atmosphere made him nervous. "Ain't so, Leah?"

Forced to respond, Leah nodded. Well, if Leah didn't want him to do the work, why didn't she just say so and save them both the time?

Clenching his jaw, he busied himself measuring, but as he worked, his annoyance began to fade. He was expecting too much. It would take time to get back to his old relationship with Leah. He couldn't rush it.

Leah had clearly thought their romance was more serious than he had. Maybe they'd been moving in that direction, maybe it would have come to that if things had continued the way they were. Maybe they'd have married. But then Susie Lehman came along.

Susie, with her sparkling dark eyes and her infectious

laugh, had been so different from the girls he knew. She'd arrived in their small community like a summer storm and created just about the same amount of damage. He'd known all the time it wasn't serious with her, but he'd been captivated. And Leah had been hurt, embarrassed, and unforgiving.

He made an effort to shove off the past. Concentrate on the present, and hope a moment would come when he could tell her how sorry he was that she'd been hurt.

So he concentrated on business. Leah showed him the front room, talking about the kind of counters she wanted, the drying racks for herbs, and the shelves for tea and other mixtures of herbs. Following her around the room, he scribbled notes.

Leah moved to the nearest window. "I've been thinking the greenhouse could go there." She pointed to the same view he'd looked at earlier from the other window.

He moved to her side to look out and found he was staring at Leah instead. She hadn't changed in a year, or had she?

She was still small and slight, her eyes as green as a spring hillside, and her oval face, usually a tad serious in expression, was now lit with enthusiasm. With a shock, he realized that if she'd been a magnet, she'd have drawn him like iron filings.

Josiah took a careful step back. None of that, now. This was strictly business. And speaking of business . . .

"Something I want to bring up before we go any further." He shouldn't sound so serious, and he tried to lighten his expression. "My idea is that this is a good project for me to get going on over the winter and early spring, before Daad's construction business gets rolling with the good weather."

She nodded, clearly not understanding what he was driving at, and he was hampered, not wanting her to guess how much it meant to him.

"Anyway, my point is that I'm not expecting you to pay

for my labor. You just take care of the materials, and that's fine with me."

She reacted with an open-mouthed gaze, as if he'd suddenly stood on his head.

"Josiah, that's ferhoodled." She recovered her voice quickly. "You can't offer that, and I certain sure can't accept it. This is business." She looked almost insulted at the offer.

He tried to treat it lightly. "Business, yah. But we've been friends since our mothers used to put us in the same playpen when they were working outside."

"That's not the point." Her temper flared, and that just made him more determined.

"It's just the point. I wouldn't be doing much except getting in Mamm's way over the winter anyway. There's not enough work to be done there to keep Daad and me and my brothers busy. I'd rather be honing my skills than sitting around."

"You mean you want to practice on me," she snapped back, turning away.

He resisted the urge to catch hold of her arm the way he used to when she was a child—a stubborn child.

"Well, why not? You're not a business owner, not yet, and I'm not a full-fledged carpenter." Not yet, though he could be if this project convinced Daad of what he could do. "But I can do the job. How about it?"

She looked away from him, and her father stared at them both and then looked away, as if leaving them to resolve it. After an awkward silence she turned back, but her gaze avoided his.

"Josiah, you certain sure can't work for free. That wouldn't be right."

"I don't need . . . ," he began.

"Yah, you do. I'd rather have anything between us on a strictly businesslike basis." She pinned him with a stare when she spoke, and her green eyes had never looked so cold.

So that was it. Leah was implying he couldn't be trusted to do what he said.

Was he never going to get rid of the reputation that followed him around? Apparently not with Leah.

"Fine," he snapped. "If that's how you want it, then it's a deal."

Leah looked startled, as if she hadn't meant to commit herself. Well, too late now. They had a deal, and he'd show her, and his daad, and anybody else who was interested, that he could be a solid, reliable businessman no matter what he'd done in the past.

WHY HADN'T SHE SWALLOWED THOSE WORDS BEFORE she'd spoken them? Leah felt as if she'd been outwitted, and she wasn't sure how. She probably would have been better off not discussing the work with Josiah at all, but she really couldn't think of any other way of handling it.

A glance at her father told her he was relieved with the result. The two families had been closer than relatives all their lives, and she knew he thought this solution best for everyone.

If she came right out and told him she didn't want to work with Josiah . . . no, she couldn't do that. Daad had been so generous and understanding about her business, so happy to help her, that she couldn't disappoint him. He probably had some idea that working together would make them friends again.

Leah could feel Josiah's gaze on her and forced herself to smile. He probably knew exactly how little she wanted to work with him. She'd seen Josiah determined before, and she knew how hard it was to change his mind. Without being flat-out rude, she couldn't refuse him now. Why was it so important to him?

The question kept niggling at the back of her mind as they moved slowly around the downstairs rooms, and she tried to silence it. She told herself it didn't matter to her what Josiah's motives were. It was enough that he had the skills she needed.

As for his ability to stick to the job and see it through . . . well, whatever he might do when it came to romancing a pretty girl, she didn't really think Josiah would desert a job once he'd started it.

"Leah." Josiah nudged her, holding out the metal measuring tape. "Hold that end while I measure for the cabinets you want on this wall, okay?"

"Yah, sorry." She felt the color come up in her cheeks. Josiah couldn't have known what she was thinking. Besides, she wasn't going to reflect on those memories anymore.

"Not there." Josiah grasped her hand and moved it another three feet along the wall. "You want to leave room for the door to open and shut, right?"

She nodded, trying to ignore his warm grasp on her hand. "Well, I might have decided to get rid of the door entirely." She didn't like to be caught doing something foolish, especially when Josiah was the one pointing it out to her.

Laugh lines crinkled around his eyes. "But you didn't, did you?"

"No." She snatched her hand away.

Daad poked his head in from the other room. "I'll find something to do a temporary fix on the back stoop so nobody gets hurt." He withdrew, leaving them alone.

Leah took a step back, searching for something to say. "Won't it be cold to be doing the work here? I don't know what kind of shape that old stove is in."

"Probably full of birds' nests." Josiah cast a disparaging look at the potbellied stove. "I can bring along a portable heater if I have to. And some of it can be done in Daad's workshop. He won't mind."

Leah had a quick memory of perching on a stool in his father's workshop, watching while Matthew taught Josiah how to use one of his saws. She'd wanted to learn, too, but Matthew had dismissed that idea.

"Does he still hang that red cloth on the door when he doesn't want to be disturbed?"

Josiah chuckled, and for a moment the memories seemed to float between them. "He gave that up once he was satisfied that all of us understood the rules about using tools safely." His lips quirked. "Although I wouldn't like to count on Paul taking the safe way with anything."

"He hasn't managed to grow up yet?" she asked, thinking about a few of Paul's more memorable pranks. He must be fifteen by now, but judging by Josiah's expression, he hadn't changed much.

Josiah shook his head. "I don't know what gets into him sometimes. He's up for any fool idea that comes along."

Leah couldn't let that go by. "Reminds me of someone else I know," she said tartly. "Paul always wanted to be just like you, goodness knows why."

If that bothered him, Josiah didn't show it. "Nope," he said. "My jokes were always funny. You can let go—"

She released the end of the tape before he finished. It snaked across the wall and snapped back into the holder. Apparently it pinched his finger, too. He muttered and shook it.

So his jokes were always funny, were they? He probably considered flirting just a joke.

"Are you sure you want to take on this job?" she asked abruptly.

Josiah stared at her, his fingers clenching the tape measure. "I said I did. We have a deal, remember?"

"I remember." She also remembered too much about those days when she'd thought she was the most important person in his life and found out otherwise.

The planes of his face suddenly showed, as if the skin had pulled tightly against them. The expression shook her. It was so different from his usual laughing look, with his brown eyes sparkling and laughter never far from his lips.

He took a step toward her, and she was aware of the height and breadth of him. He was a grown man now, not the laughing boy she'd been picturing.

"What is all this?" he demanded. "If your doubts are about what happened between us—"

"Of course not." She'd never admit that, not to anyone. "But if this is meant to be some kind of payback for Susie Lehman, I don't want it."

Josiah's face was an unreadable mask. The year she'd been away gaped as wide and deep as the Grand Canyon between them. If she'd once known what he was thinking, she certain sure didn't know now.

He seemed to make up his mind about something, and his taut muscles eased into the expression she remembered. "No payback. Susie was nothing but a short interruption in my life. If she means something more to you—"

If so, she'd never admit it. "Don't be ferhoodled. I've already forgotten about it."

"Okay. You've forgotten, I've forgotten, and as for Susie . . ." His smile flashed. "She's probably breaking hearts somewhere else by now. Or married with one and a half kids. Now can we get on with these measurements?"

They could. And she could hide anything she still felt and work with Josiah if she had to. But she wouldn't trust him. Josiah and her aunt between them had convinced her it was a mistake to count too much on anyone.

CHAPTER TWO

✦

AS THEY WALKED BACK TO THE FARMHOUSE, LEAH
tried to hide her doubts from her father. Daad was so pleased
to have helped her that she couldn't let him guess her true
feelings.

Fortunately, Daad wasn't one for looking beneath the
surface—that quality belonged to Mammi. And Grossmammi, who seemed to see everything, including things
you hadn't recognized yourself yet.

Planting a smile on her face, Leah scurried into the
kitchen and hung her jacket from the row of hooks on the
wall.

"Here you are at last." Mammi turned from the stove, a
wooden spoon in her hand, and Grossmammi looked up
from the rocking chair where she sat knitting. "Well? What
do you think about the cottage now that you've had a closer
look?" her mother asked.

"It's going to be perfect once the work is completed.
Close to the road, so people will notice it, and with plenty of
space for the greenhouse." She looked over Mamm's shoul-

der at the contents of the heavy saucepan. "Yum, chicken pot pie. I've missed that."

Judith, her fourteen-year-old sister, came bouncing into the kitchen in time to hear what she said. "Why? Didn't Aunt Miriam make it for you?"

Judith seemed to have endless questions about her big sister's time away, making Leah wonder if she was anticipating getting away herself.

"I actually did most of the cooking while I was there. And during the busy season, nobody cooked on rush days."

Grossmammi chuckled. "Busy or not, Miriam never did learn to make a gut pot pie. She had a heavy hand with the dough."

Leah exchanged glances with Grossmammi, knowing that Judith's enthusiasm would slip at the thought of cooking for someone else. At this point in her life, Judith wasn't much interested in cooking, or any other household chores, as far as Leah could see. Maybe she was more like Aunt Miriam, whose mind was always on her business, not her home.

"Did you eat out a lot?" Judith brightened at that idea. "I'd like that. Maybe I'll get a job where I can eat out all the time. Then I won't need to learn to cook."

Judith was always the bold one of the girls, jumping into anything different, but this time she'd jumped too far, catching Mammi's attention.

"As long as you live here, you'll learn whatever Daadi and I think you should," Mammi said firmly. "So tomorrow you can help me cook supper. Time you learned how to make pot roast."

Judith opened her mouth, probably to say something sassy, but the other two girls came in, diverting everyone's attention. Rebecca, who was just home from her job at Cousin Dinah's coffee shop, paused to give Leah a hug before starting to set the table.

"How was work today?" Leah asked, taking a handful

of flatware and following Rebecca around the long table. At sixteen, Becky was the closest to her of the girls in age, with their brothers falling in between.

"Pretty quiet."

Quiet described Rebecca, too. She was growing up, but still the shy, sweet person she'd always been. If Leah had a regret about her year away, it was the gap that it had made between them.

"That's how Becky likes it," little Hannie piped up, and then blushed when everyone turned to look at her. "Well, it is, isn't it, Becky?"

Becky patted her shoulder, smiling. "That's right. I get kind of rattled when it's crowded and everybody wants something at once. The other girls don't seem to mind, but I want to hide behind the counter." She turned the shy smile on Leah. "Maybe I can work in the greenhouse for you. That sounds a lot better to me."

"No fair." Judith slid off the end of the table at a look from Mammi. "You have a job. I should be the one to work for Leah."

"We could trade," Becky offered. "You could work for Cousin Dinah, and I could work in the greenhouse."

"It will be Leah and Dinah who make any decisions about who works for them," Mammi said, quelling the girls with a glance. "Finish setting the table, and then go and see if Daadi needs any help in the barn before supper."

Judith made a face at the prospect, but after glancing at Mammi, she apparently decided it wasn't wise to argue. There was a bustle of putting jackets on and doors banging, and then the kitchen was quiet.

Leah chuckled. "I see you can still quiet Judith with one firm look."

"So far, anyway." Mammi lowered the temperature under the heavy kettle.

"That child is going to get into trouble with her smart mouth if she's not careful," Grossmammi observed.

"Maybe that's what she needs in order to learn." Mammi smiled at Leah. "You were a lot easier. Raising you spoiled us. Ach, it's wonderful gut to have you home."

"And to be home." Leah frowned a little, thinking of the changes in her siblings over the past year. "Is Becky okay? She seems a little . . . well, I don't know what. It's probably just getting rattled when she's working."

Mammi shook her head. "No, you're right. Something more is troubling her, but she won't come out and say it."

"She'll talk to Leah," Grossmammi said. "They were always close."

"I'll try to encourage her, but I don't know if she'll confide in me." Once again she had the sense that she'd lost something important during her time away.

But maybe something had been gained as well. Grossmammi and Mammi were including her in their talk as if she were one of the grown women. She hadn't expected that until she was married, if then.

Or maybe they didn't think she ever would be married. Did folks already consider her an old maid?

"Girls are harder than boys to raise," Grossmammi went on, looking at Leah so intently that she immediately felt guilty. "I told your mother that when you were born. If it's not worrying about what they're doing, it's worrying about what they're thinking. And what they're feeling about boys, too."

That yanked her mind back to her little sister. "Do you think Becky is sweet on someone?" There was no reason to be surprised. After all, Becky was the age Leah had been when she'd started going to the singings and volleyball games with the other teens.

Mammi shrugged. "She doesn't talk about anyone special. I'm starting to think maybe we shouldn't have encouraged her to take the job at the coffee shop. It's so hard to know what's best for your kinder." Her glance zeroed in on Leah, and then it quickly veered away.

Leah's thoughts seemed to spin and then settle into a

new pattern. "Was that why you didn't want me to go to Aunt Miriam's?"

"I didn't . . ." Her mother clamped her lips closed for a moment, and silence pressed on Leah's ears.

Mammi took a breath and started again. "We had doubts about having you so far away. It wasn't that I didn't want you to be with your aunt."

She should never had brought this up, Leah thought, and certain sure not in front of Grossmammi. After all, Aunt Miriam was her child, too. But her grandmother didn't seem concerned.

"All you can do is what you think is best at the time," Grossmammi said. "Your aunt . . ."

Mammi put her hand on Grossmammi's shoulder as if communicating with her, and Grossmammi stopped.

"I was concerned that you were running away from Josiah and what happened between you." Her mother's eyes filled with caring. "I didn't think that would be good for you, even if it seemed easier at the time."

Leah shook her head. She could hardly deny that Josiah had something to do with her eagerness to leave home.

"Maybe so," she said slowly. "But I really did want to learn how to manage a business. And anyway . . ." A rueful smile curved her lips. "Thanks to Daad, I'll be working with Josiah for the next few months. That will cure me, ain't so?"

Both of them looked relieved. "Don't blame your father," Grossmammi said. "Josiah came to him with the idea."

That startled her, and she put it away to consider later. "I'm not blaming anyone. If it doesn't work out, I can just hire someone else." Leah wasn't sure whether that came out as confident as she'd like it to.

Mammi put her arm around Leah's waist in a quick hug. "Just remember that you and Josiah were friends for over twenty years and only sweethearts for six months. It can't be all that hard to go back."

Leah didn't believe it, but she managed to nod. If she couldn't forgive and forget, at least she'd try to look as if she had.

Forgive and forget. Those words sent her right back to those terrible moments with Aunt Miriam. The moments when she realized Aunt Miriam thought she was a thief.

JOSIAH WALKED THROUGH THE FROST-CRISP GRASS toward the cottage the next morning. Isaiah had given both him and Leah keys to the cottage before they closed the door the previous day, which was just as well, because he'd realized he needed to double-check some of the measurements. A few possible changes had occurred to him when he'd been working on plans last night that he'd like to check out as well.

Glancing across the fields, he noticed Isaiah heading toward the barn and raised his hand in acknowledgment. The Amish community might be spread out along the valley, but your neighbors still knew what you were doing. Most of the time, Josiah liked that, but sometimes a person wanted privacy.

Like last night. He'd been sitting at the kitchen table, graph paper spread out in front of him, when he realized that Daad had walked past the kitchen door three times since he sat down, looking in each time.

He'd tried to focus and found he was counting the minutes until he came back. It was a relief when Daad finally came into the kitchen, murmuring something about coffee. He came past Josiah's chair, looking over his shoulder on the way.

"Working on the plans for Leah, yah? Need any help?"

The first question was easy to answer, but the second one put his back up. Didn't Daad think he was capable of working alone?

"I think I've got it, Daad."

His father paused for a moment, then headed on toward the stove and the coffeepot. Josiah feared he'd sounded too sharp, and he hadn't meant it that way. But after all, the purpose of doing this alone was to show Daad how capable he was. Sure, he'd messed up in the past, but he was a different person now.

Well, Daad hadn't seen it that way, he guessed. And there was someone else who didn't.

Leah came walking along the edge of the road toward the cottage, and incidentally toward him. She probably hadn't wanted to get her feet wet cutting across the field. He veered to meet her, wondering how many changes *she'd* thought of since the previous night.

"Coming to check out your property again?" he asked once they got within speaking distance. Leah was bundled up against the chilly air, and her cheeks were rosy from the walk.

She smiled. Whatever animosity he'd sensed the previous day seemed gone now.

"I couldn't resist. Did you know Daad actually wants to sign the piece of land over to me?"

"That is a surprise." He stopped a few feet from her. "After all the time he's been wanting to buy it, I figured he'd never let it go."

Leah chuckled. "You're right about that. It's been a thorn in his side ever since I can remember." Her face grew serious. "I guess that makes this idea of signing it over . . ." She paused, either groping for words or thinking she didn't want to confide her thoughts in him.

"It's a sign of confidence, ain't so?" He could use one of those from his own daad right about now.

"Yah." Her face warmed with pleasure, and she looked along the road frontage, probably picturing a sign drawing folks to her business, or a parking area for customers.

Maybe he should come back later for his measuring. Did she want to be by herself to gloat over her property?

Before he could decide, he heard a familiar sound . . . an irritating one. A revving motor, followed by the screech of tires and the roar of a vehicle approaching the curve in the road.

"Best move away." He reached out to grasp her arm, but she frowned, pulling back.

"I don't see why—" The sound was suddenly louder. Her head jerked toward the bend, and she stumbled and would have fallen if he hadn't caught her and swung her away from the road.

A rusty pickup, once black but now mottled with various attempts at paint, roared into view, taking the curve far too wide, hitting the roadside gravel, and then veering away again to speed down the road.

Leah looked from the disappearing truck to the gravel that had been kicked into the grass. "Who was that? Or what?" She seemed to realize he still held her arm and pulled it away.

"Remember the Conners, down the road about a mile? That was young Jere."

"He's not old enough to drive, is he?" Her forehead crinkled.

"He's sixteen now, unfortunately. And he's dating Corrie Edwards, so this is an every-morning event. He picks her up for school and then tears down the road." The Edwards family lived just around the bend.

Leah looked annoyed at the news. "I'm surprised her parents let him drive her anywhere if that's the way he handles a pickup."

"They're both out at work at this hour, so they probably don't know. He's just showing off," Josiah added, feeling a little indulgent toward the kid.

"You mean you'd have done the same," she said, echoing his thoughts.

"Couldn't. Not with a buggy. The gelding I drove then would have come to a dead stop at the flick of the lines."

She turned toward the cottage, smiling at the image, and he fell into step with her, grateful for the truce that seemed to exist between them.

"Didn't any of your Englisch friends let you drive?" Her eyebrows lifted, lips still curving.

"You know too much about me." He paused as she stepped up on the front porch. "Do you want me to come back later?"

Leah seemed startled. "No, of course not. Just do whatever you need."

He nodded, and together they went inside. "Just a little more measuring. Then I can stop by the lumberyard for what I need to fix the back stoop first of all."

"I see." She was turned away from him, but he could hear something in her voice that wasn't quite right. Doubt?

"Is that okay? I figured it should be done before somebody gets hurt." He moved, trying to see her face, but she determinedly evaded his glance.

"I suppose. You'll want some money first, ain't so? To pay for the materials?"

Again there was doubt in her voice, and his temper sparked. "What's the matter? Afraid I'll run off with a few bucks? I'll buy it myself if that's how you feel."

She should have rushed into denying it, he thought, but she didn't.

Josiah touched her arm warily, and her gaze flew to his. Doubt, that's what it was. After all the years she'd known him, too.

His mind gave him an image of Susie. Well, that wouldn't have encouraged her to trust him. He spoke more softly than he might have.

"Look, Leah, you aren't sure about this. I get it. Your daad pushed you into working with me."

"I don't think—" she began, and he cut her off with a gesture as he strode to the door.

"So take your time." He couldn't completely erase the

annoyance in his voice, but he could try. "You'll let me know when you decide." More disappointed than he would have expected, he walked out.

LEAH TOOK A STEP AFTER HIM AND THEN STOPPED. What was wrong with her? She was flitting back and forth like a dandelion in the wind. One minute she was convinced she had to go through with the arrangements Daad had made, and the next she was backing away from the very thought of working with Josiah on something that meant so much.

It was past time for her to face facts. She might find it awkward to see so much of Josiah, but they were next-door neighbors, members of the same church district. She couldn't live on bad terms with him, or risk creating a rift between families that had been so close since before she was born.

A rebellious voice in Leah's heart insisted that Josiah was the one who'd created the rift. He was the one who had courted her and then turned away to follow the first pretty girl who came along.

The church said to forgive, but how could she forgive when he didn't even seem to think he'd done something wrong?

This was getting her nowhere. She knew what had to be done. She had to hide her feelings and follow through with the plan Daad had inadvertently set up for her. No more questioning. If it meant nothing to Josiah, she'd make sure it meant nothing to her.

She flung open the back door, intending to go after Josiah, and nearly fell on the boards Daad had stretched across the hole. The momentary delay gave her time for a second thought. Maybe it was best to let them both cool off. She'd go over later in the day and take the tea mixture she'd made for Josiah's mother. She could see him then.

After sketching out a few more ideas for her workroom, Leah headed for home, wondering why the family buggy was sitting at the back door, hitched up. Mammi hurried to intercept her before she could take off her jacket.

"Ach, gut. You're just in time. Dinah needs Becky to go in to work, but James has the two-seater, and Daad doesn't want the family buggy tied up in town all day."

"No problem," Leah said quickly. "I'll take her in. It'll give me a chance to chat with Dinah for a few minutes." She took her bonnet from the rack, not having bothered to put it over her kapp for the short walk to the cottage. "Is she ready . . . ," she began, but then heard her sister running down the stairs.

"Denke." Becky slung her jacket on, and she sounded a little breathless. "Dinah left a message on the answering machine in the phone shanty, and none of us saw it right away."

They climbed into the buggy. They headed down the lane, and Leah could feel her sister's nervousness. She took a second look, noticing the tension around Becky's eyes and the way her hands were clasped tightly in her lap.

"I'm sure Dinah won't scold you for being late," she said, hoping to comfort her. If working in the café made Becky this nervous, maybe she'd best find something else to do.

"Oh . . ." Becky seemed to realize how much she was fidgeting, and she pressed her hands flat. "She won't . . . she's wonderful gut to work for." Her voice hurried over the words. "I just didn't expect to go in today."

Mindful of her mother's worries, Leah reached across to pat her sister's hand. "Well, then, why . . ." She hesitated, not sure how to ask what she wanted, and Becky hurried into speech.

"I told you. I just get upset when we're busy. That's all." The snappish tone wouldn't surprise Leah coming from Judith, but gentle Becky rarely snapped, too sensitive to the possibility of hurting someone if she did.

Clearly it would be a mistake to pry, so she contented herself with a nod. "Perhaps it will get easier after a time," she murmured.

Becky looked doubtful, but she didn't speak the rest of the short drive to town.

As she pulled up to one of the parking spaces reserved for buggies, Leah gave it another try. "You know, if you ever want to talk, I'm here."

"Yah." Tears seemed to glisten briefly in Becky's blue eyes. "I . . . I'm glad you're home, Leah." She hopped down and ran for the back door of the coffee shop.

That hadn't worked very well. Moving more slowly, Leah clipped the mare to the hitching post. Snuggling her hands into her mittens, she headed around to the front of the building.

One side belonged to Dinah's café, while the other was occupied by her husband's harness shop. Jacob actually owned the whole building, but he'd rented half to Dinah back when her first husband was still alive.

Poor Dinah had gone through a difficult time when her husband died, leaving her childless, but she was obviously happy now with Jacob, and together they were raising Jacob's small nephew.

Dinah's business seemed to be thriving, too. Many of the tables were filled by midmorning coffee klatches, and several people stood in line at the counter for takeout. Becky was already scurrying out to join Cousin Dinah behind the counter.

At a whispered word from Becky, Dinah glanced back, saw her, and waved, indicating she should sit at a small table that was in the corner by the counter. Nodding, Leah wove her way through the other tables. What with stopping to speak to those people she knew, by the time she reached the table the line at the counter had dissipated. A moment later Dinah joined her, setting a tray containing coffee and crullers down to hug her.

"Ach, it's wonderful gut to see you." She held Leah back at arms' length to scrutinize her. "You look too thin. Have a couple of crullers."

"Don't tempt me," Leah said, laughing. "On the other hand, you look happy. Marriage and motherhood agree with you, ain't so?"

Dinah flushed, nodding. "You must come to the house and meet our little man. He's staying with his grossmammi today."

Leah promised, listening while Dinah talked about how smart and how strong little Isaac was. And while she listened, she kept an eye on Becky, still wondering what lay behind her discomfort. Now that no one stood waiting, Becky stayed busy, restocking the glass-topped counters that displayed baked goods.

Still, Leah couldn't help noticing how she kept an eye on the door, looking up quickly at every shadow that paused before the glass. Odd. She must be looking for someone, but Leah couldn't tell whether it was someone she was eager to see or someone she dreaded to see.

"You know the aunts were all guessing that you'd come back with a husband in tow."

That pulled Leah's attention back to Dinah in a hurry. "Whyever did they think that?"

Their generation always used the term *aunts* to include all the aunts and cousins and second cousins who were their parents' and grandparents' ages, and especially the unmarried ones. "The aunts" were always matching people up like so many matchmakers.

Dinah shrugged. "You know how they are. It seems you mentioned in a letter the name of a man you met. That was enough for them to build on."

"Thomas Esch." She filled in the name without any difficulty. "He was in and out a good bit, being a neighbor. He always wanted to help Aunt Miriam with any heavy work. But he certain sure wasn't courting me."

"No?" Dinah asked the question with a quirk of her lips and a raised eyebrow.

"No," Leah said firmly. Actually, she'd wondered about Thomas's attentions once or twice herself, but nothing had ever come of it. It had almost seemed he'd been waiting for something.

Anyway, the last thing she was looking for was a husband.

"I'll pass the word along if anyone brings it up," Dinah promised. "But you know that won't stop them talking. And what's this I hear about Josiah converting the cottage for your new business?"

That grabbed Leah's attention all right. "How did you hear about that? I've just barely made the decision." She was still a little wary, but she'd decided, and it was high time.

Dinah shrugged. "The Amish grapevine works quickly. Isn't it true?"

"I guess." She may as well commit herself openly. Then she couldn't back out. "We haven't settled everything yet. There's so much to think about. Well, you run a business. You know what it's like."

Looking with satisfaction around her coffee shop, Dinah nodded. "True. Lots and lots of details to settle. I had the advantage that I didn't have to start full-on. I'd been running it as more of a bakery just a few days a week." She glanced around again, smiling. "It grew."

"I guess it did." Her gaze was caught by Becky, refilling coffee cups for a trio of Englisch ladies. She looked as if only half her mind was on them, while the rest waited for something. Or someone.

The bell on the door jingled, and Becky glanced at it quickly. And flushed. She looked away at once, but it was too late. The Englischer who stepped inside was clearly the person she'd been watching out for.

Leah eyed him as he took a table near where Becky stood. He was youngish, probably not out of his twenties, well-dressed, and good-looking. And he was clearly interested in her little sister.

"Well, with your daad behind you and all you learned from Aunt Miriam," Dinah went on, "I'm sure you'll be successful. It's good that you . . . well, got over whatever you felt about Josiah." Dinah hesitated. "You did get over it, didn't you?"

"Yah, for sure," she said quickly, feeling her cheeks grow warm. It was on the tip of her tongue to ask Dinah about the man.

"Gut." Dinah rose, patting her shoulder. "Stay here as long as you want. I have to check some things in the kitchen." She took a step and then turned back. "Because if you weren't over your feelings for him, working together on a project like that should cure you."

Dinah moved off toward the kitchen, leaving Leah sitting there with a red face. Was she really being that obvious? First Grossmammi, with her talk of forgetting their sweethearting interval, and now Dinah, proposing a cure. If only everyone could ignore the whole subject, she probably wouldn't have an ounce of trouble with Josiah.

And as for Becky . . . that was going to take some careful handling.

CHAPTER THREE

❧❧❧

WHEN SHE REACHED HOME, LEAH WAS DETERMINED to settle the business she had with Josiah immediately—or, at least, as quickly as she could. Unfortunately quickly meant putting the buggy horse in the paddock, hanging up the harness, going inside to report to Mamm that Becky was at work, and then getting caught up in the usual chatter that went on with that many people in the house.

Funny, at first she'd really enjoyed the quiet at Aunt Miriam's. Soon, though, she'd begun to miss the noise of home . . . the talk and laughter and even the spats that were bound to erupt.

"We've got to figure out where we're going to seat everybody for dinner on Christmas. Second Christmas will be easy with just the Burkhalters, but Christmas Day is another story."

Mammi sat at the kitchen table with a note pad in front of her, organized as always. Mammi's lists were notorious in the family—Daad sometimes teased that Micah had gotten married in order to get off the list.

"Well, it's your side of the family this year, so how many people is that?" Leah set a basket on the table to pack with several boxes of her herbal tea for Josiah's mother.

"Thirty-three, no, thirty-four," Grossmammi said, ticking them off on her fingers.

"Yah, but some of them are babies. We don't need an extra chair for a baby." Mamm drew a large rectangle that was probably meant to be the dining room table. "Did you know that in some of the western states the Amish don't celebrate Second Christmas? Just Christmas Day and Old Christmas."

"I'd rather have three celebrations than two," Grossmammi said. "I'm glad we have an extra day for getting together with the neighbors after having the whole extended family here."

It suddenly struck Leah as Grossmammi said the words that Mamm's extended family included Aunt Miriam. Her heart sank at the thought of seeing her so soon, and with the whole family here.

Giving herself a shake, Leah brought her mind back to the current problem.

"What about opening the partition between the living room and the dining room and putting extra tables there?" she suggested. "Just as we do for hosting church."

After all, there was nothing she could do about it if Aunt Miriam came, so she'd have to pretend their relationship was unchanged. When she was a child, she'd anticipated Aunt Miriam's visits like the arrival of her birthday. Not now.

"If we get out the folding table we use for piecing quilts, there will be room for another table beside that," Grossmammi said. "And we can use it for the children when the Burkhalters come the next day."

Leah smiled, wondering which of them would be relegated to the children's table this year. Tradition had it that the two families got together on Second Christmas, but her sisters and Paul were the only ones she'd consider children now.

"Yah, but . . ." Mammi suddenly noticed what Leah was doing. "Are those for Hannah Burkhalter? Get a couple of jars of that blackberry jam from last year and take over. We have plenty."

It was a good thing neither of her brothers was around to hear that, Leah thought. They never considered any amount of jam was enough.

"Will do." Leah zipped into the pantry and grasped the jars of jam, popping back into the kitchen in less than a minute. "And if you think we won't have enough seats, what about borrowing a table and benches from the church wagon?"

Before Mammi could explain the difficulties that would entail, Leah had pulled her jacket on. She really needed to see Josiah and settle this before she started doubting again. "I'll be back soon."

She whisked out the door and headed quickly for the path along the edge of the field to the Burkhalter farm. Surely Josiah would be there, and she could take care of both things at once.

Her thoughts slipped back to Becky. Should she say anything to Mammi about it? Not that she really knew all that much yet.

As she approached the house, Hannah emerged onto the porch and waved at her. "Ach, Leah, it's wonderful gut to see you." She swept Leah into an embrace, basket and all, leading her into the kitchen.

Leah hugged her back, feeling an outpouring of love for the neighbors who were as close as family. "I'm so glad to be here."

Hannah released her, wiping her eyes and beaming. "Now tell me, did you come to talk business with Josiah or to visit with me?"

Leah smiled at her ability to be right on target. "Both, I think."

"He's out at the barn, so why don't you catch him there while I put the kettle on. It looks as if we can have some of your wonderful herbal tea," she said after a glimpse in the basket.

"Right you are. The tea is from me, and the jam is from Mammi."

"So sweet, the both of you." She gave Leah another hug. "Go, get your business done, and then we can talk."

Hannah turned to the stove, kettle in hand, while Leah headed for the barn. Now that she was keyed up to do this, she wanted to get it over with.

The warm air of the barn, smelling of hay and grain and horse, closed around her as she went in, and she paused to let her eyes get adjusted to the dimness. She and the boys used to play hide-and-seek here, scrambling up the ladder to the loft and crouching behind and under the bales of hay.

"Leah." Josiah straightened from where he was apparently mending a stall board, putting a hammer down. "What brings you here?"

She marched toward him, determined that, this time, she wouldn't let him rattle her. And she certain sure wouldn't let the emotions she had once felt trickle into her thoughts.

"I have something for you." She held out an envelope. "This is a down payment to cover whatever you need to fix the back stoop. I think we decided to start there."

"Did we?" He moved toward her, a teasing note in his voice. That was Josiah . . . a teasing answer and a twinkle in his eyes for everything.

Well, she wasn't in the mood right now.

"You said to let me know when I was ready for you to start. I'm ready, and Daad says we'd best get the stoop fixed before someone breaks a leg on it."

"Like me?" His brown eyes always seemed the color of milk chocolate when he teased her, and she never had understood why that was.

Leah took a grip on her temper. He'd always teased her, and she'd always responded. If she didn't want this to degenerate into a childish spat, she'd have to control herself.

"I think you already had a try at that, didn't you? You came away with your leg in one piece."

"True. I could give it another try, if you want."

"What I want . . ." She heard her voice rise and stopped, taking a deep breath. "What I want," she repeated politely, "is to have you start on whatever you can do before it gets too cold to work out there."

"Sounds like a gut plan." He frowned, apparently deciding it was time to talk business. "Okay. I guess I can get started with the back stoop. At least that's not something you'll be changing your mind about, ain't so?"

Leah crumpled the piece of paper she had in her hand, pressing her hand into the folds of her skirt. "What makes you think I'll change my mind about anything?"

"When didn't you? I remember when you and your mammi bought blue material for a dress and you spent the whole evening moaning because you hadn't picked out green."

He moved a bit closer, the lines around his eyes crinkling in the way they always did when he smiled. Her breath caught.

"Green . . . green matches my eyes," she murmured, and ran out of something to say.

"Yah, it does." His voice was equally soft, and he seemed to be studying her eyes. "Green with a bit of gold flecks in them."

For just a moment she seemed to be back in the courting buggy next to him on a warm summer evening when the stars clustered thickly and the Milky Way traced a pale swatch across the sky. There'd been the scent of the wild roses along the lane where they'd stopped coming home from a singing, and she seemed to inhale it again.

Ridiculous, she told herself. It was December, and there were no wild roses in bloom here or anywhere else in the state. She couldn't be smelling them.

"Anyway . . ." She tried to think of something else to

say and forced herself to remember how he'd chased off after Susie. That brought her back out of daydreams in a hurry. "It probably would be best for us to go over the plans for the counters and shelves together before"—she was running out of breath in spite of herself, and that wouldn't do— "before we make a final decision. You might have some suggestions."

For an instant she thought he'd say something else in that warm, teasing manner, but instead he took a step back. "Sounds like a gut idea. Let's do that soon." He was still too close for comfort, but she managed to nod in agreement.

Before she could say anything, the barn door rattled and Paul appeared, eyeing them curiously.

"What do you want?" Josiah almost snapped.

Paul's lips twitched as if he suppressed a grin. "Mammi says the tea is ready and she's cutting the coffee cake so come fast before we eat it all."

Leah walked toward him, hoping she looked casual. What had Paul seen when he walked in on them? Paul was the youngest, only fifteen, and he'd grown what seemed ten or twelve inches in the past year. He was all long legs and arms that stuck out of his jacket sleeves. And he still had that irrepressible twinkle in his blue eyes.

"Lead me to the coffee cake," she said, linking her arm with Paul's and trying to eliminate any trace of emotion from her voice. And her thoughts, for that matter.

IF PAUL TRIED ANY OF HIS UNFUNNY JOKES ON LEAH, Josiah decided he'd teach his young brother a lesson he wouldn't soon forget. And whatever Paul thought he saw between him and Leah, it wasn't any of his business.

Josiah followed Paul and Leah across the yard to the back door, noticing that Leah was talking to Paul with a lot more ease than she had talked to him. Paul's face flushed so easily, the redness rushing under his pale skin. He had all the young teenage male's awkwardness where an older woman was concerned.

Older woman—that sounded ridiculous applied to Leah, who so often seemed the skinny kid with long braids from his childhood. Maybe he ought to remember that she was grown and not give in to the temptation of teasing her. The thing was, lighthearted teasing had always been part of their relationship, and he wanted to get back to normal with Leah.

When they reached the kitchen, Mamm began raving about the tea and the jam Leah had brought over. "Just smell that." She waved the teapot under their noses before swirling it and starting to pour.

"I'll just take the blackberry jam," Paul said, snatching it as Benjamin reached for it.

"You can't have it all," Benjamin complained, sounding as if he were six again instead of twenty.

Mamm swooped in, taking the blackberry jam into her own control. "If you boys want blackberry jam so much, where were you when I was trying to get someone to go pick blackberries last summer? I can't make the jam without the berries."

Josiah heard Leah's soft chuckle and grinned at her. "Mamm knows how to handle them, all right."

Leah nodded and then turned as Mammi asked a question about her time working with her aunt. Josiah found himself studying her profile as she replied. In the past year she had changed. There were shadows under her eyes that he'd never seen before, and as she talked about working with her aunt, her increasing tension seemed obvious.

To him, maybe, but not to his mother, as far as he could tell. She was reminiscing about how much Leah had wanted to be like Aunt Miriam.

"You started your first herb garden when she was here for a visit. I still have the oregano plants you gave me all those summers ago."

"Yah, once oregano gets a good start, it keeps coming back. It's the tender plants that give you all the trouble. I have some basil in that sunny corner of the sewing room that I'm trying to nurse through the winter."

When she spoke about the plants, her usual enthusiasm filled Leah's face. It was just mention of her aunt that brought the tension. What had happened between them to spoil the closeness they'd always enjoyed?

"You'll be excited to have your greenhouse, yah?" Mammi went on. "Too bad you have to wait on the weather. But Josiah says you're going to have herbal crafts for sale, so you don't have to wait to work on those."

Leah glanced at him as if wondering how much he'd talked about her. Or why. "Yah, I'll be working on those all winter. Expect to get an herbal pillow from me for Christmas," she added, smiling.

"What's an herbal pillow?" Benjamin looked doubtful. "I've heard of goose feathers and down, but why herbs?"

"So you'll smell nice," Paul retorted, and Benjamin flicked tea at him from his spoon.

"Stop that, you two," Mammi said automatically.

"Tradition says putting a little herbal sachet under your pillow helps your sleep. Rosemary to keep nightmares away, mugwort to help you remember your dreams—"

"I don't want to remember mine," Benjamin said, grimacing.

"Then you need extra rosemary," Leah said. "Or maybe some wood betony. I'll make you one with a mixture of both."

"Denke," Benjamin muttered, flushing a little and making Josiah wonder what on earth he'd been having nightmares about. Benjy had always had them, waking up anyone sharing a room with him by shouting and flailing his arms around.

Mammi seemed intrigued with the idea of herbal pillows. "My grossmammi used to have one under her pillow.

A little cloth bag that she'd crinkle to make the scent come out."

The scent was one thing, but when they started talking about different ways to make the pillows, Josiah had to speak. "You don't really believe that, do you? About smelling the herbs helping you to have restful sleep? Isn't that an old wives' tale?"

"It so happens old wives know a lot that you don't," Mammi retorted. Her head came up, and her expression changed. "Something's burning." She dove for the range, where a pot of soup bones had been simmering. No doubt that was where the scent of burning was coming from.

He moved to help, but he had just begun to shove his chair back when Mammi snatched off the lid. Something popped loudly and flew into the air, narrowly missing Mamm's head. It hit the wall and fell to the floor. A grinning clown's face looked up at them, and an acrid stench filled the air.

With one accord, all of them turned to look straight at Paul.

He turned scarlet. "I didn't—I mean, yah, I set it up, but I didn't know it would burn the pot or make such a stink. Honest, Mammi."

"Of all the stupid things . . ." Josiah glared across the table at him. "Will you for once think about what you're doing? Grow up, will you?"

He'd been as startled as all of them. That didn't matter, but Mammi could have been hit in the face by that thing. What if it had been blazing instead of smoldering? Even now the edges were turning black and curling. And why Paul had to do it in front of Leah he didn't know.

"I'm sorry, Mammi. I didn't think—"

"You didn't think is right!" Josiah snapped.

Mammi brushed the clown face away. "Paul, apologize to everyone. And then take this pot out and scrub it until there's not a spot of burning. Not there!" she barked when he headed for the sink. "Outside."

Red in the face, Paul muttered apologies, especially to Leah as a guest in the house. Josiah saw Leah's lips twitch, but she received his apology gravely.

"Wait a minute," Mamm said as he reached the door. "Where are my soup bones?"

"In the oven." Paul's voice squeaked, and he darted out, the door slamming behind him.

Just in time, because Leah couldn't control her giggles. They erupted from her, bubbling over as she put her hand over her mouth in a futile effort to stop.

After one glance at her face, Mammi started to laugh as well. Josiah caught the contagion and even normally serious Benjamin managed to smile.

"That boy." Mammi shook her head, wiping away tears of mirth.

"That's all very well," Josiah said, trying to control his own laughter. "But we shouldn't laugh at him. It's time he outgrew this foolishness."

"At fifteen?" Leah shook her head. "I seem to remember a few tricks you played, like putting Joe Fisher's buggy on the roof of the farmhouse the night before his wedding. You were considerably older then."

"That was different," he protested, but his mother just shook her head.

"Ach, well, forget about it," Mammi said. "Leah, will you have a fresh cup of tea?"

Still smiling, Leah rose. "I'd love it, but I really need to get going. Mamm has things in mind for me today."

"Yah, I'm sure, with Christmas right around the corner. Your mammi ought to lend me a daughter to help with the baking." She was smiling, but they all knew Mammi would love to have had a daughter. There'd been no more babies after Paul.

Given how Paul was turning out, maybe that was just as well. Who knew what tricks he'd want to play on a younger sister or brother.

He trailed Leah to the door, but once they were clear of the house he stopped, and Leah stopped with him.

"Denke," she said. "I'm glad you're going to do the work."

"Me, too." His hand brushed hers. "You see what I mean about Paul's jokes? They always backfire."

That made her smile again. "They're even funnier that way. Are you sure you're not jealous?"

"Not of that." For a long moment they stood, their gazes entwined. Then Leah murmured something he couldn't hear and walked quickly away.

BY THE NEXT DAY, LEAH HAD TAKEN SO MUCH INPUT from her family about the design of her shop that she was thoroughly confused. She'd decided the best thing to do was to consult with Josiah on the spot, finalize the plans as much as possible, and then stop her ears to all the alternative ideas.

When she reached the cottage, she found Josiah already there, unloading some planks and a kerosene heater from a wagon while the horse looked on.

"Can I carry something?" She patted the gelding's neck, and he blew lightly into her hair.

"I think I've got it all." Josiah hefted the heater to carry it inside. "The boards for the back stoop are already cut, so I'll just stack them out here until I get started. I figured it was simpler to do whatever I could in the workshop."

"That sounds as if you have your plans all made." She held the door as he carried the heater inside and followed him. "I wish I was that far along. Whenever I think my plans are complete, someone suggests something else."

His lips quirked. "You know what they say. 'Too many cooks spoil the broth.'"

"Definitely." She set everything down on the old wooden table in the back room. "I thought maybe the two of us could look at the plans and make a final decision. That way I can tell everyone it's too late for changes."

"Right. Blame me," he said, his eyes twinkling.

She flipped open the pad that contained all of her scribbled notes as well as a sketch of each room. Opening it to the plan of the back room, she smoothed it out. "How does this compare to what you were thinking for this room?"

Josiah spread his sheet of paper open beside it. His was much more professional, she had to admit. Done in pencil on graph paper, it showed the sizes of each table, counter, shelf, and cabinet.

"Now I'm embarrassed about mine." She put her palm over the page. "How did you learn to do all this?"

"Did you think we built a wing to a house or a chicken coop without any measurements?" He was laughing at her, but it was friendly laughter, the kind they used to share. He pushed her hand off her sketch. "Let's see what we've got."

Josiah bent over the table, leaning on his hands, nodding as he assessed her scribbles. He put his pencil down on one counter. "Take a look at that wall." He pointed from the plan to the wall between the back and front. "I'd suggest you might want to put a counter here instead of a wall of shelves."

"Why?" Her forehead wrinkled. Did Josiah think he knew better what she needed than she did herself?

He seemed to read her thoughts. "You should suit yourself, that's for sure. But if you're potting plants in here and then taking them into the other room for display, you might want sort of a staging area next to the door. Someplace to park things when you're carting them back and forth. You could always have some extra shelves underneath if needed."

"I don't think . . ." She stopped. What Josiah said made a lot of sense, so why was she automatically rejecting it?

"Like I said, suit yourself. Doesn't matter to me." He didn't look offended, but his face had tightened at her refusal.

"No, wait. That a good idea." She suddenly realized what she'd been doing, and she shook her head. "I was copying what my aunt had, but there's no point in that when the cottage is laid out differently."

Josiah turned to face her, propping his hands on the table as he studied her. "She was the expert, I guess. You always said so. But this is your place, not hers. You should have it the way *you* want it to work."

What was he seeing when he looked at her? Was she giving away the mixed feelings about her aunt that had replaced her childhood admiration?

"Yah, I should." Leah said the words firmly. "If I make a mistake, at least it'll be my mistake. Like you said, this is my place."

"Good for you." He turned back to the plan, probably not seeing the relief she felt at his words. If was freeing to think that the business was hers.

"Funny." She spoke almost to herself. "If I'd taken over Aunt Miriam's nursery, the way I'd thought I might, I wouldn't have dared to change anything."

He chuckled. "She sounds like Daad. It's his way or nothing."

It was her turn to study his face. He'd said it lightly, but his eyes had darkened a little, despite his laugh. "Is he giving you trouble about how to run the business?"

Josiah shrugged. "As far as Daad's concerned, I'm just a hired hand. He doesn't ask my advice."

There was a thread of bitterness in the words, and she didn't know how to respond. Before she could think of the right thing to say, they'd both heard the sound of a car pulling off the road in front of the cottage.

"You expecting company?" Josiah walked through to where the front windows gave a view of a shiny black van parked on the verge of the road.

She shook her head. "Maybe they're lost." She moved to the door and opened it as footsteps sounded on the front porch.

"Hello there. You'd be Ms. Stoltz, I guess. I'm Bart Lester. You might know my name."

The man moved forward, as if sure of his welcome, and said the words with an easy confidence that made Leah feel inept for not knowing him.

She scoured her memory. Probably in his forties, he had a square, tanned face and wore a baseball cap and jeans like most of the Englischers in the area. Other than that, there was nothing familiar about him.

"Yah, I'm Leah Stoltz, but I'm afraid I don't know you." A little flustered, she stepped back, glad Josiah was there with her.

"There, that'll teach me to go around thinking I'm some-body." His cheerful grin seemed to show that he didn't take offense. "Well, Ms. Stoltz, from what I've heard around town, you're the owner of this little piece of property, and I want to talk business with you."

"I . . . I'm sorry, I don't understand. What kind of business?"

"Well, it's this way. I've been keeping my eye open for a small parcel of land somewhere along this road for a new drive-in restaurant. Bart's Drive-Ins, that's who I am. Seems like this spot might be about what I need. I can't be sure, of course. I'd need to see the exact measurements, make sure it would pass all those new regulations they have about land use in the township, that sort of thing."

He didn't seem to expect an answer to any of that, as he walked around the room, peered out the windows, and even took a look through the door into the back room.

"Look, Mr. Lester . . ."

"Call me Bart." He turned that hundred-watt smile on her again. "We just might be able to do a deal that would be good for both of us. I'd have to knock down this place first, of course. Make room for one of my drive-ins, put parking lots in front and in back . . ."

His mention of drive-ins finally permeated. She'd seen the bright red-and-yellow drive-in out by the highway, and there was another over toward Wilford. But it didn't matter, because she wasn't going to sell the land. More to the point, Daad wasn't, and it really belonged to him.

"Mr. Lester," she said again, louder than she intended. "Are you saying you're interested in buying this property?"

"Yes, that's what I'm talking about. Make you a good offer for it, too. It's important in my business to get the right location, and this is a good possibility, close to town, with plenty of space for parking—"

"It's not for sale." The only way to deal with the man seemed to be to talk over him. "If someone told you it's for sale, they were mistaken."

"Now, we haven't even started talking price yet. You never know what you might do when there's money involved. How about letting my surveyors do some measuring . . ."

She shook her head and went on shaking it. "I'm not interested," she said. "You're wasting your time."

"Time's never wasted when it comes to getting what I want. That's what I always say. You just let me sit down and work up some figures, and then we'll . . ."

"No." What was it going to take to make him stop talking and go away?

"No? Now don't be hasty. I wouldn't cheat you, not me. Anyone'll tell you that I'm an honest businessman."

"I'm still not interested." She sent a pleading glance toward Josiah. Maybe he could help her convince the man.

"Sorry you've had the trip out here for nothing." Josiah held the door open. "We've got work to do, and we'll have to ask you to leave now."

Annoyingly, Lester took it seriously when it came from Josiah, she thought, and then scolded herself. What did it matter as long as he left?

Lester reached the door and then stuffed a card into Josiah's hand. "You call me if you have any questions. And I'll be seeing you again, Ms. Stoltz. Don't you worry about that."

She wanted to tell him not to bother, that the property wasn't and wouldn't be up for sale, but she was afraid if she said anything he'd start talking again. She just shook her head, and Josiah ushered him out, closing the door firmly.

"Goodness." She let out a breath of relief. "What brought that on? Why would he think this property was up for sale? Daad just bought it a couple of months ago."

"Well, one good thing," Josiah said, watching through the window as the van pulled out. "You know this is a good site for a business if he wants it."

"I already knew that." She shivered and rubbed her arms. "I didn't like it."

Josiah moved closer, focusing on her face. "Why? He can't make you sell if you don't want to. Forget it." Apparently not liking what he saw in her face, he took her arm and steered her back toward the plans.

She moved with him, trying to calm her jangled thoughts. Josiah's grasp was firm and his hand warm. It seemed to carry assurance, making her able to dismiss the man from her mind. Of course Josiah was right.

She wasn't going to start relying on him. But she was glad he happened to be here today.

CHAPTER FOUR

❧❧❧

AFTER A FEW MOMENTS DISCUSSING THE PLANS, Leah found that the butterflies in her stomach had decided to take a nap. She stared at the plans absently, still trying to make sense of her unexpected visitor. His visit had been odd, and even odder to her mind was that he hadn't given any explanation of why he believed the property was for sale.

"Was ist letz?" Josiah asked her what was wrong without looking up. She guessed that was a testimony to how well they knew each other. He knew when she was troubled, even if she didn't speak.

"Nothing's wrong, exactly, but I'm still wondering how that man even knew the cottage was here. He isn't from Promise Glen, or we'd know him."

She stated the simple fact. When you'd spent your life in the same small area where your parents and grandparents and even great-grandparents had lived, if someone new came along, you were aware of it.

Josiah stopped frowning at the plans and turned to her,

his long frame balanced against the rickety table. "He's not exactly a stranger. I've heard of him. He's got a chain of those drive-in restaurants across central Pennsylvania." He shrugged. "I'd guess he's been thinking about starting one near Promise Glen."

"Maybe, but why would he stop *here*? Daad owns the place, even if he did say he was giving it to me. If Lester wants to buy, he'd have to make a deal with Daad."

"He would, but what are you worrying about? Your father isn't going to sell it out from under you after promising it to you."

The words might have been arrows, aimed right at her heart. "It's happened before," she muttered, and then wished she hadn't.

Josiah's face cleared. "You're talking about your aunt's place. Is that what she did?" His voice was filled with disbelief.

She shrugged, not meeting his eyes. "Something like that. We didn't have any formal agreement, after all."

"You wouldn't expect one, dealing with someone right in the family. She must have given you reason for believing it. You're not one to imagine things. What got into your aunt?"

Leah winced away from that question. She wouldn't talk about what caused the change in her aunt's attitude, not to her own parents, and certain sure not to Josiah. She wanted to close the door on it and never think of it again.

Too bad that wasn't working.

"It was her business, built up by her own hard work." It took a huge effort for her to sound casual and convincing. "She changed her mind, that's all."

He seemed to study her face for a long moment. "It's for the best, anyway. You didn't want to move that far from home, ain't so?" She could hear the strain in his voice at his attempt to sound reassuring, and she also knew that it didn't convince either of them.

"I went up there to learn how to run a nursery business," she said firmly. "I learned. So it was time to come home again. That's all."

Now if only Josiah would let the subject alone . . .

He'd turned back to the plans, but then he tossed his pencil on the table. It promptly rolled to the far corner and fell off.

Leah couldn't restrain a watery chuckle. "I think this whole place has a mind of its own."

"It won't when I get through with it," he said firmly, making her smile grow.

"It *would* be nice if my plants didn't fall off the display racks."

He grinned. "I promise they won't. Satisfied now?"

She nodded, relieved that he'd apparently decided to leave the subject of her aunt alone.

Josiah's next words showed her how wrong she was. "I remember how excited you always were when your aunt was coming for a visit. You wouldn't do a thing with the rest of us when she was here. You were too busy following her around. And when I did see you, you just repeated everything she'd told you."

"I was learning," she protested. "Just like you, working with your daad."

"I was never as obsessed about it as you were. You had a bad case of hero worship."

"You sound jealous," she teased.

"Do not," he said promptly, with the comeback so automatic in their childhood.

"Do, too," she said, starting to laugh. In another minute they were both laughing so hard they leaned against the table, which groaned ominously.

Josiah straightened. "It's not my business what went on between you and your aunt, I guess. But I'll go on thinking she was unfair." He gathered up the plans. "Now I'll get some work done on the back stoop. You want to give me a hand?"

That was a peace offering, she thought. She wouldn't have believed it, but it seemed Josiah didn't like the breach between them, either.

Then why had he rushed off to flirt with Susie Lehman when he was supposed to be courting her? That still rankled.

Brushing away the thought, she followed him out to the back stoop. It was her place he was working on.

After half an hour of helping to move boards and hold them in place while Josiah secured them, her cheeks were rosy and her worries, such as they'd been, had vanished. Whatever happened in the past, this was now, and she was headed for a satisfying life with family and friends who believed in her and work that she enjoyed.

She stopped to rub cold fingers, and Josiah grinned. "Not used to working out in the cold, yah?"

"You have gloves on," she protested. "That makes a difference."

"You had a pair of mittens on when you came, ain't so?" As he spoke, he straightened and pulled off his work gloves.

"Not ones that I wanted to snag on rough boards. I'll have to get some work gloves if I'm going to be the carpenter's apprentice."

He took her hands as if measuring them against his. "I might have an old pair that would work." He glanced at her, and the teasing left his eyes as he pressed her hands between his. "I'm sorry, Leah. Whatever happened with your aunt, I'm on your side. Always."

Leah didn't want him to see how much his simple statement of faith meant to her, so she stared down at their clasped hands, remembering other moments. She pushed back the warmth that flowed through her.

Forget those months of courting, she reminded herself.
Just focus on the years of friendship.

IT WASN'T UNTIL LATER IN THE AFTERNOON THAT
Josiah had time to start work on the shelves for Leah's cottage. He'd decided the best option was to build them piece
by piece in Daad's workshop and then assemble them on
site, and he was glad to have some time alone. Paul had
been in one of his sillier moods at lunch, teasing Benjamin
until he thought even calm, quiet Benjamin would lose his
temper.

Josiah had caught his father watching Paul, and he'd been
able to read Daad's expression easily. *When is that boy going
to grow up?* He should be able to . . . he'd seen that look di-
rected at himself too often to misinterpret it.

Daad had finally sent the boys off to do some chores,
and Mammi had disappeared into her sewing room, probably to work on Christmas gifts. Despite the fact that she'd
been working on things for months, she would still keep at
it until late on Christmas Eve. It wouldn't be Christmas
without Mammi sneaking off to her sewing room every
time she could.

He'd been working alone for some time before he heard
the door creak open and felt a short burst of cold air before
it closed. Daad came in and stood for a moment, watching him.

Josiah straightened. "Am I in your way?"

Daad shook his head. "I have some work to do on your
mother's Christmas present, but I'll use the other end of the
bench."

Watching, Josiah saw him lift a canvas-covered bundle
from a cabinet and set it on the bench. The canvas slipped
off to reveal a walnut plate rack, the back formed of carefully shaped pieces to set off the special plates that had
belonged to Great-Grossmammi.

"She's going to love it." The admiration in his voice was the real thing. Josiah had wondered sometimes if Daad still had the fine control needed for the detail work, but here was proof that he did.

"Yah." Daad didn't say anything else, but he didn't need to. His love was clear in every inch of the piece.

They worked in silence for a time, and Josiah let his mind stray to that odd incident earlier with the drive-in owner. He'd played it down to Leah, but it had been strange. The cottage and the plot of land had never even been advertised . . . Leah's daad had snatched it up the instant the previous owner decided to sell. So what brought Lester there? He surely didn't go driving around making offers on any random piece of property.

He glanced at his father. "Have you ever heard tell of a guy named Bart Lester? Owns a chain of drive-in restaurants?"

Daad frowned slightly. "Lester. Yah, I've heard something about him. He set up one of his restaurants over near Millerton, but he didn't give any of the local builders a chance at it. He brought in an outfit all the way from Harrisburg."

"That couldn't have made him popular with the local people."

"Not with folks in the business, that's for sure. And that sort of thing makes people annoyed even if they don't have a stake in it. You know what I mean."

Josiah knew quite well. Old-timers in Promise Glen, Amish or Englisch, stuck together.

"If you're an incomer, you have to prove yourself. And he's not even that—sounds like he just wants to make money off us."

"Yah." Daad showed all the characteristics of someone whose ancestors had been here for four generations. "Sid Fuller told me that when I was talking to him at the Millerton Fair."

Sid was an old competitor of Daad's but a friend as well. They'd often given a hand with each other's projects if someone was running late or they'd lost a few workers.

And Sid was a talker. "What else did he have to say about Lester?"

Daad grimaced. "According to Sid, he never pays the going rate for land. Seems he has the reputation of finding people he thinks he can push into making a quick decision. Sid wouldn't deal with him, he said." His father stopped smoothing the finish of the plate rack to focus on Josiah. "Why are you interested?"

"Lester stopped by the cottage today when I was there. He told Leah he heard the place was for sale, and he wanted to buy. She doesn't want to sell, and anyway, her daad owns the place, and he wouldn't want to sell. That drive-in would annoy him more than the deteriorating cottage. But Lester was really pushy. Fast and loud."

Fast and loud was the opposite of the way the Amish spoke, and he, like his father, equated it with someone who wanted to sell you something you didn't want. Or in this case, wanted to buy something you didn't want to sell.

"She said no, didn't she?"

"Yah. Several times. Leah didn't like the way he kept pushing."

Daad nodded in agreement. "I wouldn't, either. Who wants a place like that right next door?"

"Anybody who likes soft ice cream." Paul stood in the doorway. He must have caught the last thing Daad said.

"If you want ice cream, you can get out the ice cream maker," Daad said. "You do enough running around as it is. We don't need a place for teenagers to gather right next to us."

"Leah won't sell," Josiah said soothingly. "Don't worry."

"You know all about it, ain't so?" Paul came over to hold the end piece Josiah was attaching. "You're spending a lot of time with Leah."

"I'm doing some work for her." Josiah tried not to sound annoyed at his brother's interest. Knowing Paul, showing annoyance would just encourage him to tease.

"That's a good thing," Daad said. "You tell Leah that any of us would be glad to help. Especially Paul. Seems like he doesn't have enough to do."

Paul grimaced. "I'm working. See? I'm giving Josiah a hand. 'Course he'd probably rather it was Leah helping him."

He shouldn't overreact, Josiah told himself firmly, and he bent over the work so that Paul couldn't see his face.

"Maybe so. At least Leah doesn't talk as much nonsense as you do."

"Yah, and she's sweeter, ain't so?" It didn't take much to hear the laughter in Paul's voice.

"Enough." Daad's voice was sharp. "Go and help your brother with mending that stall door in the barn. You're not doing much here." When Paul didn't move immediately, Daad gave him a look that sent him speedily out the door.

"Denke." Josiah hesitated, not sure what he wanted to say. "I don't mind his teasing, but if Leah heard him, it might hurt her feelings."

Daad looked at him steadily. "You owe it to Leah to spare her feelings, that's certain sure."

"I didn't . . ." Protesting didn't do any good. "There wasn't anything serious between us, Daad. I'm sure she knows it as well as I do."

Daad made a sound that expressed without words his doubts and turned back to the plate rack.

It would take time, he guessed, for people to stop watching him and Leah for signs of either romance or ill feeling. Well, tomorrow was Worship Sunday, and if he had his way, he and Leah would demonstrate to the entire Leit that they could stop wondering. He and Leah were back to being friends again. Weren't they?

* * *

LEAH GLANCED AROUND THE CROWDED ROOM WHERE people were finishing lunch after worship the next day. She carried a tray laden with desserts for her parents and Grossmammi, and she sure didn't want to drop anything down someone's neck or crack a head with her tray.

Lifting it higher, she started edging around the tables and benches, watchful to be sure the way was clear. She was nearly there when someone right ahead of her shoved back his chair to rise, and she found herself inches away from Josiah.

Don't react, she ordered herself. Not with everyone watching. She assumed a friendly smile and slid past him, her back against the wall to keep from touching.

"Need some help?" Just friendly and polite, he seemed better able to do this than she was.

"No, denke. I have it."

His breath brushed her cheek as he moved by, and then he was gone. Relieved, she paused, ostensibly to adjust the tray while she pushed Josiah out of her mind and shut the door on him.

It should be easy. She'd been doing it for over a year. But push as she did, there was always something that slipped back—the way his eyes laughed as he teased her, the black look of his rare anger. It would stop hurting eventually, but it seemed to be taking a long time.

Leah took the desserts to where her mother and Grossmammi were sitting.

"Ach, Leah, you didn't need to bring this much," Grossmammi said, surveying the array of cake on the tray. "I don't eat like I used to."

That was true. Leah had seen it quickly enough on her return, and when she put her hands on Grossmammi's shoulders, they felt so frail it seemed a breeze would blow her grandmother away.

She patted Grossmammi's shoulder lightly. "I wanted you to have a choice," she said, and glared at Judith, who was already reaching for a piece with peanut butter frosting. Judith withdrew her hand quickly, and Grossmammi chose a devil's food piece with inch-high fluffy white frosting.

Smiling, Leah unloaded the tray to the middle of the table and then used it to start cleaning up. She wasn't on the cleanup crew today, but it made a good reason to keep busy, and the hosts always appreciated an extra hand.

An hour later people had started to drift away, and some of the boys were setting up for the singing that night. Leah stood on the back porch, out of the way, enjoying the chill air after the noise and busyness inside. Before she could get too relaxed, the door opened, letting out several members of the Miller family, who passed with a cheerful goodbye.

Behind them Josiah moved toward her, and she stiffened. "Wouldn't it be best not to have any little talks here if we want people to stop wondering about us?" she said, before he could speak.

He made a business of leaning on the railing and looking out at the line of buggies. "Is it possible to stop people from wondering? I'm beginning to doubt it."

She turned as if to leave, but he shook his head. "You're more jittery than I am. Listen, I'm trying to tell you something."

Leah looked up at the gravity in his voice. "What?"

"I ran into Becky in the hallway. She was on the verge of crying and trying to keep anyone from seeing her. So I pushed her into the pantry, shut the door, and said I'd get you."

"Denke," she muttered, her mind whirling. She'd been right . . . something was going on with Becky.

She headed inside with Josiah a few steps behind her.

"I'll try to keep anyone from opening the door," he said. "Don't tax my ingenuity too far, though. I can't come up with much of a reason."

Nodding, she wove her way through the kitchen, aware that Josiah had grabbed his brother Benjamin and was tugging him along. Maybe she was about to find out what was really going on with Becky.

She scurried into the pantry and closed the door behind her, hoping Josiah could think of several good reasons not to let anyone in.

Becky stood in the corner of the small room, her face to the shelves, clearly trying to look occupied. Leah crossed to her and put her hands gently on her sister's shoulders.

"Komm now. It's just me. Tell me what's wrong."

Becky looked down, seeming to study the jars of tomatoes on the bottom shelf. "Nothing. N-nothing. I just wanted to be by myself."

Leah turned her around so she could see her sister's face. *Woebegone*—that was the word that came to mind. Becky tried to smile, but her face crumpled instead, and she leaned against Leah, hugging her tightly. She sniffled, her face pressed into Leah's shoulder.

"I can see that," Leah said lightly. "You always hide in the pantry at worship and cry all over my shawl."

"I'm sorry. I'm all right, really. I just . . ."

She hesitated when outside the door, Josiah could be heard talking to Benjamin about repairs to the barn. The door creaked, and Leah could picture Josiah leaning against it.

"They'll delay anyone who tries to come in," Leah assured her.

Becky nodded, wiping her eyes with her fingers. "I guess I don't feel too good today."

"Try again," Leah said, keeping her voice soft. There was no need for Josiah and his brother to hear this.

"It was just something the bishop said." Becky seemed to be gaining control. "You know how sometimes a hymn or a scripture makes you want to cry."

Leah had hoped Becky's problem was more about a boy she liked who was talking to some other girl and not her.

Leah could speak to that. But if Becky was upset about her faith, Leah's instant reaction was that she wasn't wise enough.

But she was here. Right now, being here was probably more important than being wise. Leah patted her sister's cheek, still as soft as a baby's, and tried to look as wise as Grossmammi.

"Yah?" She waited, hoping for more.

"He said about how we had to obey the spirit as well as the letter of the law, the way Mary did when the angel came to her . . . willing to do whatever she was supposed to, no matter what it brought. And I thought about how young she was . . . maybe about as old as me."

Mary . . . the Annunciation, that was what she meant. Panic gripped her, and just as suddenly disappeared when she looked at her sister's innocent young face. She clearly didn't even guess at the fear Leah had leaped to.

She framed a question carefully. "Do you feel as if there's something God wants you to do?"

Becky looked at her blankly.

"Or something God doesn't want you to do?" That got a response. Becky sniffled again. Her head drooped as she studied the floor.

Leah felt out of her depth, and it was probably only minutes before Mamm was looking for them. She took a breath and plunged in.

"You know, when I was little, I thought it was very easy to know what our faith asked of us. We all knew the rules. But when I got older, I saw that it wasn't so easy. Sometimes when I tried to follow one requirement, I ended up breaking another."

Becky nodded. "Yah. Me, too. I . . . I don't know what to do."

There was a soft tap on the door, and Josiah's raised voice. "Hello there, Doris Ann. Looks like you're in charge of putting things away today. Those go in the pantry, yah?"

Doris Ann, about ten and as shy as a mouse, didn't make a sound, but she must have nodded, because Josiah went on.

"You've been really helping your mamm with the meal today, and here we haven't done much at all. Why don't you let Benjamin put those away for you? He'll be careful, I promise. Won't you, Benj?"

There was an embarrassed mutter of agreement from his brother, and Leah heard the clatter of dishes.

"I'll get the door for Ben. You go tell your mother that you're all finished. Maybe she'll let you quit, ain't so?"

There was a giggle from Doris Ann, and the sound of footsteps leaving as the door opened. Ben sidled in, carrying a stack of serving bowls. His cheeks were red, and he carefully didn't so much as glance in their direction.

Suppressing a smile, Leah took the bowls and slid them onto what looked like the right shelf. "Denke, Ben." A quick look at her sister told her that Becky looked all right except for being a little pink around the eyes.

The door opened a bit wider. "The coast is clear," Josiah said. Benjamin hurried out, and Becky was right behind him.

Leah caught her before she reached the door. "You don't have to talk to me, but you should talk to someone about what's worrying you . . . Mammi or Daadi or Grossmammi."

Becky pressed her lips together, then gave a half-hearted nod and fled. Leah went more slowly, but still found Josiah waiting for her, his brown eyes carrying that twinkle she remembered.

"Denke," she muttered, brushing past him but unable to stop from meeting his gaze when he clasped her wrist.

"Reminds you of how difficult it all was when we were that age, ain't so?"

She didn't answer, because there were too many memories dancing in her thoughts. Josiah didn't seem to mind. His lips quirked, he squeezed her wrist warmly, and then he let it go.

"See you tomorrow."

She nodded, hurrying off after her sister.

Great, now she had even more memories to shut out. To say nothing of a host of worries about her little sister. Life kept getting more and more complicated.

CHAPTER FIVE

ON MONDAY MORNING, LEAH GOT UP DETERMINED to find some way of unraveling the mystery of her sister's tears after church. She'd hoped Becky would confide in her, but Becky clung tight to her secret. Still, Mamm was counting on her. The eldest sister in a big family was expected to be a kind of second mother to the young ones.

Something in the worship service had triggered Becky's tears, and Leah had spent half the night thinking through the two sermons without a clue. The story of the Annunciation and the telling of Mary's visit to her cousin had been the subjects—they were common scripture passages for the weeks before Christmas, focusing thoughts on preparing your heart for Christmas.

Leah carried a box into Mamm's sewing room. That room was especially busy in December, as family members worked on gifts for each other, usually accompanied by shrieks as they tried to hide their projects when anyone came in.

She had to smile, remembering some of the gifts she'd made for Mammi and Daadi over the years. And Grossmammi still displayed the calendar Leah had made the year she was ten, despite the fact that it was years out of date.

Lifting a roll of butcher paper from the box, she rolled it out on the table. Just the sight of someone working in here should be enough to draw her siblings in. She'd checked Mamm's calendar of everyone's commitments for the week. Any mother of six kinder had to be organized, and Mammi kept track of everyone and everything. Becky didn't have to be at work until eleven.

Leah expected one of her sisters to appear, but Grossmammi was the first to follow her in. "Ach, Leah, you're staring at that paper as if you expect it to talk back to you."

Leah was surprised into a laugh. "Not that, Grossmammi. Just wondering how much gift wrapping paper we'll need this Christmas."

Grossmammi was using her cane this morning, which meant that her joints were bad. Leah hurried to bring over the padded bentwood rocking chair that was her grandmother's favorite and helped to ease her into it. Grossmammi's bones felt as light as a bird's, but enthusiasm and spirit sparkled in her faded blue eyes.

"Christmas seems to come faster every year. But you wouldn't know about that yet." She glanced toward the open door. "Judith, Hannie," she called. "Help us make wrapping paper."

A thunder of feet answered her as the younger girls came downstairs at their usual gallop.

"And Becky will want to help, too," Leah reminded, but Grossmammi shook her head.

"She's gone to work."

"Already? But she'd not been on the schedule until eleven."

"Your daadi had to go in to the hardware store earlier,

and she decided to ride with him." Grossmammi peered at her, probably reading her expression easily. "You hoped to involve her, ain't so?"

She nodded. "I thought it would be a good chance to talk to her. She's still . . ." She let that trail away as the other girls made an appearance.

"She works until four." Grossmammi gave her typical brisk nod. "You can go and pick her up. You'll have all the way home, yah?"

Hannie's big blue eyes were fixed on her grandmother's face as she leaned against the rocker. "Way home for what?"

"For a quiet talk, you nosy little schnickelfritz." Grossmammi put her arm around Hannie, squeezing her.

But before she could pursue the point, Judith leaned across the table. "We can't do stamping, Leah. We used up all the red ink when we made a poster for Valentine's Day. Remember, Hannie?"

Hannie's little face fell. "I'm sorry, Leah. We didn't mean to do it."

"As a matter of fact, I noticed that, and I have a new box of all colors of ink pads." She set them on the table. "And some brand-new rubber erasers to make printing blocks."

"So we don't have to use the old one of the star with only four points." Judith snatched at an eraser, and Hannie did as well, resulting in three erasers flying across the room.

Leah put her hand firmly on the rest. "Go and find those before we start," she ordered. "This time we'll draw before we cut."

Stamping the plain paper with trees and bells and other signs of Christmas was a favorite activity of the young ones, and Leah still enjoyed it as much as they did. Despite the failure of her plan, Grossmammi was right. She could talk to Becky later, and this was fun to do with kinder.

Hannie, who was named for Hannah Burkhalter but

hadn't grown into the adult version of the name yet, put the found erasers on the table. She leaned heavily against Leah to watch her drawing a star on the flat surface of an eraser.

"Becky will be sad she missed it to go to work. She likes drawing and stamping."

Leah tapped her littlest sister on the tip of her pert nose. "We'll save some for her to do, all right?"

Hannie nodded. "Then maybe she won't cry anymore." The words were barely out before Hannie clapped her hand over her mouth, eyes widening.

"I told you! You were dreaming!" Judith's face was red as she glared at her little sister.

"I was not!" Hannie glared right back.

"Hush now." Grossmammi tapped on the floor with her cane. "When was Becky crying?"

Leah felt instantly guilty. She hadn't told anyone yet about what happened after worship yesterday. She intended to, but now wasn't the time. Anyway, that wasn't the point. Hannie couldn't have heard that. She must be talking about another time.

Hannie looked about ready to cry herself. "Last night. I woke up and I heard her through the wall. And I wasn't dreaming."

Grossmammi looked at Judith for an answer. She shrugged a little. "I guess it could have been that. But it wasn't our business." She glared at her little sister again.

Leah didn't feel capable of teaching her sisters about when it was or wasn't appropriate to tell. And Grossmammi was looking both sad and tired. That tiredness seemed to come on so much faster now than it once did.

"All right, stop fussing about it." Leah frowned at both of them, but she was more upset about her grandmother than she was angry at them. "It's up to Mammi and Daadi to take care of Becky. You two just try to be nice to each other."

They both nodded, intimidated by this new, take-charge

version of their sister. Still, this was not at all how she'd imagined the morning going.

"Let's get on with the paper, yah? We all like to make it. And after our noontime meal, we'll go out and cut some greens to put in the windows. But only if I don't have to listen to arguing," she added.

A flurry of activity followed her words. Hannie brought her eraser and one of the small sharp knives to Leah to get her help in cutting, and Judith settled down next to Grossmammi. With another glance at Grossmammi, Leah decided she should try to get her grandmother to take a little rest soon.

Grossmammi, Becky, now Judith and Hannie. Everyone had changed in one way or another since she'd been away. Her thoughts skittered to Josiah.

He hadn't changed. Or had he? She couldn't quite make up her mind.

JOSIAH STOOD ON THE BACK PORCH AFTER LUNCH, glancing around. The afternoon was warmer than this morning, but all the same, the sunlight slanting across the porch was weaker every day. Winter wasn't far off. Beyond the barn and the pasture, the ground swept up toward the woods, bare now of leaves but still thick with evergreens, and the air was brisk and chilly.

Across the field between the farms, he spotted activity. Leah came out of the house, and the two youngest girls spurted past her. They ran to the barn and reappeared a moment later with a wagon and what looked like pruning shears. The three of them started up toward the woods. It looked like Leah was taking her sisters to collect evergreen branches.

He'd thought, or maybe even hoped, that she'd turn up at the cottage sometime this morning, but she hadn't. He'd like to know what all the mystery had been about yesterday after worship.

Despite the fact that he'd helped, Leah had seemed determined to get away without saying anything about it. She'd been upset, he guessed, but maybe by now she'd be ready to talk. It was worth a walk over to find out, anyway.

By the time he reached the three of them, they were at the edge of a thick grove of spruce and white pine. Unaware of his approach, Leah was standing on her tiptoes, trying to pull down a branch of spruce, while Judith held the clippers at the ready and Hannie looked on.

Leah wasn't having much success, only able to touch it with her fingertips. "Maybe if I stood on the wagon—"

"That sounds dangerous," he said, and reached above her head to grab the branch and pull it down. "Greens to decorate the house?"

Leah let go of the branch in a hurry, gasping. "Ach, I didn't realize you were there." She smiled, her cheeks rosy from the chilly air . . . or maybe with embarrassment. "Yah, Mammi and Grossmammi always want candles and greens in the windows once Christmas is near."

"We're helping decorate," Hannie said, too small to reach the branch.

He pulled it closer to her. "Do you think this one will do?" He kept his voice serious, consulting her like the grown-up she wanted to be.

Hannie studied it closely and then nodded. "I like it. See how many little cones it has? They look just like the big ones. I think they're babies."

Josiah checked with Leah by way of a raised eyebrow. When she nodded, he turned to Judith.

"*Now* can I cut?" she asked with elaborate patience.

"Yah, now," Leah said. "But don't get the clippers close to Josiah's hand."

Judith looked ready to take offense at the caution, so he smiled at her.

"I need all my fingers," he said, winking.

Mollified and a little flushed, she poised the clippers. "There okay?"

He nodded, and she snapped them together. The branch fell at their feet.

Hannie clapped, bouncing a little. "It's so pretty. Can I help put it in the wagon?"

Judith nodded, and the two young ones seized the branch to pull it to the wagon.

"You know that spruce will fall off faster than the pine would." He grinned at Leah.

"You know it, and I know it, but Hannie really wants the 'baby cones,' so we'll let her have them."

"What'll she say when they fall off before Christmas? Let me guess. You'll replace them, and she won't notice a thing."

"Certainly not." She looked affronted. "That would be like lying to her."

Did she assume he'd lie to his siblings, just because of what he said? "Relax, Leah. I'm teasing."

"Sorry." She stared down at her feet, and it seemed to him that she took the whole exchange too seriously.

"You used to be able to tell when I was teasing." That was one change he didn't like.

"I said I was sorry." She turned away, reaching for another spruce branch. Then she hesitated, turning back slightly but still not looking at him. "I'm a little sensitive on that subject."

The young ones were struggling to find a way to fit the branch in the wagon and weren't looking their way. They might as well be alone here. Maybe this was his opportunity to ask.

"Is this about what happened yesterday with Becky?"

She studied his face as if she'd never seen it before, and

her eyes had turned nearly navy with some emotion. Finally her gaze fell. "Thanks for your help, but I don't really want to talk about it. Not with the kids here."

"Or not to me? Look, I won't pry into something you don't want to tell me. But we used to tell each other all kinds of things. I'd just like to get back to that friendship, that's all."

Leah stared at him, and he thought she was puzzled by something. But before he could ask, the others came running back.

"We'll need some more, won't we? Will you help us get the very best one, Josiah?" Hannie was jumping up and down with eagerness.

He glanced at Leah, and she nodded.

"I'll try, if you can tell me why we put branches and candles in the windows at Christmastime." He squatted next to her so she'd know he was serious and waiting for her to talk about it.

Hannie's forehead wrinkled as she thought, and for a moment she looked very much like Leah at that age. She looked at Judith, as if to ask for help, but Judith seemed to have withdrawn from them.

Why were teenage girls so changeable? And for that matter, it wasn't just girls. It was women, too.

"I know!" Hannie's face lit up. "It's to remember all the people who came to Jesus that night, like the shepherds and the angels and . . ."

"And maybe some of the people around, don't you think? If your mammi heard someone had had a baby in the barn, don't you think she'd go right away?"

Judith's attention seemed caught by that. "She'd go and take food, ain't so?"

"And blankets," Hannie chipped in.

"And diapers for the baby." Judith looked, for a moment, as if she were about Hannie's age and had forgotten about being a teenager.

Leah chuckled. "That's what Mammi would do, all right. And Grossmammi, too."

"Well, we'd best get back to work," Josiah said, reaching up to pull down another branch that was well provided with cones.

"Yah, yah. Pick me up so I can see it."

"Hannah!" Leah sounded horrified. "What would Mammi say if she heard you talking that way to a grown-up? Ask nicely if you want something."

"Please?" Hannie wheedled, looking up from under her eyelashes as if she'd been practicing ways of getting her way.

"Okay." He caught hold of her and swooped her up above his head. "What do you think? Judith? Is that one okay?"

"Looks okay." Judith stamped her feet. "Let's get it done, yah? Before my feet freeze." She lifted the clippers.

Josiah pulled the branch down so that Judith could reach with the clippers, and in a moment the two younger ones had dragged it to the wagon. He glanced at Leah.

"Will that be enough?"

"For now, maybe." She smiled. "I'll have to make a couple more trips when Mammi decides she wants more. Funny, how much I missed little things like this when I was away."

"I guess so." He hesitated. "I'm glad you're home, Leah."

She studied his face for a moment and seemed to come to a decision. "About Becky . . . we've noticed that she hasn't been herself for the last few days. Maybe longer." She shrugged. "At her age, that usually means a boy. So far, that's normal. But yesterday she got very emotional after worship. Well, you saw her. You know."

"Did you get any explanation out of her?"

"All she'd tell me was that something in the sermon made her want to cry. So I still don't know."

Josiah thought of Sunday's sermons and ran right into the

lesson about the Annunciation. A moment's thought told him how unlikely that was.

"Ach, Leah, I know what you're thinking." He caught her hand as they started to walk in the wake of the girls. "You know how foolish that is. Why, she's barely started on her rumspringa, and she doesn't go anywhere that family isn't around."

"Yah, I know that." She colored. "Silly of me. I'm making a mountain out of a molehill, right?"

"Right," he said firmly.

But as they walked back down the hill, he began to wish he hadn't been so intent on finding out what was going on. Some things he really didn't want to know.

LEAH WAS GLAD TO ESCAPE THE DECORATING PARTY when she finally left to pick up Becky. Not that she didn't enjoy decorating for Christmas, but Hannie and Judith made enough noise for ten. Hannie had tried to drag all the branches right into the middle of the kitchen, and Leah had to persuade her they should leave them on the porch until the dampness was off. By then, Judith was trying to remove the plant pots from the windowsills.

Mammi, calm as ever, took the plants away from Judith, sent the children back to remove their wet boots, and insisted that the windows and windowsills must be washed before decorating. At the sound of groans, she had a simple reply.

"We do this to celebrate the coming of Jesus. We can't greet Jesus with dirty windowsills, can we?"

Without a word, Judith went to get the bucket while Hannie searched for the white vinegar Mammi used as a window cleaner. Leah watched, standing by Grossmammi's rocking chair.

"Mammi gets results without raising her voice, ain't so? I had to yell before they listened to me."

"It will come to you." Grossmammi's eyes twinkled as she patted Leah's hand. "When you're a mammi yourself."

"I guess." Maybe it would be best to say *if* she was a mammi herself. The chances didn't seem very great at the moment.

For some reason her thoughts slid to Josiah, helping the girls cut the evergreens. He'd been remarkably patient with them, listening to Hannie and restraining Judith when she wanted to plunge ahead.

Kindness and patience were wonderful good qualities, but through her mind ran the old saying, *Once a flirt, always a flirt*. How could a woman ever be sure with a man like that?

The thoughts so occupied her that she was pulling up at the hitching post by Dinah's building before she knew it. Becky wasn't waiting, so she tied the mare and went inside.

Becky seemed to be busy with a customer at the cash register, but Dinah saw her and came to greet her.

"Come in, sit down a bit. Becky will be ready in about ten minutes, all right?"

Nodding, Leah followed her cousin to the table by the counter. By the time she sat down, Dinah was already pouring coffee. "You'll take some pastries home for your family, yah? I'll tell Becky to fill a box for you."

"Denke, but don't . . ."

Dinah had already leaned over to whisper something to Becky, who glanced at Leah and smiled, nodding.

After a word to someone in the kitchen, Dinah came to sit down with her. Leah grabbed the chance to alert her to their concerns.

"Has everything been all right with Becky? I . . . we thought she might find it hard to relate to all the Englisch you get in the shop."

Dinah seemed surprised. "I've been keeping an eye on Becky, like I always do with the young girls, and everything seems fine as far as I can tell. She's really doing very well . . . getting better all the time at taking orders and staying calm."

"Denke. I appreciate it." Maybe Becky's troubles didn't have anything to do with work, but she couldn't help remembering the man she'd seen here.

"Ach, it's what I always do when the girls start work."

"No issues with any . . . well, male customers?" she ventured to say.

"Not that I could see." She smiled. "The Amish boys don't hang around here, you know. If they're in town, they'll be at the hardware store or the harness shop."

If the problem was with one of the congregation, it wouldn't be here. But that still left some space for trouble. "What about any Englisch?"

"Not so far as I've noticed, and you can believe I keep an eye out for anything of that kind." Dinah sounded so militant for a moment that Leah had to smile at how unlike her it was.

"You've gotten very brave, ain't so?"

"Mostly because Jacob is right next door," she said, her eyes crinkling as she nodded toward her husband's harness shop in the other half of the building. Her face sobered. "It is a responsibility to hire the young girls for their first jobs. I'd hope Becky would tell me if she had trouble with a customer."

Leah nodded. "Maybe I'm making too much of it. I guess when we were that age, our emotions were all over the place, too."

"She was upset after worship yesterday, ain't so? I noticed."

"I'm sure half the church noticed," Leah muttered.

Dinah patted her shoulder as she rose. "It wasn't that bad. I just happened to be in the kitchen when she came through. Don't worry. I'll tell Becky she can go."

Not worrying was easy enough to say but not so easy to do. When she and Becky reached the buggy, Leah started automatically for the driver's side, but Becky stopped her with a gesture.

"Want me to drive home?"

Encouraged by the normalcy in her tone, Leah grinned. "Help yourself. After gathering greens with Judith and Hannah and helping them wash windows, I'm ready to relax."

Becky looked dismayed as she picked up the lines. "But I love to do that."

"Don't worry," she said quickly. "You didn't miss much. We ended up only getting a couple of windows done because I was watching the time. We'll make sure there's some for you."

"Gut. I'd like that."

They passed the front of the bank building, and a man who was just coming through the double doors paused and waved. Leah glanced at him, looked around, and then studied him more seriously. It was the same man she'd noticed before.

She looked at her sister, noting the flushed cheeks. "Who was the man that waved at you?"

"What man?" Becky rushed the words, and her cheeks grew a little redder.

"Komm, Becky. There was no one else he could have been waving at." She hesitated, searching for words. She didn't want to say the wrong thing and upset Becky, but she shouldn't miss an opportunity to help her little sister, either. "The man who was coming out of the bank."

Becky shrugged. "Just . . . just someone who comes into the coffee shop." She was quiet for a moment, but Leah sensed she wasn't finished. "He's a gut customer. Dinah wouldn't want to lose him."

"No, of course not." She considered it, hoping she understood why Becky had added those words. Was she wondering whether she should speak to Dinah about him?

Or afraid he might complain about her? It was hard to be sure.

Maybe it was a simple misunderstanding that had her worried. "When I first started working out among the Englisch, I found it hard to understand what they meant sometimes. I think they must talk and, well, joke different than we do."

Becky let out a sigh of relief. "Yah, that's it. He's always very nice to me, and he gives me a big tip. More than any of the ladies do. I just don't know what to say when he teases me."

"What kind of thing does he say?" Leah asked cautiously, hoping Becky would say a little more.

"Well, like he'd laugh about how he got lost trying to find a place, and then he'd say I probably never did and maybe I should show him how to find his way around."

Leah felt a sudden urge to grab the man by his striped tie and shake him. She suppressed the idea. He might mean nothing at all, and Becky was so eager to do well at her first job. "Did you think he was trying to get you to do that?"

"I'm not sure." Becky frowned, shaking her head. "Maybe he was just talking, or maybe he did. How could I tell?"

That was a good question. "Maybe it's best to say nothing, then. Just smile and maybe shake your head." A thought hit her, sending a bone-grabbing chill down her spine. "He hasn't tried to get you to meet him anywhere, has he?"

Becky's eyes widened. "Ach, no."

"Well, fine. If anybody should do that, you say no and tell Dinah right away. Okay?"

"Okay."

Leah felt her sister relax. Becky wanted to be perfect at her first job—that was clear. Leah wanted that for her. But how could she tell if she'd said enough but not too much?

Sometimes Amish girls seemed to have a special appeal for outsiders. Becky was young for her age, and maybe vulnerable.

Leah didn't want to break a confidence, but she'd have to speak to Mammi about Becky's concerns. She'd know far better what to do. After all, she'd already gone through these adolescent years with Leah, and that couldn't have been easy.

CHAPTER SIX

❧❧❧

IT WASN'T UNTIL FAIRLY LATE THAT EVENING BE-
fore Leah was able to manage a private talk with Mammi.
The difficulty of accomplishing that in a house crowded
with a noisy, sociable family was something else she'd forgotten during her time away. Aunt Miriam's house had been
quiet with just the two of them living in it. Too quiet. At first
she'd reveled in the privacy, but eventually it had become
depressing, even lonely.

No, she'd take the normal chaos of a house full of growing kinder over a place so still she could hear a leaf fall to
the ground. But family noise did cause problems at times.

Finally she caught her mother alone in the kitchen. When
she described the man Becky had seemed to watch for,
Mammi looked distressed. "You don't mean she's mooning
over a stranger? And an Englischer at that?"

"Ach, Mammi, I don't know that she's attracted to him.
I just saw that she seemed to notice him especially. She'd
mentioned something to me about having trouble understanding whether one of the customers was joking with her

or not. He's a newcomer, I'm sure, and maybe it was just a misunderstanding."

"Maybe." Mammi didn't look relieved. "But what if he's . . . well, trying to get her to go out with him?"

"She knows better than to do that," Leah said quickly. "I did warn her about anyone asking her to meet them someplace, but I don't think she'd do that anyway."

"No, no, she wouldn't." Mammi looked a bit relieved. "Goodness knows she's so shy she can barely talk to strangers, let alone go anywhere with them."

"That's right." Leah patted her arm. "Even if the man were foolish enough to ask her, she wouldn't do that. And Dinah told me that she always looks out for that sort of trouble."

Her mother nodded, seeming content to let the subject rest at that point. But there was still a shadow of concern in her eyes that Leah couldn't ignore. Both of them were worried, and both of them were trying to make light of the situation for fear of alarming the other person.

On her way up to bed, Leah paused outside her sister's door. Not a sound broke the stillness. She was about to move on when some lurking concern made her pause. She closed her hand over the knob, turned it, and pressed the door open softly.

With a sense of relief, she recognized the sound of Becky's easy breathing, and she relaxed a little. Whatever had led to Becky's crying in the night, she seemed to have forgotten it for this night, at least. Maybe she had been reassured by Leah's words on the ride back from town. Clinging to that hope, Leah went on to bed.

Looking back on it the next morning as she walked along the road toward the cottage, Leah had nearly convinced herself the whole thing had been just one of those flare-ups of complicated emotion that come so easily to a girl in her teens. She remembered moments when the whole day was ruined because someone hadn't smiled at her, or the teacher had spoken sharply. A person just had to grow through those challenges. But still she ached for Becky, with her sensitive spirit and her shy, hopeful heart.

How did Mammi manage to understand each member of her big family, all so different, and all at different stages? Judith had the temperament that would charge through any obstacle in the way of what she wanted. And Micah went single-mindedly without fuss from one task to another, while James switched from interest to interest like a toddler trying to pick a lollipop flavor. As for their little Hannah . . . who could say yet what she would be?

Given the problems kinder brought, it was a wonder anyone wanted to be a parent. But Leah had to admit that just the sight of someone with a new baby could make her long for the little ones she might have one day.

Reaching the fence row that marked the boundary between the farm and the cottage, she glanced toward the back. She couldn't see Josiah from where she stood, but she heard the sound of his hammer, tapping away at the back stoop.

She took a step toward the sound and then swung back at what was becoming a frequent annoyance—the noise of Jere Conner's old rattletrap roaring along the road. Coming from behind, it was on her side of the road, so she took a few more steps back, mindful of his habit of taking the curve too widely.

The pickup passed her, thumping off onto the berm as usual and spraying up gravel. But instead of zooming off to his girlfriend's house, Jere made a U-turn, swung back past her, then turned again and pulled up right next to her. Before she had a chance to react, he'd jumped out of the pickup and headed toward her, his young face scowling.

"It was you, wasn't it?" He stopped in front of her, planting his hands on his hips. He was trying to look tough, she guessed, but the still-soft curves of his face and his crop of freckles denied it.

"Hello, Jere." She remembered him as a small boy, leaning out the window of his dad's truck to wave at her. "How are you?"

"I'm ticked off, that's what. It was you, wasn't it? Nobody else would do it. You Amish think you own the roads with your horses and buggies."

Leah shook her head, mystified. Had she delayed him driving her buggy? But when?

"I don't know what you're talking about. Hadn't you best move your truck off the road? If someone came along—"

"That's just what I mean. It's none of your business. Telling my parents that I'm a reckless driver just because I came too close to you, making them mad for no reason."

The light dawned on her. Apparently someone had complained about Jere's driving. It was hardly surprising, as far as she could see. But it hadn't been her.

"Jere, listen to me. I haven't even talked to your folks since I got back in town. If someone complained to them, it wasn't me." She smiled at him, remembering the little boy he'd been such a short time ago.

"I figured you'd say that. But I know what I know. Nobody else would. This road is too darn narrow. Anyone can take the curve a little wide. You had no right—"

"I didn't!" She raised her voice, catching sight of Josiah appearing around the corner of the cottage. She didn't want to admit that she was relieved to see him, but it was good to know she wasn't alone out here. "Ask your parents if you don't believe me."

Doubt crossed his face, but then it hardened again into something like a sneer. "I'm not gonna put up with it, so you'd better watch it."

He edged close to her, and she could almost feel the haze of baffled anger that surrounded him. A shiver of fear went through her, but she shook it off. He was a kid, when all was said and done, just a few months older than Becky.

Besides, Josiah was headed toward them, picking up speed as he came.

"You'd better get off to school or you'll be late," she said calmly. "Your parents wouldn't like that, either."

She probably shouldn't have said it, because temper flared in his face again.

"You leave me alone. You think I need you telling me what to do? I'll show you." He took a quick look at Josiah, then jumped back into the pickup and roared off down the road again.

Her knees were wobbly. How silly. He was just the neighboring kid he'd always been, even if he had grown a bit in the last year. But she was still glad to see Josiah.

Leah amended that thought quickly. Not Josiah especially. Just anyone she knew. That was what she meant.

JOSIAH CROSSED THE GRASS TOWARD LEAH IN A RUSH. His heart had been pounding since he'd seen that boy looming over her with what seemed a threatening look. He heard it now, thudding in his ears.

"Was ist letz? What did he say to you?" He rushed the words out, and then he felt a little foolish when Leah turned a calm, smiling face toward him.

"Who? Oh, Jere Conner. It was nothing."

He clasped her arm firmly and moved with her toward the cottage. "It didn't look like nothing."

At that moment she stumbled over a clump of icy grass, and he tightened his grasp to hold her steady. She wasn't as calm and cool as she'd like him to believe, he decided.

"Komm now. You might as well admit it—your knees are wobbly. If you can't tell an old friend like me what's going on, who are you going to tell? Anyway, if Jere Conner is declaring war on pedestrians, I'm involved, ain't so?"

That brought the hint of a smile to her lips. "Not pedestrians in general. It's the Amish. Did you know we hog the roads?"

He raised an eyebrow. "Jere never got that from his parents. They're good people and good neighbors, too."

"Yah, I think he just threw that in to be obnoxious. Apparently someone complained to his parents about his driving, and he thinks I was the one."

"You didn't, did you?" He remembered her annoyance the last time the boy had ripped past.

"Of course not. I know better than to start trouble with the neighbors. Anyway, like you said, he's just a teenager feeling his oats."

"Did I say that?" He led her around the cottage to the back stoop.

"Words to that effect," she said, smiling. "You were remembering your own risky behavior at that age, I think."

"Guess I was." The indulgence he'd felt earlier toward the boy had disappeared. The idea of him confronting Leah, maybe frightening her, had washed away any softening.

But it seemed Leah, who'd been thoroughly annoyed earlier, somehow didn't seem so bothered now. Or didn't want to admit it, anyway.

"Just as well someone did complain to his parents," he muttered. "They can't be everywhere, and the way he's been taking that corner makes him a danger."

She didn't respond, and when they stopped by the back stoop he turned her to face him, looking steadily into the depths of her green eyes. "You can't put one over on me, Leah. You were rattled."

For a moment her eyes darkened, and he knew he was right.

"Yah, okay, I guess I was . . . having someone jump out of a vehicle and start yelling at me has that effect." She shrugged. "But then I looked at Jere and remembered him as a little boy. He was trying to put on a tough act, but it's not easy with those round cheeks and his freckles."

That surprised a laugh out of him. "I almost wish that boy would have a little fender bender, just so he'd take it seriously. But to be safe, maybe you'd better cut across the field for a few days, even if you do get your feet wet."

Leah nodded, smiling. "I'll give it some thought. Now tell me what you've been doing here."

He had to push down the longing to ask for her promise to be careful. What was he doing, acting like a mother hen where Leah was concerned? She wouldn't appreciate it, that was certain sure. He'd best follow her lead and talk about the job.

"There you have it." Josiah waved his hand toward the back stoop. "All finished and guaranteed not to collapse no matter who steps on it."

"I didn't imagine you'd have it finished already." Leah ran her hand along the railing as she went up the two steps and then bounced at the top as if testing it. "It's fine, Josiah. Denke."

The words didn't exactly overflow with praise, but her smile was reward enough. "Fine." He repeated her word as he picked up his toolbox. "Let's go in. I want to show you something."

They went in, and he closed the door firmly. It was plenty cold inside, but at least they were sheltered from the wind that was blowing ragged clouds across the sky.

"If it's okay with you, I'll start on the cabinets around the sink." He nodded toward a broken door that sagged from one hinge. "You want all of these replaced, I know. What about the sink?"

Leah took a look at the rust-stained sink and made a face. "I'll want a new one. But do we need to get a plumber in?"

We, she'd said. It sounded like old times. "Not unless you want the sink moved to a different location. Otherwise it's a simple matter of reconnecting the pipes."

"Gut. Let's go ahead with it, then." She stood staring at the sink and surrounding cabinets, but he knew she wasn't seeing the stained, dirty reality. Her eyes shone because she envisioned the gleaming new sink and the polished wood of the new cabinets.

"Right. I'll bring over a kerosene can and get busy, then."

Leah came abruptly back to reality and gave him a questioning look. "I thought you planned to put things together in your father's workshop and then bring them over."

He didn't miss the question in her voice. He shrugged, remembering Daad's curiosity over what he was working on, his eagerness to offer advice . . . no, not advice. Direction.

"Yah, well, there's too much interference over there. Folks in and out all the time."

Leah studied his face, and he had a feeling she saw everything he didn't say. This business of knowing each other worked both ways.

"Folks? You mean your daad?"

He evaded her gaze, but it was no use. "I guess."

She didn't speak, but her serious gaze demanded more from him.

"All right, I have a problem with my own father . . . always looking over my shoulder, wanting to tell me what to do and how to do it. It seems like he doesn't trust me to finish a job on my own."

The instant he said the word *trust*, he knew he'd reached the heart of the matter. Knew, too, that it was a word that would resonate with Leah. After all, she didn't trust him, either.

But right now she was looking at him with a puzzled frown. "But you and your daad—you've been working together since you were a little boy. What makes you think he's not just interested?"

He saw it then . . . the thing he'd pictured a hundred times in his mind and never did actually see. And maybe never would.

"Yah . . . since I was a kid, right? He used to talk about putting up a new sign out on the road. Instead of just saying *Burkhalter Carpentry* it was going to say *Burkhalter and*

Son. You've seen that sign since you got home, ain't so? You noticed any change? No, you haven't. And the way things are going, you never will."

He stopped, and it was so silent in the small house that his ears seemed to ring, echoing the absolute stillness.

Finally Leah moved, and he could feel her eyes on him. "So that's why."

For a second the words didn't make any sense to him. Then he understood. She'd figured out why he was so eager to do this job for her . . . and to do it by himself.

"Yah, that's why." He could hear the bitterness in his tone but he couldn't seem to do anything about it. "I'm using you to prove to my daad that I'm capable—that it's time. Trouble is, I could build you a . . . a castle, and he still wouldn't be satisfied."

Quiet again . . . so quiet he could hear Leah's indrawn breath.

"I guess it's a gut thing I don't want you to build me a castle, ain't so?" Her voice was light, but he sensed the seriousness behind it.

She caught his hand in hers as if to comfort him or to assure him that she was on his side.

"Ach, Josiah, what does it matter? Our parents never want to admit that we're grown up. You're doing the job I need to have done. If your only reason is that you want to impress your father, that doesn't matter to me."

He wanted to tell her that it wasn't the only reason. Maybe it had started out that way, but it wasn't now. But he couldn't find the words, and even if he did, she wouldn't want to hear it.

Leah, like his daad, had already made up her mind about him.

WATCHING THE GRIM LINES TIGHTEN ON HIS FACE, Leah longed to wipe them away with a touch. But she couldn't. Whatever the truth was about Josiah's relationship with his father, there was nothing she could do about it.

"Sorry," he muttered. "Don't mind me. I've got no reason to be feeling sorry for myself."

"When has that ever stopped anybody from feeling that way?" She tried for a lightness she didn't feel. "Believe me, I know how parents can be."

"Yah, but still, whatever I think, I shouldn't be saying it out loud."

Leah shook her head. "Only to me. Grossmammi reminded me that we were good friends all of our lives, and sweethearts for only six months or so. That should mean there's nothing we can't say to each other."

But even as she said the words, Leah couldn't help but think about all the things she hadn't told him—hadn't told anyone.

Josiah's lips quirked reluctantly. "Your grandmother's a smart woman. I guess I do feel a bit better for saying it out loud."

"There. See?" She patted his arm, feeling the strong muscles beneath the wool of his jacket. She looked for something else comforting to say.

"Maybe . . . maybe you're wrong . . . misinterpreting your daad's feelings. Or maybe he just hasn't thought about the fact that you're ready for more responsibility. Fathers are like that."

She tried to shrug it off like something normal, but he didn't seem to be buying it.

"Your daad isn't," he said. "Here he is, buying a piece of property for you to start a business, helping you every way he can."

Leah considered. "It's different when it's a girl, I think."

"How?" he challenged. "If anything, I'd think they'd be more protective of girls."

She tried to find a way to explain the feeling that seemed so clear to her. "I guess if it seems like a girl isn't going to marry, then her parents feel an obligation to help her take care of herself."

"So you're saying I helped you out when we broke up?"

He was being sarcastic, Leah guessed, but it hurt anyway.

"Yah, well, not on purpose anyway. You were too captivated by Susie's bright eyes."

Leah was sorry when the words came out. She hadn't intended to mention Susie ever again, and here she was blurting out her name.

Josiah's color deepened, and she hurried to try to wipe out the effects of her remark. "Anyway, forget it. It's all over, and we're friends again. I'm not looking for anything else."

He studied her for a moment, his face serious. Then he nodded. "Okay."

"Okay," she agreed, feeling as if she could breathe again. "So you work on the cabinets wherever you want to. It doesn't matter to me, so long as they get done."

"You want a spring opening, ain't so?" He seemed relieved to get back to a neutral conversation.

"As much as I can anyway. The plants in the greenhouse won't be ready as soon as I'd like, but at least I can get things started."

"Right." He knelt by the front of the sink cabinets and opened his toolbox. "I'll just get this dismantled first." He paused, looking up at her. "Did you hear about our rumspringa group Christmas party at Ruthie's house?"

"Next week, isn't it?" She'd heard, but as nice as it would be to see some of her old friends, she didn't feel like meeting them all in one large group.

"You don't sound too enthusiastic." He pulled one door free and started on the other one. "Don't you look forward to being the only one still single?"

He was trying to tease her, but two could play at that game. "I won't be, not if you're going."

He flung up his hand. "I give up. And actually we're not

the only ones, I'm glad to say. But the numbers are dwindling."

"Yah, from what I heard, there was at least one wedding a week in the fall. Maybe it's just as well I was away."

Not that she didn't like weddings, but it was strange to see the girls she'd run around with settling down one after another.

"Well, we could always go together." His eyes twinkled. "That would give them something to talk about."

"I don't think . . . ," she began, and then stopped at the sound of a vehicle pulling up in front of the cottage. For just an instant she fought down a flicker of fear. If it was Jere Conner coming back, at least Josiah was still here to support her.

But the figure she saw prowling around the outside of the cottage wasn't Jere. Instead it was Bart Lester again.

Josiah, standing, saw the man a second after she did. "I thought you got rid of this guy," he said.

"So did I." He was heading toward the back door now, obviously having seen them through the windows. "I guess I'll have to talk to him." She tried to smile. "This seems to be a day for unwelcome visitors."

"Right." Josiah moved to stand next to her, and she was glad to feel his solid presence beside her as she opened the door.

"Mr. Lester," she said, resigned to the fact that she'd have to talk to him. "I'm afraid I haven't changed my mind."

She hadn't invited him, but he came in anyway, his ruddy face and bullet-shaped head thrusting forward.

"Well, now, don't say that until you hear what I have to say. I'll tell you what I've been doing," he swept on. "I've been scouring the township trying to find a better place than this, but there's not one."

She was shaking her head already. All she had to do was keep on shaking her head. He couldn't force her to sell to him, could he?

"Come now, Mr. Lester." Josiah pushed his way into the

conversation. "That's hard to believe. There are plenty of small parcels around owned by folks who'd be only too happy to sell."

"Not with this access to the road and only a couple of miles out from town," he countered. "I'm telling you, this is the perfect spot. If you'd just think about it. Wouldn't it be nice to have a drive-in right next door, where you could pop in for ice cream whenever you wanted?"

"Popping in next door isn't something we care to do," she said. Before she could continue, he'd carried on.

"Hey, everybody likes ice cream, even the Amish. You can't say they don't."

"No . . . I mean, yes, everyone likes ice cream, I guess, but we don't want a business right next door. It would be . . . disruptive." That, she thought, was just what Daad would say.

"You haven't heard my offer yet." He beamed at her. "I've been checking on costs. It seems like the average cost of an acre of farmland is right around six thousand. But because it's got just the road frontage I want, I'm willing to go to seven thousand. And you won't get a better offer from anyone else, I promise you. What do you say to that?"

For an instant her mind spun. That was far more than she'd have thought, if she'd thought anything about it. Before she could answer, he went on.

"Take your time. Think about it. Talk to your father. From what I understand, he's the actual owner of the property anyway."

"He has given it to Leah for her business," Josiah put in. "He's not going to change his mind."

"Well, we'll see. Seems like you ought to think about it." He zeroed in on Leah again. "You wouldn't want to put your father in a position where he'd lose that money just because he wouldn't want to disappoint you."

Josiah straightened, taking a step forward to put himself between her and the man. "I think Ms. Stoltz doesn't care to talk anymore just now."

"Sure, sure." He backed toward the door. "I understand. You just talk it over. And talk to your dad, too. I just know we're going to make a deal."

Leah held her breath until he was out the door. He was so overwhelming that a person almost felt helpless against him. But the door closed firmly, and Josiah turned to her.

"Don't look like that." He clasped her cold hands warmly between his. "Your dad isn't going to disappoint you."

Leah stared at him, hoping he was right but unable to dismiss the fear in her heart. "But, Josiah, what if Daad doesn't feel that way? What if he thinks that the money is too good to pass up?"

Josiah tried to give her an encouraging look, but beneath it she saw the uncertainty. He didn't know, any better than she did. What if Daad let her down, just the way Aunt Miriam had?

CHAPTER SEVEN

∽♥∾

LEAH HAD EVERY INTENTION OF TALKING TO HER father that evening about Lester's offer for the property. The trouble came, predictably, when she tried to catch him alone. In their busy house, no sooner did she start having a conversation with him than someone else came in—either one of the kids wanting something, or having a problem, or simply eager to join in whatever talk was going on.

She was used to hearing everyone's opinion on everything, but in this instance, she and Daad needed some privacy. If she came right out and said that, people would leave them alone, but they'd be endlessly curious. They might not ask, but the question would linger in the air. Sometimes she wondered how her parents ever managed to have a private conversation— waited until everyone was asleep, she supposed.

In any event, it wasn't until after breakfast that Leah managed to catch her father enjoying a second or third cup of coffee in the kitchen. She slid into the chair next to him.

"Finally," she said. "I've been trying to talk to you since yesterday."

"I noticed," he said. "You've been looking like a hen trying to find a place to lay her eggs. What is it? A Christmas secret?"

She had to laugh at his description. Of course he'd noticed—he noticed everything, even if he didn't say anything.

"Not Christmas this time, but I do need to talk to you." She frowned, twisting her fingers together as she always did when she was nervous.

Daad put his square work-roughened hand down on hers. "Just say it, Daughter. Nothing seems as bad once it's shared."

"It's not bad at all, I guess. Just surprising. You remember when I told you about that Mr. Lester stopping by the cottage when we were working?"

"The Englischer who owns those drive-ins? Yah, I remember." His face didn't show anything but mild interest.

"Well, he came back yesterday." She paused for a moment, distracted by the thought of Jere Conner's visit, too. But there was no point in telling her father about it. "He said that he's been looking all over for the best spot to put a new restaurant, and he really wants the cottage and the land around it. So I thought you'd best know."

He eyed her seriously for a moment. "No point in it, Leah. I already told you. The cottage is yours, the land, too. It's up to you. If you want to sell—"

"Ach, no. It's perfect for what I want. You know that. But . . . well, you paid for the land. He's offering so much money that I didn't feel right not telling you."

His hand squeezed hers. "The property is yours," he repeated firmly. Then he grinned. "But I am curious."

Leah smiled at his expression. "You want to know how much, don't you?"

"You know me too well, ain't so? Yah, what did he offer?"

"Seven thousand."

At his startled expression, her heart sank a little. Maybe, now that Daad knew how much money was at stake, he'd have second thoughts.

"That surprises me, I admit. Lester has the reputation of being a sharp dealer when it comes to negotiating. I'd have expected him to offer less than the average cost, not more."

She wasn't surprised that Daad knew the current price of farmland. Farming was his business. But what was he really thinking of the offer? It wasn't that often that money would drop into a farmer's lap.

"I know you said you wanted me to have that piece of property, but really, Daadi . . ."

"Ach, Leah, don't be so foolish. Your mamm and I are not putting prices on what we do for our kinder. We gave it to you because we wanted you to be able to have your business right here next to us, instead of . . ." He paused, as if he wasn't sure he wanted to go on with what he was saying.

"Instead of what, Daadi?" He and Mammi had been supportive of her working with Aunt Miriam. Hadn't they?

Rising, he patted her shoulder. "You couldn't expect us to like the idea of you spending your life so far away, now could you? If you weren't . . . that is, if you wanted a business, we hoped it could be right here, near us."

He took his jacket from its hook and paused at the door. "Just forget about Lester. Let him put his restaurant wherever he wants, as long as it's not next to us."

Smiling, she watched him go and then filled a pitcher with water and went to the sunny corner where her plants lived. She knew very well what it was Daad had started to say. *If she weren't going to marry . . .*

It hadn't occurred to her that her parents had probably been just as eager to see her married to Josiah as she had.

Shrugging it off, she finished tending the plants, talking to them softly as she did so. Silly, she guessed, but they were part of God's creation, too.

Once she'd finished with the plants, Leah settled in the sewing room, seizing the momentary quiet to work on the sachet pillows she planned to give for Christmas. There was no reason for her to go over to the cottage today, after all. She probably ought to give Josiah the peace and quiet to get started on the cabinets.

Her sympathy went out to him over his father's attitude toward the carpentry business, but the more she thought of it, the more convinced she became that it was a simple misunderstanding. If they could just talk with each other about it . . . but most likely his daad didn't even think it was necessary, and Josiah was too proud to ask for what his father would probably be eager to give. Loving someone didn't seem to mean understanding him.

Light footsteps in the hallway were quickly followed by Hannie, leaning against the back of Leah's chair and breathing on her neck. "What're you doing?"

"Working on presents. What are you doing? Why aren't you in school?"

"Teacher Anna is having a day to plan with some of the other schools." Hannie pressed her cheek so hard against Leah's she thought it would leave a permanent mark. "I don't know what they're planning. What do you think?"

Leah swung around in her chair. "Oof, don't hug so hard." She patted Hannie's round cheek, still chubby and babylike despite the fact that she was in school now. "How's your sewing coming? Do you want to make one of these?"

Hannie touched the quilted design Leah was working on, tracing it with her finger. "I'm not very good at the quilting stitches yet," she said wistfully. Unlike her next older sister, she never claimed to do something she hadn't mastered.

"This is just a design I'm trying out. You could make a plain one and then put some ribbon on it, if you want. Just pick out a fabric square and ribbon." She gestured to the plastic box where she stored fabric remnants.

"Oh, goody." Hannie seized the box and carried it over to the window where the light was better. "Maybe I could do a green one and then put mint inside it."

"Sounds like a great idea." Leah started hunting out a needle and thread for Hannie, when a sound from her small sister made her glance that way.

"Leah, I thought I saw—yah, I did. I did! There's a snow-flake. Look, another one." She pranced over to grab Leah's hands and tug her to the window. "It's snowing. It's really snowing. Look, Leah, look."

"I see." Leah put her arms around Hannie, and they watched the snow together, reveling in watching the first snowfall of the winter. The flakes came, just a few at first, and then increasing as if in a hurry to cover the ground. "It's going to be a real snow, I think."

"It is." Hannie bounced, bumping the top of her head against Leah's chin in her excitement. Leah rubbed it. Loving her little sister could be painful.

"Look how it's starting to cover the ground already. We can make snow angels, and a snowman, and . . ." Hannie caught Leah's hand. "Go out with me, Leah. Please?" She tugged. "Please, please?"

Looking out, Leah saw that they weren't the only ones to be captured by the sight of the first snow. Josiah had come out of the cottage and stood looking up at the snow starting to gather on the branches of the spruce tree. After a moment she saw him open his mouth, and she giggled. She knew exactly what he was doing. He'd always insisted that it was good luck to catch some flakes of the first snow-fall on your tongue. Where he'd gotten that superstition she didn't know, but it seemed he still abided by it.

"Come on," Hannie repeated, dragging out the second word. "We're missing it. Let's be first, before Judith sees it."

Laughing, Leah grabbed her hand and they raced for the coat pegs. After all, who would want to miss the first snow-fall of the winter?

* * *

JOSIAH TILTED HIS HEAD BACK, ENJOYING THE LIGHT kiss of snowflakes on his skin. He figured he'd never get too old to have this special feeling about the first snow. He might be tired of it by the time February was dragging into March, but he wouldn't want to lose this feeling.

He glanced toward the Stoltz place just in time to see Leah and Hannie run outside, hand in hand. In a few seconds Judith came slamming out to join them. Leah and Hannie were already spinning around, their arms spread out, their faces tipped up to the falling snow.

Josiah grinned, seeing that Leah hadn't lost her excitement at the first snow, either. He could hear her laughter as she grabbed Judith's hand and pulled her to join them.

What was he waiting for? There wasn't anything he had to do that couldn't be put off a little. He trotted back inside to get his jacket and gloves, hesitated, and then turned off the kerosene heater. He probably wouldn't be gone that long, but no sense in taking chances.

He headed across the field toward the girls, his boots squeaking on the fresh, fluffy snow that was coming down fast. Little Hannie saw him coming first. She waved, then scooped up an armful of snow. As soon as he came within range, she smooshed it together into a snowball and threw it at him.

Grinning, Josiah ducked, and the snow just fluttered over his shoulders.

Leah turned then and saw him. "Looks like a wonderful gut snow, right?" she said. "We couldn't stay inside, not when it's so beautiful out here."

"Yah, me, too. Besides, I could see that this young woman needs a lesson in making snowballs." He bent over Hannie, who wiggled with excitement.

"Show me, Josiah." She scooped up a big armload again.

"Here, not that much."

She blinked up at him. "But I want it to be a big one."

"Yah, but you start small and build it up, like so." He began squeezing a small amount in his hands, letting their warmth melt the snow just enough to stick together. "Here, you try it."

She took the clump of snow he handed her, trying to model his movements. He spoke to Hannie encouragingly, but his gaze followed Leah, who was helping Judith bring several snow saucers from the shed. The round plastic toys had become very popular with the younger ones in the past few years. They could slither down the bank even without much snow on the ground.

Before Hannie could be distracted by the saucers, Josiah whispered to her, nodding to Leah. "Let's surprise Leah. Here's another snowball for you."

She took it, giggling at the idea of a secret, and he packed another for himself.

"Wait until I say go, yah?"

Hannie nodded, grinning, and Leah shot them a suspicious look.

"What are you two plotting?"

"Ready, set, go!" Josiah and Hannah pelted her with their snowballs, and she shrieked very satisfactorily, making Hannie giggle so much she could hardly stand up.

He steadied her on her feet and looked up just in time to get a snowball full in the face. He sputtered, wiping his face while the others laughed.

"You think I don't know you started it?" Leah said, packing another snowball.

"Yah, and I'll finish it, too," he threatened, scooping up snow.

In a moment the snowballs were flying thick and fast. Paul came running from the barn, armed with several snowballs. Without picking sides, he pitched one at Josiah, then two more in quick succession at Judith, who took off after him.

Josiah glanced at Leah's face, rosy and laughing, and was caught suddenly in a swirl of memories . . . her face, rosy and laughing, in other years, in other snowball battles. He blinked, disoriented, and she slung another one in his face.

"Now you've done it," he said. "I'll have to wash your face with snow for that."

The threat of having your face washed with snow had always been the direst thing that could happen in their battles. He pursued her, grabbing up snow as he went, and chased her down the slope toward the barn, both of them laughing so hard it was a wonder they could run.

He slipped, slid, nearly fell, and then caught up with her. Grabbing her, he pulled her around, managing to get a handful of snow in her face before they both collapsed with laughter.

"Ach, let me up, you silly thing. I'm getting soaked." Leah pushed back at him, their eyes meeting.

Once again he had that sensation that time had slipped, tumbling backward to those months when they'd been sweethearts. He seemed to see so deeply into the clear green of her eyes, feeling as if he could see right into her heart.

Leah's eyes widened, grew darker, and there was a stillness between them, a silence that shut out the laughs and squeals coming from the others.

Tires shrieking, a pickup rattled into the curve. Then it was the brakes that screamed . . . it was Jere Conner, of course. His head jerked up.

The accident that had been looming over Jere had arrived. It was now, and they could do nothing but watch, helpless, as he lost control on the snow-slickened road, bounced over the berm, and careened straight into the trunk of the huge oak tree at the end of the pasture. The cry of crushing metal was echoed by a scream from Judith and a sob from one of the others.

He felt Leah shudder, but she regained control in an instant. Hannie ran to her, crying, and she hugged the little one.

"Judith, run fast as you can to the phone shanty. Call 911. Tell them quickly just where it is.

"Say they'll need an ambulance," he added, and then tugged his brother's arm. "Come with me." He ran toward the pickup, hearing Paul right behind him. His thoughts spun, and he sent up a wordless prayer. It looked bad . . . very bad.

Behind him he heard Leah giving quick instructions to Hannie to run and get Daadi, her voice as calm as if it was any other day. Then she was running after them. He wanted to yell at her to stay back, but it would do no good. He knew his Leah better than that.

LEAH'S HEART THUDDED AGAINST HER RIBS AS SHE ran toward the accident. Should she have stayed with Hannie? The poor child had never seen anything like that before, and she was frightened.

Still, she'd be better off with Mamm and Daad, and Leah's having a job to do should calm her. If Leah could be a help to the boy who might even now be dying in the crumpled metal . . .

No, she wouldn't let herself think that. She focused her mind on prayer, instead. Jere was in God's hands, as they all were.

Ahead of her, Josiah and Paul had nearly reached the truck, climbing over the mangled fence. They'd be in time, wouldn't they? Even if all they could do was comfort Jere until the paramedics came, that would be better than being alone.

She reached the fence in her turn and scrambled over it, stumbling when her foot caught on a broken piece of fence post. She forced herself to stop and untangle herself. She wouldn't be any help if she wrenched her ankle on the way.

In a moment she was free, and she took a quick look back. Judith wasn't in sight—she must have already reached the phone shanty. Help would be on its way. And Daad, carrying Hannie, had come out of the barn.

She was wonderful relieved to see him. Just the fact that he was on the way made her feel even better than thinking about the ambulance. Daad would know what to do.

The toppled pickup loomed ahead, lying on its side with the front crumpled against the oak. Josiah and Paul moved slowly around it, trying to peer inside. The front was such a tangle that she wasn't sure they could see anything. How could they possibly get Jere out? Was he alone?

"Is anyone in there with Jere?" she called out. "Can you see them?"

"He's alone, I think." Josiah hefted himself up a bit against the metal, craning to see. "I don't know. There, I saw him move! Jere, can you hear me?"

A sound little more than a murmur answered, and Leah's heart twisted. It sounded like a small child or an animal, hurt and whimpering.

"Paul, give me a hand to get up higher," Josiah said, and his brother, his face white as the snow, hastened to boost him up until Josiah was perched precariously atop what would be the driver's side door. "Gut. That's enough."

He peered inside for what seemed like forever, and Leah's nerves stretched to the breaking point. "Is he moving? Can we get him out?"

Josiah leaned back, looking down at them. "I think he might be stuck. Maybe we shouldn't try. The paramedics will have the equipment—"

A moan, nearly a cry, came from inside the truck. "I want . . . get out . . ."

"Easy, Jere. Can you move your arms? Your legs? You might be safer there."

What Josiah said made sense. Leah knew it. But she also

understood the boy's feelings. He was helpless, hurt and frightened like an animal in a trap.

She glanced around and her breath caught. From under the front came a small gray curl . . . not dust, smoke! The engine must be on fire. She didn't know much about vehicles, but enough to know that was bad.

"Josiah." It took all her strength to keep her voice calm. "Look. There."

Josiah and Paul both glanced down, seeing what she had. She couldn't say the words and risk panicking poor Jere. But they couldn't wait for an ambulance that might have trouble getting there through the driving snow. They had to get the boy out.

"Here, Paul, you're skinnier than me. See if you can wiggle down there and reach Jere's hand."

As they exchanged places, Paul struggling out of his jacket, Leah moved as close to the smoke as she could. A flame licked out at her. She had to do something . . . if she could just slow it down . . .

Scooping up an armload of snow, she threw it toward the source of the smoke. Anything was better than doing nothing, wasn't it?

An instant later her father and her brother James were there next to her, each carrying a heavy blanket. Daad began to beat at the flames, and James joined him. "Get back, Leah. I've got this. Stay back."

Josiah's father was there now, too, reaching up behind him. "We'd best get him out quickly."

Josiah nodded, not looking back. "We've got him. Now, Jere, we're going to pull you out as gently as we can. You say if it hurts too much."

"Just get me out." Jere's words were punctuated by a sob.

"You'll be fine." Josiah spoke as calmly as if he were sitting at the kitchen table instead of perched atop a burning pickup. "Ready, Paul? Now."

Slowly, painfully slowly, they pulled. She could see Jere's hands, then his arms, and finally his tear-streaked face was visible.

"Here." Judith shoved the end of a plastic snow boat into her hands. "To lift him with," she added.

Leah nodded, and together they raised it up as high as they could. One part of her was filled with surprised admiration that Judith had thought of it while the rest of her uttered anxious prayers for safety.

Above her, Josiah grabbed the end of the plastic boat-shaped sled, sliding it right under Jere as they dragged him clear of the cab. In another moment, eager hands reached up to lift the sled and its burden gently to the ground. Josiah and Paul followed, jumping clear as flames ate hungrily toward them.

"Hurry, get him farther away," someone said. Leah, wiping away tears with her mittens, heard a siren wailing down the road, red lights barely visible through the whirling snow.

She felt an arm around her. "Here, move," Josiah said. "You're not fireproof, are you?"

"You'd think so, the way she was shoveling snow into the flames." Paul put his arm around her from the other side, and all three of them moved down the road.

"You two were up there taking chances," she said, scolding a little because she'd been so frightened. "I couldn't just do nothing, could I?"

Josiah hugged her a little closer. "No, you couldn't," he murmured, his voice close to her ear.

She didn't dare meet his eyes, afraid of what he might see, afraid of what they both might expose to Paul's keen gaze. Afraid, even, to look at her own heart too closely, not knowing what she might see.

And then the ambulance rumbled to a stop next to the little group by the road. A police car followed, then a fire truck just in time to wet down what was left of the pickup.

In what seemed hardly more than a moment, the paramedics gave them a quick thumbs-up sign, and they were loading Jere, on a regulation stretcher now, into the ambulance.

CHAPTER EIGHT

IT SEEMED LIKE A MINUTE TO LEAH BUT WAS ACTU-ally over an hour since the crash had sent them running to help. Now everyone was crowded into their kitchen, while Mamm and Josiah's mother poured coffee and hot chocolate into mugs and Grossmammi slid a platter of warm-from-the-oven chocolate chip cookies onto the table.

Leah's heart warmed as she looked from face to face around the table. A call from the hospital had been reassuring, and that had drained the tension from the faces. Each one seemed intent on denying that he or she had done anything special, and yet together they were united with the sense of a job well done.

That was it, Leah realized. They had been challenged, and they'd done the right thing . . . not a subject for praising themselves or each other, but for gratitude.

"I'm wonderful glad that truck has been taken away." Mammi shuddered as she sat down next to Leah.

"I know what you mean," Leah said softly.

The flames had left a smoldering heap of metal on the

side of the road. It was too great a reminder of what might have been. If they hadn't been right there when it happened, if they hadn't managed to pull Jere free in time . . .

She didn't want to think about that possibility. They had been there, in the right place at the right time.

Josiah, sitting on her other side, nudged her with his elbow. "Why are you looking so serious? Jere's going to be all right." His gaze darkened for an instant. "When I think I wished for him to have a fender bender just to teach him a lesson, I'm ashamed."

"Don't," she murmured, patting his hand under cover of the table. "If it hadn't been for you, getting him out in time . . ."

"And Paul, and Judith, and my daad, and your daad," he said lightly.

Hannie squeezed between them and shoved herself onto Leah's lap. "What are you talking about?"

Josiah smiled at her. "About how everybody helped, that's all."

Her small face clouded. "I didn't do anything."

"Sure you did." Leah wrapped her arms around her, squeezing. "You ran fast and got Daadi, didn't you?"

Hannie considered that in the solemn way she had. Then she smiled, looking up at Leah. "Yah, I did. I ran as fast as I could."

"You see?" Josiah said. "You helped, and so did everyone else. We each did what we could, and all together it was enough, ain't so?"

Hannie nodded. "Yah. Even Judith."

Judith bristled. "What do you mean, 'even me'? I'm the one who called the paramedics."

"And you brought that plastic sled, too," Paul said. "It worked great. How did you think of that?"

Judith flushed a little, not accustomed to a compliment from a boy. "I saw something about . . . I mean, I heard about it somewhere, and it just popped into my mind."

Hiding a smile, Leah swallowed a mouthful of the creamy hot chocolate. *Saw something* was probably closer to the truth. Judith babysat for an Englisch family on the edge of town, and she'd probably been watching television while she did.

Josiah leaned over, whispering something to Hannie that made her smile, his eyes warm with laughter. The look squeezed Leah's heart. Why had she never realized before that he could be so good with the younger ones?

Her thoughts went back to those moments when he'd been on top of the wrecked truck. She'd always known he was brave, for sure. No one could have tried all the daring things he had without physical courage.

But his cool control had surprised her. The boy she'd known had been quick as a flash of lightning, jumping from serious to silly in two minutes, with a temper as noisy as it was short-lived.

Today he'd stayed so calm. She heard again his unhurried tones as he'd explained what to do to Paul, as he'd reassured and calmed Jere. Maybe he'd always had those qualities hidden, ready to come out when called upon.

The sound of a car outside pulled her out of her introspection. Someone was coming. Daad hurried to the door, and a moment later they heard the rumble of male voices. Daad ushered in Frank Conner, Jere's father.

Mammi was already on her feet, hurrying to pour a mug of coffee as subdued voices welcomed him. They all probably had the same anxiety she did, Leah realized. Was there bad news from the hospital? Frank's face was tight with worry, but it seemed to relax at the warmth of their welcome.

"I wanted to stop and tell you . . ." He broke off to accept the mug of coffee and drained it thirstily. "Doctors say Jere will heal. He's got a concussion and a badly broken leg, but could be a lot worse."

"Ach, that is gut news." Mammi spoke for all of them.

"When I think of how that truck looked . . ." His face seemed to crumple for an instant, and he struggled to bring it under control. He was fighting back tears, Leah realized, and her own eyes grew wet. "I don't know how you got him out."

"We all helped," Hannie piped up, and turned bright red, making everyone laugh and relaxing the tension.

"Yeah, you sure did," Frank said. "Drat the boy—we just told him yesterday that if he couldn't be more careful we'd take that pickup away from him." His face twisted again. "Guess we don't have to worry about that now."

Leah couldn't help but be relieved that Jere wasn't going to be out risking his life on the road, but it was a hard way to learn a lesson, poor boy. She thought, not of the sulky teenager, but of the grinning boy who used to wave to her every time he went by.

"At least he'll be all right," she murmured.

He seemed to catch her words, because he nodded. "Thanks to all of you." He silenced their protests with a raised hand. "I know about it. The paramedics told us." He looked from Josiah to Paul. "If you hadn't got him out before the fire—"

He stopped, choking on tears that he tried to suppress.

Daad patted him on the back. "Doesn't help to be thinking that. How is your wife?"

"She's okay. Upset. She's going to stay the night at the hospital. I'm just going to pick up a couple of things for her and take care of the stock, then I'll head back over there."

He shifted, as if to rush out.

"Here, wait." Daad's hand tightened on his shoulder. "Take a couple of the boys along and show them what you want done. We'll look after the animals until things settle."

"Yah, that's right," Josiah's daad put in. "Here, Paul, you and James go with Mr. Conner." He'd picked the two youngest boys from each family, and they got up, making an effort to look responsible.

"Thanks," Mr. Conner muttered. "You . . . well . . . thanks." He went out, Daad and the boys following him.

Leah brushed away a tear, sensing that Josiah was watching her, and managed a smile.

"You did a gut thing," she murmured to him under the cover of other voices.

His mouth quirked. "So did you."

Leah glanced around, hoping no one was watching them and reassured by the talk bouncing around the table. Then she glanced down and found Hannie's huge blue eyes fixed on her solemnly, as if she knew something was happening but didn't know what.

That was only fair, Leah told herself. Because she didn't know what was happening, either. She just knew that something had changed between her and Josiah.

JOSIAH FOUND THAT MEMORIES OF THE ACCIDENT continued to pop into his head that afternoon while he was working. Going over that moment when he'd looked into the cab, not knowing whether Jere was alive or dead, was useless. He had to push it away, if he didn't want it to haunt his dreams.

Better to remember how they'd worked together . . . his brother's quick, brave actions, Judith's resourcefulness, Leah's calm, confident voice as she kept them all steady. It was surprising what an emergency could bring out in people . . . surprising and sometimes enlightening.

He ran his hand along the shelf he'd just installed, then reached for the level to double-check. The cottage door opened, distracting him.

"So this is where you are." Paul came in, stamping the snow off his boots. "I thought you'd be working in Daad's workshop."

Josiah shrugged, not wanting to get into his reasons for preferring to be in the cottage. "Fewer interruptions here."

"You mean Daad won't keep telling you how to do it if you're here." Paul grinned, squatting next to his improvised workbench.

Paul saw more than Josiah had given him credit for.

"Something like that." He darted a glance at his little brother, seeing how he studied the cabinet with his eyes, first, and then with his hands. Just like Daad had taught them.

Josiah began to set up the next shelf, then frowned, aware of Paul next to him. "How about not breathing down my neck when I'm working?"

"Sorry." Paul moved back, then started prowling around the room as if he'd never seen it before. Come to think of it, maybe he hadn't. Well, let him look around. If he wanted something, he'd come out with it sooner or later.

The silence drew out, broken only by Paul fidgeting around the room, touching things. It sometimes seemed he was never entirely still. If nothing else, his fingers moved, almost as if he played an invisible piano.

"Did you get everything taken care of at the Conners' place?" Josiah asked when he couldn't stand the fidgeting any longer.

"Oh, yah, we did. We figure we'll go down in the morning and take care of things, too. They only have the two horses and the chickens, besides the dogs." He picked up a plane, felt the edge, and put it down again. "Funny thing. Mr. Conner kept saying about how upset his wife was, but he was restless enough for ten people."

"About like you," Josiah said, just as his brother dropped a screwdriver on the floor.

He picked it up. "Yah, I mean no. He was really stressed out about Jere, but it was like he didn't want to admit it."

"Parents are like that about their kids," Josiah pointed out.

"I guess. And Jere's parents only have him. Maybe that makes it harder. I mean, with Mamm and Daad having a bigger family, it's not as bad if one is hurt or . . ."

Josiah finally gave up trying to steady the shelf. "I don't think it works that way. If you have five dollars and you lose one, you're still not broke. But I have a hunch parents feel about each of their kids as if he or she is the only one."

Paul made a sound that might indicate agreement. Josiah supposed thinking about things like life and death meant his little brother was growing up . . . something he'd begun to think would never happen.

Paul began tossing the screwdriver from hand to hand, as if his fingers could never be still. Or maybe that helped him talk.

"When you told me to climb up where you were on the pickup today," he said abruptly, "I didn't want to."

Studying his face, Josiah saw the way his eyes darkened and his mouth trembled.

"You did, though." He hesitated. "That's what's important. I didn't want to look, because I was afraid of what I'd see. But we did what we had to."

"Yah." Paul smiled, looking relieved. Whatever was going on in his head right now, at least he seemed to have found an answer.

"Seems like a good idea to keep busy right now. How about holding this shelf steady for me?"

"Sure." Paul scooted over to grasp the shelf, holding it while Josiah put in the screws. "It's going to be nice. Leah's going to have all new cabinets, yah?"

"Yah. There's not much worth saving after this place being empty for so long."

Paul seemed to consider that. "Listen, how about if I help you with the work for Leah? You could use an extra pair of hands, ain't so?"

Josiah straightened, staring at his brother. Paul didn't often volunteer to do anything extra.

"I'm trying not to take any money from Leah, you know. I couldn't pay you."

His brother looked offended. "I'm not offering for money. I just want to help."

"Why?" Maybe it was wrong to be suspicious, but he was, given Paul's reputation for practical jokes.

"What do you mean, why? I want something to do. Seems like I could learn a few things by helping you. Do I have to have another reason?"

Josiah didn't immediately answer. He looked absently at the flame of the kerosene heater. "Leah's serious about this business of hers. If you're planning some elaborate practical joke—"

"No! Can't I just want to help? Why does everybody think everything's a joke to me?"

The words raised an uncomfortable echo in Josiah's head, but he ignored it. "Is that really so surprising, given how you like to play jokes?"

"Not on the *job*." Paul said it with emphasis. "I know the difference. I'm not a kid anymore."

He suppressed a smile. Paul wasn't an adult, either, but it seemed as if that day's events had pushed him a little further on the way.

"Okay," he said finally. "If Leah agrees."

Paul broke into a wide grin. "Hey, that's great. It'll be okay with Leah, you'll see. And I'll do good work, I promise."

"Just remember, one practical joke and you're done. And no teasing Leah. Like I said, she's really serious about this."

"Whatever you say." Paul eyed him. "You tease her, though. I've heard you."

"That's different. And don't ask me why it's different. It just is."

Paul, seeming impressed, nodded. "What can I do first? Do we put another shelf in this unit? When do we put it in place? What about doors?"

Josiah closed his eyes for a moment. Was he crazy, agreeing to this? Maybe so.

And as for the question that Paul was probably burning to ask, Josiah didn't have an answer. *He* could tease Leah, gently, about things that didn't matter. He always had, and he wasn't going to change now.

THE KITCHEN TABLE WAS COVERED WITH COOKIES in various stages of completion the next day, and the air smelled of sugar, molasses, and baking. Judith reached over Hannie's head to pick up the red sprinkles, inciting a wail from her little sister.

"I was just going to use that. Mammi . . ."

Leah tapped her on the nose, leaving a bit of flour on the tip. "You weren't using it, though. Judith will give it back as soon as she finishes, won't you, Judith?"

"Yah, sure." She crinkled her nose and muttered, "Baby," loudly enough to be heard.

Hannie clouded up again, but before she could say anything, Leah grabbed one with each arm, shaking them playfully. "Listen, you two, that isn't the proper spirit for making Christmas cookies. Maybe Grossmammi and Mammi and I should do it by ourselves."

"No, no." Hannie wailed again, but Judith elbowed her.

"Quiet, silly. You don't want to be kicked out of the kitchen, do you?"

Hannie shook her head, clamping her lips tight.

"Wise girl," Grossmammi said. "Never argue with your elders."

"That's right." Leah let them go, turning back to the big yellow bowl where she was mixing the next batch.

Hannie looked confused. "But, Grossmammi, Leah isn't my elder, is she? I thought that meant like you or Mammi or Daadi. Old people."

Mammi turned from the stove, where she was pulling a hot cookie sheet out of the oven, looking outraged. Grossmammi began to laugh, and Leah couldn't help joining her.

"Denke, Hannie," Leah managed around giggles. "I'm glad I'm not old."

"Yah, you are." Judith looked from her to Grossmammi. "I mean, you are Hannie's elder. That just means she's older than you are, schnickelfritz."

Leah glanced at her grandmother and saw that she was enjoying it all just as Leah was . . . the warmth, the teasing, the laughter, and over all the smell of Christmas baking. Funny. When she'd realized that she'd have to come home instead of taking over the herb business, she'd felt terrible. But now . . .

Grossmammi nodded, as if she knew what Leah was thinking. "Sometimes a door closing seems bad, but it really means that God will open another, even better."

Leah's heart swelled. Yah, Grossmammi was right, as she so often was. Grossmammi had a sharp tongue, but she only ever exercised it on those she thought guilty of unkindness. Anything else she would love people through.

The grinding of gears and the crunch of tires on snow drew Leah's attention to the window. A truck was pulling up to the back door, and Leah recognized it as one that was often hired by Aunt Miriam and other business owners to make deliveries. Not sure what was going on, she swung her jacket around her shoulders and hurried out, followed by the others.

She reached the back steps as the driver clambered down from the cab. Seeing them, he touched his cap. "You're Ms. Miriam's niece, aren't you? I remember seeing you at the greenhouse."

"That's right. Were you looking for me?" She tried to think of anything she'd left behind but couldn't come up with any idea.

"Yup." He pulled a folded paper from his jacket. "I've got an order from your aunt to you, but it says on it to deliver to your herb business." He glanced around, questioning.

She exchanged glances with her father, who'd just walked over from the barn.

"How big is it?" he asked sensibly. "Something we need room to store?"

"Yeah, I guess." The driver unlatched and opened the rear doors, standing back so Leah and her father could look inside.

She stared, more than a little surprised. Why? After what had happened between them, she didn't see that Aunt Miriam had any cause to send her such a gift. And what a gift . . . the back was filled with tables that had been in her aunt's greenhouses—things she'd assumed Aunt Miriam would sell to the new owner, not give to her.

"That's a wonderful good surprise, ain't so?" Daad put his hand on one of the tables. "For your greenhouse, I guess. We'll have to find someplace to put them until that's built, though. Maybe if I moved things around in the loft . . ."

"Ach, no. We don't want to be hoisting them up to the loft. Anyway . . ." She toyed for a moment with the thought of sending them back. Did she really want to accept such a present from the person who believed her a thief?

But a moment's thought convinced her she couldn't do that, not unless she wanted to start everyone talking. "I think they'll fit in the cottage okay for now. They can go in the front room while Josiah is working in the back."

Daad nodded, turning to the driver. "Right over there, by the road." He pointed. "We'll meet you there and unload." He started yelling for her brothers to come and help.

Buttoning her jacket to follow them, Leah wished for the opportunity to stay away from Josiah for a while. Maybe Josiah wouldn't be at the cottage today.

That hope dissolved quickly. As soon as the truck drew up by the cottage, Josiah came out onto the front porch, with Paul right behind him.

A few more minutes and they'd caught up.

Daad hailed Josiah. "Leah's aunt sent along some things for the greenhouse. We'll have to store them inside for now."

"Nice gift," Josiah commented. He looked over the plant tables. "Guess we can stack them all on one side of the front room for now."

Leah caught his glance at her and pinned a smile to her face. Nobody needed to know what went on between her and Aunt Miriam. So she'd have to act the way people would expect.

She realized Josiah was still studying her face and tried to conceal any betraying expression with busyness. She reached toward one of the rough-hewn tables. "Let's get them inside."

Her father pushed her gently away. "You can open the door for us. We'll bring them in."

Anything, she decided, that would get her away from Josiah's inquisitive gaze was fine. She scurried toward the porch.

With a lot of the usual chaffing and teasing, the boys soon got the first couple of tables inside and stacked. Paul elbowed James. "Come on. We can stack them faster than Josiah and Micah, ain't so?"

"For sure." James joined him in trotting after their next load.

While reflecting that males seemed able to turn anything into a competition, Leah had a closer look at the tables, now stacked one atop the other. They were definitely the heavy, sturdy plant tables that had filled Aunt Miriam's greenhouse, holding plant seedlings to grow into salable plants. Aunt Miriam had had three greenhouses, but Leah was starting with one. If her business flourished, she might add another one the next year.

With all of them working, it took no time to unload everything. The truck pulled out, then Daad and her brothers went toward home, her brothers still agitating each other. She turned to Paul.

"Denke, Paul. Aren't you glad you came over to see your brother just in time to help unload a truck?" she asked lightly.

Paul looked awkward for an instant, glancing toward his brother. Then he shrugged. "Just my luck."

"He came over and offered to help me. It'll keep him in shape to work once it's construction season," Josiah explained.

"That's fine." She just hoped Paul wouldn't decide this was an appropriate place to set up one of his practical jokes. Still, that was up to Josiah. He'd be responsible.

"You can go ahead home, Paul." Josiah began putting away tools. "See you at lunch."

When the door closed behind him, Leah hesitated. Stay or go? She made a quick decision. "I'll be off, too. Thanks for helping."

"Hold on a minute." Josiah moved, his step putting him between her and the door. "What's going on? Why don't you want those things your aunt sent?"

She gaped at him for a second. "I . . . I don't know what you're talking about. Aunt Miriam—"

"Don't bother telling me any stories, Leah. I know you too well, and you're too transparent for that. Something is wrong between you and your aunt, ain't so?"

A quick flare of temper was her only defense. "It's none of your business."

"It is if your problems with her affect the job I'm doing for you." His voice changed, growing softer. "Come on, Leah. If it's something you can't tell your folks, then tell me. You know enough of my secrets, ain't so?"

For an instant she held back. And then the words she'd held locked inside her for the past month welled up and burst out.

"I don't want anything from my aunt—not when she thinks I stole from her."

She waited for Josiah's eyes to turn cold with doubt, and her heart cringed at the thought.

But his gaze was warm, even understanding. He clasped her hand, wrapping his fingers around it securely. "Gut. It's out. Now tell me the whole thing."

Her tension slowly unwound, and the clamp it had on her throat vanished. She had said it, and the world hadn't ended. He hadn't believed it.

CHAPTER NINE

֍

LEAH SEARCHED HIS FACE, NEEDING TO BE SURE SHE wasn't mistaken. His eyes, brown and shining as horse chestnuts, held nothing but warmth and belief.

"You believe in me." She hadn't really doubted it, but somehow . . . well, questions crept in, no matter what she told herself.

"What do you take me for? Of course I believe in you. I've known you all your life. You're as honest as . . . well, I'd sooner believe I'd taken something myself than think for a minute that you'd turned into a thief. Your aunt was wrong."

The outrage in his face made her want to laugh with relief. She shook her head, blinking back tears. "I told myself you'd believe me, but still, I guess I doubted. If my own aunt could believe I had stolen from her, who knew what other people might believe?"

Josiah just shook his head, but at least he wasn't angry. "So how did all of this happen? I mean, did she add up the receipts wrong and jump to the conclusion she'd been robbed?"

"Not exactly. Actually, she was really good at adding up the amounts in her head. I couldn't do that—I never did learn. I just kept a tally on a piece of paper. It wasn't that she was mistaken. There really was money missing from the cash box. But it wasn't me."

If there was a challenge in the way she said the words, his answer was prompt. "Sure you didn't. So who could have taken it? Who had access to the cash box? It was a cash box, not a cash register?"

She shook her head. "Just a metal receipts box with a little lock on it. Almost anybody who came in could have gotten to it. It sat right out in plain sight most of the time."

"Anyone?" He leaned back against the table, still holding her hand as if he'd forgotten about it. "You mean customers, or other people who worked there?"

Leah shrugged helplessly. "Anybody, really. There were customers in and out, and it just sat on the end of a table at the front of the first greenhouse. And a couple of other people took turns working there besides me and Aunt Miriam."

"So why pick on you?"

"I don't know." Tears prickled her eyes, and she rubbed them furiously. "She took me completely by surprise—just announced one day that money had been missing from the cash box for the last couple of weeks." She took a breath. "She said she knew I'd taken it but she forgave me."

"But you . . . you denied it, ain't so?"

Leah made a helpless motion with her hands. It had been so shocking she'd been completely stunned. "I tried. But she ran right over me. Said she was sure of her facts, and she didn't want to talk about it. She kept saying, 'Least said, soonest mended.'"

"That's . . . well, I guess that would be generous if you really had done it. But you didn't." His voice rose. "You mean she didn't even give you a chance to defend yourself?"

"It was like I said." Leah rubbed her forehead, where an

ache was beginning to build. "It was forgiven and forgotten, she said. And I . . . I was so shocked I couldn't find a way to make her listen."

She felt exhausted suddenly, as if she'd been running a very long way and just couldn't run anymore.

Josiah was silent, frowning down at her hand, clasped in his. "Seems to me that she didn't really forget about it, did she?"

"What . . . what do you mean? She never said a word about it after that."

"Maybe not. But she didn't pass the business on to you, either, like you expected she would." His tone had sharpened, and it added to the clamor in her head.

She rubbed her temples. "Please, Josiah. You insisted on knowing, so I told you. But I don't want to talk about it any longer."

His grip on her hand tightened until it was almost painful. "Not talking about it is what got you into this pickle to begin with. What did your parents say when you told them?"

"I . . ." She fell silent, unable to go on. "Please, Josiah. Drop it."

"You haven't told your parents, have you?" He stood up, holding her arms so that she faced him. "What ferhoodled idea do you have in your head now, that you wouldn't tell your own parents?"

"It's not ferhoodled," she insisted, trying to pull away from him and not succeeding.

"You can't possibly think they wouldn't believe you."

"No . . ." It came out uncertainly.

"Leah, wake up." He shook her, very lightly, the way she'd waken one of her little sisters. "What did that woman do that made you doubt your own parents?"

"I don't doubt them," she snapped, becoming rational. "But what happens if I tell them? They go right to Aunt Miriam and want to know what she means by accusing me.

And then next thing you know there's a big family fight, and a breach between my mother and her sister. And Grossmammi. Does she have to choose between her daughters? I can't be the cause of that."

Josiah's frown was fierce, and she could feel the tension in him that was on the verge of exploding. But at the same time, he seemed to grasp the thing she feared.

"It's still not right. This way, you're bearing all the hurt by yourself. Isn't it better to get the truth out, no matter who gets hurt?"

She shook her head and went on shaking it. "It would be a nightmare, don't you see that?"

"It's a nightmare now," he snapped. "You've got to think. If we could find out who really did take it—"

"That's foolishness," she snapped right back at him. "If I couldn't figure it out when I was there, I'm certain sure not going to find out now." Before he could say anything else, she jerked her way free of his grip . . . and then felt cold and lonely when he wasn't holding her.

"I'm going home before my head explodes. Just leave it alone, Josiah. There's nothing anyone can do. It's over and done with."

She hurried to the door, wiping away tears with the back of her hand. Before she could get outside, she heard his voice behind her.

"Leah, at least talk to me about it." The edge was gone from his voice, and he was very nearly pleading.

She couldn't, no matter how much she might want to. She should never have been so weak as to tell Josiah. Longing to get away and hide, she darted out and slammed the door behind her.

SUPPRESSING HIS DESIRE TO GO AFTER HER, JOSIAH stalked to the window, then gripped the sill with both hands so tightly that his knuckles turned white. Her slight figure, her jacket dark against the snow, was bent, making him think she was crying. He clenched his fist and slammed it hard against the windowsill. It rewarded him with an ominous creak.

Couldn't Leah see that the only way to stop agonizing over what had happened to her was to clear it up? Suffering in silence wasn't a solution. She was beating herself up for something that wasn't her fault—or her responsibility.

For an instant, Josiah had a glimmer of understanding. Why should *she* have to prove herself innocent? If that precious aunt of hers accused her, she should bring the proof for Leah to see.

Forgive and forget . . . yah, he believed in it. But Leah hadn't done anything that warranted forgiveness, and clearly her aunt hadn't forgotten, either.

His fist clenched again, but deciding the window wouldn't hold up to any more temper displays, he walked back to the cabinet he hoped to finish this afternoon.

At first he had to force himself to concentrate, but soon his fingers began to move automatically, leaving his mind free to worry at the issue. If something like that had happened here, he figured he could find out who was responsible . . . not because he was any kind of an expert but because it mattered so much he'd never let it go.

But it hadn't, and he didn't know enough about her aunt's community. A few people here had relatives there, but his family didn't. A trusted friend or cousin would be a useful source of information right now.

He couldn't think of a way to free Leah from the burden of that unearned guilt. But he wouldn't give up, that was certain sure. Once he could get her to talk to him, he'd find out who else had access to that cash box. And Leah must know things she didn't even realize she knew.

Mealtime had come and gone without him when his brother Paul came in, stamping snow from his boots. He held up a lunch box.

"I persuaded Mammi not to come out and drag you in to eat, but I couldn't keep her from packing you a lunch." He handed over the lunch box.

"Denke." How had Paul known how much he wanted to be alone? He must have sensed something in the air between his brother and Leah. If so, Paul was a lot more noticing than his brother had given him credit for.

Paul shrugged off his jacket, warmed his fingers briefly at the kerosene heater, and came to squat next to the cabinet. "It's coming along, yah?" He reached past Josiah to steady the door.

"It's fine." He wasn't in the mood to talk.

"Yah, but—" Paul shifted position and was even more in the way.

"Move back, can't you?" Josiah frowned at him.

"Okay, okay." Paul had the air of someone who knew better, but he obeyed orders. He took his hand away, and the door, secured by only one loose screw, fell off.

Silence for a moment, while they both looked at the door.

"Ahh . . . that's what I wanted to tell you." If Paul wanted to smile, he managed to control it.

Josiah let out a long breath, then another, and finally sat back on his heels and chuckled. "Okay. Sorry for my bad temper."

Paul's face relaxed. "If you want to tell me whatever it is, well, I know how to keep my mouth shut."

Josiah studied his little brother's face. There was no hidden agenda, and he wasn't teasing. His little brother honestly wanted to help.

"Denke, Paul." His voice was gravelly but not curt. "I would, but it's not my secret." He paused, then rested his hand on his brother's shoulder for a moment. "Here, let's get this put together. You hold it in place while I mark the hinges."

They worked together in silence for a few minutes.

"I told Daad I was giving you a hand," Paul commented.

Paul was never one to keep quiet for long. "He says the more I learn, the better."

Josiah had tensed a bit at the mention of their father, and he pushed himself to smile. "That's true enough. I'm glad he trusts me to teach you."

His brother's blue eyes widened. "Why wouldn't he?"

That was a mistake. He shouldn't involve Paul with his own frustration. "Ach, well, I just thought he'd want to teach you things himself."

"I figure he got too discouraged when he tried it with Ben," Paul said, grinning.

"Yah, Benjamin will never make a carpenter, that's for sure. Remember the birdhouse he tried to make for Mammi?" He chuckled at the thought. "No self-respecting bird would even try to nest in it."

Sharing a laugh over the family memories was one of the best things about working with kin. He couldn't imagine working with a bunch of strangers.

Paul straightened, glancing around the back room. "So this goes over next to the sink?"

He nodded. "I figure to wait until the new sink goes in to install it, though. Leah says she needs plenty of counter space for working with seedlings, but once we get the greenhouse up in the spring, she should have more than enough."

They both looked through the window to where the greenhouse would be. "I guess Leah is wonderful glad to be home and building up her own business," Paul said. "She's better off with folks who know her. Especially after all the problems she had up there with her aunt."

At first, the significance of Paul's words didn't register with Josiah. He was so used to hearing Paul rattle on about anything and nothing that he only listened with half an ear.

But finally it penetrated. He spun toward his brother, grabbing his arm.

"Ouch. Hey, what . . ."

Paul looked shocked, but no more so than Josiah was at the surge of anger that shot through him. How could his brother know anything about it? "What do you mean? What problems?"

"Well, I don't know . . . I mean, not exactly," Paul stammered. "I mean, everybody said she was going to stay up there and take over her aunt's business, but something went wrong with that, ain't so?"

Speculation tumbled through his mind. How could Paul know anything? And then a bigger fear overtook his thoughts. If Leah heard him say anything like that, she'd assume Josiah had told him.

He forced himself to stay calm. If he vented his feelings on his brother, he wouldn't learn anything.

"Maybe Leah just decided she'd rather be home. Didn't you think about that?"

"Well, I guess. But somebody said there was more to it than that."

"Who?" he snapped, any semblance of calm vanishing in a second.

Paul made an instinctive movement back. "Hey, take it easy. I wouldn't say anything bad about Leah. You know that."

Josiah took a deep breath. "Yah, I know. But if somebody else is hinting about things . . . well, you know how hurt Leah would be."

"I wouldn't repeat anything. Honest." He paled. "I wouldn't want Leah to get hurt."

"No, I guess you wouldn't. But if someone else is thinking that, I want to know about it before they start spreading rumors all over the place."

Paul nodded slowly, his face sober. "Well, I think it was Jamie Miller. Or maybe his sister, Dora. You know how Dorie jabbers. And their mother's cousin or something lives in that community where Leah's aunt is."

"What exactly did this cousin say?"

His brother shrugged. "I don't know. I mean, nobody listens to Dorie that much. She never shuts up."

Like you, Josiah thought, but he was too concerned to find it funny. "You must remember something."

"Well, I think it was something about a fuss between Leah and her aunt, and how the cousin said that she wouldn't work for Leah's aunt for anything, because the aunt was so picky. But then she started babbling about her job at the restaurant in town, and I stopped listening."

Apparently that was all there was to get from his brother. Josiah felt as if he were walking on a tightrope. What to do? If he probed any more, Paul would start suspecting something. But if he didn't find out what that relative had actually said, who knew what kind of gossip would flow through the Amish grapevine?

Leah would hear about it, that was certain sure. If something like that started flying around, getting worse as it went, she'd be hurt and humiliated. And how could she fight something so shapeless and indefinite?

He had to do something, but he had a feeling that no matter what he did, Leah was going to end up getting hurt.

DRIVING INTO TOWN TO PICK UP BECKY THAT AF-ternoon, Leah realized how quickly the snow had melted. While it still lay untouched on the fields and pastures, the roads and driveways were clear, and slushy water ran in the ditches. A watery sun shone down on her.

If the weather held, the rest of the snow would be gone in a day or two . . . not surprising, because it was early to have it accumulate. But no matter how abnormal, just about everyone enjoyed the first snowfall and longed for another one for Christmas.

Except for the occasional car, the road was empty, and the only sound the clop of the horse's hooves and the creak of the wheels. In the quiet, her conversation with Josiah came flooding back into her mind.

How could she have told him the whole story? She'd promised herself that no one would ever hear it from her. And then at the first reminder of her aunt's accusation, it had burst out of her mouth, and to Josiah.

Maybe it wasn't so surprising that it had been Josiah, though. Who else could she tell? Certainly not anyone in her own family . . . she could easily see where that would go, with Mamm and Daad defending her. And Aunt Miriam . . . well, the result would be a painful split in the family, and she couldn't bear to do that to them.

Still, she couldn't help but be heartened by Josiah's instant belief in her. He knew her far better than Aunt Miriam, and from what she could see, there hadn't been a second when he'd doubted her.

But satisfying as it was to feel that belief, his idea that she could somehow prove her innocence was just impossible. Even when she'd been there she couldn't think of an explanation, and at this distance of time and miles, it was clearly impossible. Whoever had stolen from Aunt Miriam, he or she had gotten clear away with it.

She was a few minutes late, and she spotted Becky on the sidewalk, waiting for her. Good . . . that meant she could pull up and get her instead of parking and going inside. Normally she loved talking to Dinah, but the day had just been too upsetting.

A car drew out, leaving space right in front of the coffee shop for her to stop. Becky came rushing across the sidewalk and scrambled in, very much in a hurry.

"I'm sorry I kept you waiting in the cold." Leah scooted a little closer to her, holding out the edge of the lap robe. "Share this with me, and you'll warm up in a minute."

"That's all right." Becky was glancing away, and her voice seemed muffled. "I should have gone back inside, I guess. Let's just get home."

Checking the traffic, Leah clicked to the horse. "Off we go."

They hadn't gone more than a block when she glanced over at Becky to see her looking back the way they'd come, as if watching for something. She must not have seen it, whatever it was, because she turned around again and settled back on the seat. She tucked the lap robe across her, but a moment later she pulled her hands free again, twisting her fingers together as if she intended to tie them in knots.

Taking the lines in her left hand, Leah reached over to clasp those frantic fingers in her own. "Becky, whatever is wrong? Did you forget something? Should we go back?"

"What? No, no. I . . . it's all right."

She tried to pull her hands free, but Leah wouldn't let go. "Komm now. If you don't tell me what's wrong, I'll have to pull over, and we'd get awfully cold just sitting there, ain't so?"

Leah tried to cover the anxiety by keeping her words light, but she didn't think she succeeded very well. Something was clearly the matter. Trouble with her job?

"I don't . . ." Becky's voice wobbled. "Don't tell anybody," she said, all in a rush.

"Hush, now. It's all right." She patted the cold hands. Daisy would take them home whether Leah drove her or not, that was certain sure. "I won't say anything if you don't want me to, but you have to tell me what's wrong."

Becky blew out a long breath, forming a mist in the air, and her tense hands seemed to ease off their straining. "It was him . . . the man I told you about. The Englischer at the coffee shop."

"Did you tell Dinah?" She'd felt relieved after talking to Becky and having a word or two with Dinah. That must have been a mistake.

Becky shook her head. "I couldn't . . . I mean, it wasn't in the coffee shop. Usually one of the other girls will take his table, or Cousin Dinah will. So that was okay. But then, while I was waiting for you, he pulled up in his car."

She took an instinctive glance back. "You mean the one that pulled out—"

"Yah." Becky rubbed her forehead. "It . . . he probably didn't mean anything. I mean, he just asked if I needed a ride home. And I said no, my sister was coming. But then he said to get in, and he'd drive me to meet you. And he kept urging me."

Guilt flooded through Leah. She'd been late. She'd been engrossed in her own problems, and she'd left her little sister standing there.

She shook her head irritably. What good did blaming herself do? Becky had to learn how to manage herself when she was away from her family. And anyway, she could have stepped back inside the shop.

"If you were upset, why didn't you just go back inside?"

"I . . ." Becky sniffled a little. "I was kind of embarrassed. I mean, he was being friendly, and joking, and everything. I didn't want to . . . to make a scene." She rubbed her nose vigorously. "I know it's dumb, but I just sort of couldn't find any words. But then you came, and I said here you were, and he just said bye and drove away."

"It's all right. You're okay."

Becky shook her head. "I knew I should go back inside, but I couldn't seem to do it. Why? It's like I was frozen."

"I understand." Leah put her free arm around her, snuggling her close. "I know."

And the strange thing was that she did understand. At Becky's words, she was back in her aunt's greenhouse, listening to her accusation of theft, and standing frozen, unable to speak or defend herself.

Because she understood, she had to be the one who could help Becky. It couldn't be more clear if it was written on a sign in front of her. She could only hope she knew how to do it.

The horse clopped on patiently as Leah breathed a silent prayer.

"You and I might find things easier if we were like Judith. You can't picture her ever being without words, can you?"

At Becky's nod she went on, feeling her way. "We're not like her, though. We're just ourselves, you and I. The hardest thing for us to do is to confront someone . . . to come right out and say what we think. We'd always rather run away or give in or anything to get out of an embarrassing situation, yah?"

"Yah." Becky squeezed her hand. "I . . . I didn't think you were that way."

No, of course not. She was Becky's older sister, the one who did everything first, the one who went places. Becky didn't see the person she hid inside herself. The person who'd run off to Aunt Miriam's rather than stay and confront Josiah. And then she'd run off home, rather than confronting her aunt and saying loud and clear that she hadn't taken anything. And if she weren't careful, she'd go on running away the rest of her life.

It was such a startling thought that she really wanted to stop and consider it further, but right now, Becky came first.

"You know, I'd have saved myself a lot of grief if I'd spoken up for myself." Her throat contracted on the words, and she had to push them out.

Becky looked at her wonderingly. "You mean with . . . with Josiah?"

"Yah, with Josiah. And some other times, too, but I didn't. I'm going to try to figure out how to stop doing that." She held her sister's hand tightly. "Maybe together we can figure out how to confront your problem, too. Okay?"

Becky's face held a hopeful expression. "Yah. I'd like that."

They were in agreement. Now all she had to do was to come up with a solution. She had an idea how to help Becky find her voice, but her own answer was still lost in a fog of what-ifs.

CHAPTER TEN

BY THE TIME THEY REACHED HOME, LEAH HAD A plan that she hoped would help Becky deal with her annoying customer and maybe give the younger ones a guide to future problems. As for her own problem, she still didn't know.

She couldn't go back and change what her fear had made her do in the past, but at least she could change how she confronted problems in the future. If only she could be brave enough . . .

The first step was to clear her plans with Mammi. The opportunity came when she found herself helping Mamm roll out the dough for homemade noodles.

Leah patted a small ball of dough on a floured bread board. Mammi was doing the same at the other end of the table.

"It takes an awful big amount of noodles to feed this family." Leah pressed the dough down and began rolling it out gently.

Mammi smiled. "I've never made too many. Sometimes

I think there will be leftovers, but the more we have, the more they eat. Your brothers, especially. Ach, but that's a wonderful gut thing, yah?"

"For sure." She turned the board to roll in the other direction, creating a bigger, flatter circle with each stroke. Mammi was doing the same, and they worked almost in rhythm.

"You know, I was thinking that it might be good for me to talk to the girls about how to deal with people like . . . well, like some people I ran into when I was traveling by myself. People who get too friendly."

By making it sound as if it was about her, she might be able to divert attention from Becky. But she quickly found she was wrong.

"Becky," her mother said quickly. "Has she talked with you? What is troubling her?"

She had to proceed carefully now. "Becky did talk with me a bit. But—"

"Ach, I know," Mammi interrupted. She brushed her lips as if to brush away the question she'd asked, leaving a smear of flour on her cheek. "She asked you not to say anything." She seemed to struggle with the words. "It's all right. Go on."

Leah nodded, feeling as if a lot could be said between the two of them without the need for words. Mammi was having the fear lots of Amish mothers had these days . . . that their young daughters might not be prepared for the outside world intruding on their safety. Too many bad things had happened, some right here in Pennsylvania, at least one in their mother community in Lancaster County.

"I think I could help them know what to say and what to do, and maybe they'd . . ."

"They'd take it better from their sister than their parents," Mammi finished for her. She hesitated a moment, pondering before she spoke. "Yah, I think they might."

Mammi dusted her hands together, came around the table, and hugged her tightly. "Denke, Leah. Let's do it."

So with considerable doubts, after supper Leah popped an enormous mixing bowl full of popcorn, chased her brothers away, and led her sisters upstairs to her bedroom. She shut the door and plopped the bowl and a stack of napkins in the middle of the bed.

"Was ist letz? What's wrong?" Judith was the first to ask. "What's going on?"

"We're having a girls' party," Leah said firmly. "Have a seat."

In a minute they were all sprawled on the bed surrounding the popcorn bowl. "This is a gut idea," Hannie got out around a mouthful of popcorn, some of it spurting back out.

"Yuck, how gross." Judith threw some of it back at her.

"Quit it or I'll tell Mammi you said a bad word," Hannie threatened.

"Let it go, you two." Leah toyed with a handful of popcorn, unsure how to start now that she had them here. Would Becky understand that what she said was for her?

"Go on, Leah." Becky glared at the younger ones. "Don't mind these kids."

"Right." She took a breath and prayed she could find the words. "You know, when I went up to Aunt Miriam's place, that was the first time I'd ever gone on a bus by myself. Lots of times with Mamm and Daad, but never by myself. How would you feel about doing it?"

Hannie wrapped her arms around herself. "I wouldn't. Not unless someone was with me. That's scary." She shivered, and Leah pulled her onto her lap and hugged her.

"What's to be scared about?" Judith said scornfully. "I'm not a baby. I'd like to do it. I'd go clear to Niagara Falls if I could. I'd like to see that." Her eyes sparkled.

"How can you think of that?" Becky was almost as upset as Hannie was at the thought. This might be harder than Leah had thought it would be.

"Well, sometime you might have to go somewhere on

your own," Leah said. "And it was kind of fun at first. I had a window seat so I could see everything we went past."

"That would be nice," Becky acknowledged.

Leah nodded and went on. "But after a bit an older man came and sat down in the seat next to me. He seemed okay at first, but then he kept moving closer and closer to me, like he wanted to see out the window."

She looked from one face to another. Mostly this was true, and it made a good object lesson.

Hannie wiggled, uncomfortable at the thought. "I'd be scared, Leah. Weren't you scared?"

"I was, a little bit. But he seemed really nice, and we were right there with other people around. He was laughing and saying funny things about what he could see out the window. But I was uncomfortable, too. I didn't want to hurt his feelings or make a scene, but . . . I didn't know what to do."

They were all very still, eyes wide, watching her. Becky's lips trembled for a moment.

"So what did you do?" Judith said, for once not sure she had all the answers.

"I just sat there, feeling like I was frozen, and he kept leaning against me. And then I saw an Englisch woman a couple of rows ahead looking at me, like she knew what was happening. I saw her get up, and then she came back and spoke to the man." She paused for breath and saw that they were completely engrossed.

"So this lady told him she wanted to sit there, and he could take her seat by the window, next to her husband. At first I thought he was going to say something nasty to her, but she just stared at him. And then she said the same thing, only louder. Some other people turned and looked, and her husband stood up. And the man got up right away and did what she said."

"What else did the lady say?" Hannie wiggled and

helped herself to more popcorn, apparently relieved. "Did she ride with you then?"

"Yah, she stayed with me all the way to Aunt Miriam's. And she said something I thought I should remember. She said, 'If somebody makes you feel uncomfortable, you have a right to say no. And if they don't listen, say it again, louder. That usually embarrasses them enough to make them back off.'"

"Did you say that yourself?" Becky asked.

Leah shrugged, knowing she had to be truthful. "Sometimes I did. But sometimes I wanted to but I didn't. I guess I should have practiced it, ain't so?"

"Practiced?" Becky said, doubtful.

"Sure. Just like this. No! No! No!" She looked at them, making sure they understood she was serious. "Say it with me. No!"

"No," they chorused.

She shook her head. "That wasn't very determined. Try it again. Said it nice and loud. *No! No! No!*"

This time it was more convincing. "Komm on. Louder. Loud enough to shake the roof."

"No! No! No! No!" Their four voices really did seem loud enough to shake the roof. Hannie started to giggle, and in a moment they were all collapsing on the bed, making it creak with their laughter.

She glanced at Becky. Her face was pink, and she was laughing as loud as the others.

Would it help? She didn't know. She hoped so. That Englischer had a job in town. He couldn't afford to have a sweet little Amish girl shouting no at him. And maybe practice would give Becky the nerve she needed to stand up for herself.

JOSIAH WAS WORKING ALONE THE NEXT MORNING, Paul having been sent off on an errand to town. He'd welcomed the privacy, hoping that Leah would show up, giving him a chance to smooth over whatever ill effects had followed her unexpected confidences the day before. But it was midmorning, and she hadn't shown up yet.

He checked the level of the shelf he was replacing in the small entryway at the back of the cottage. There wasn't much space there, but a little extra storage was always useful. And he could easily glance out the small window and see if anyone was coming. Not that he was eager to see Leah, or anything. But he'd gotten used to seeing something of her every day.

Most likely, Leah was embarrassed to be around him after what she'd told him. She'd been keeping her secret pretty well since she'd returned, but he could tell that it had been wearing on her. She'd been ready to explode with it, and he'd been handy.

He still didn't entirely buy Leah's reason for keeping such a secret. After all, her family would support her, and they would be just as sure as he was that the whole thing had been a misunderstanding.

Some misunderstanding—her own aunt behaving like that. Worse, it had been the aunt she'd spent her life looking up to. The woman sounded like one of those self-righteous people who'd never done a wrong thing and was eager to lecture someone else.

A surge of anger went through him at the thought. He whacked at the nail, missed, and hit his finger. Dropping the hammer, he muttered under his breath, clutching his finger. Maybe that was meant to be a lesson to him to control himself.

He picked up the hammer and secured the shelf with a few taps before glancing out the window. And there was Leah, almost to the porch. Reaching for the doorknob, he gave himself a firm warning to be tactful. He'd let Leah take the lead and try to keep his opinions about her aunt to himself.

Leah came in, her cheeks rosy, bringing with her a warm scent of cinnamon.

"You smell like baking." He said the first thing that popped into his head.

"Good guess." If there'd been any tension in Leah when she'd stepped inside, it was gone now. "We were making cookies for the school Christmas program. Hannie has been so excited she doesn't know what to do with herself, so this should make her happy."

He gave a pointed look at the basket she carried. "By any chance did you bring some for us?"

"Yah, I did." She glanced around. "Is Paul not here this morning?"

"He'll be back later." He grinned. "Don't worry. I'll save one for him."

"More than one. He's a growing boy, ain't so?"

"Well, so am I. Let's go in where it's warmer." He held the door to the back room, then picked up his toolbox and followed her.

Leah held out her hands to the kerosene heater. "Maybe I should get someone to check out the stove. It'll have to be done at some point anyway."

He shrugged. "Paul and I can do it, if you want. There's nothing he'd like better than to poke his head into a chimney."

Leah hung up her bonnet and coat. "Don't you mean that you don't want to?"

"Hey, the youngest gets the dirty jobs, didn't you know that?"

She seemed to be considering that. "I wouldn't say that applies to Hannie. Maybe it's different with a girl." She hesitated, her face growing sober. "Anyway, I wanted to say something to you."

But then she didn't speak, and he could actually feel her tension deepen, even though they were three feet apart. He tried to think of something to say to make it easier for her . . . it had to be about what happened the day before.

"Leah . . . ," he began, but she shook her head.

"I didn't intend to say any of that." The words came out in a rush, as if she'd lose her nerve if she didn't speak right away. "I want to be sure you understand that it's . . . well, private. I wouldn't want—"

"You wouldn't want me blabbing it around like the worst blabbermaul?" He was annoyed that she'd even think he would. "You should know me better than that. I won't repeat it, but I want a few answers."

Her eyes widened. "Answers? What is there to answer? I told you what happened, but I didn't mean to."

"Because I'm such a blabbermaul?" He took a step closer.

"All right, I know you're not that. It's just that it was so embarrassing I don't want to think about it, let alone talk about it."

"You told me the bare bones of it . . . your aunt said she knew you'd taken money from the cash box and then said that about forgiving and forgetting. And you just walked away."

"Yah, I know. You're thinking I should have argued, or insisted I didn't, or tried to find out who did. But I just couldn't. I was so shocked and upset and embarrassed that I just froze." Something changed in her face when she said the words . . . as if she saw something she hadn't seen before.

"Yah, well, I get that it was a shock. But didn't you want to know why she thought it was you? And was there really money missing, or did she just make a mistake?"

Leah rubbed her arms with her hands, as if she were cold despite standing right next to the source of heat. "I told you. No mistake. I'd noticed it a few days earlier. I was the one who drew her attention to it. Ten dollars, that's what was missing that day. And then twenty another day."

"Funny she thought it was you, since you're the one who noticed it. Isn't it?"

She didn't seem to have thought about it. "I guess it was. But the cash box hadn't been tampered with, and the only time it was unlocked was when we were actually using it. So who else could have done it? Anyway, that's what she figured."

"Weren't there people who helped? Maybe some people who were in there regularly?"

"Some, I guess. Some cousins who lived next door that helped . . . Jenny and Alice. They're sisters, thirteen and fourteen. And their brother, Alfred. Freddy, they called him, about ten. And Thomas Esch."

Something changed in her face when she mentioned that last name. What was it?

"Who's Thomas Esch?" he asked, surprised by the edge to his voice.

She shrugged. "Just . . . another neighbor's son. He often came over, and he'd help with any heavy work that had to be done."

"How old?" He wanted to know why she got that funny look in her face.

"I guess about our age. What difference does it make? He couldn't have done it."

It almost sounded as if she wanted to protect him, who-ever he was.

"Friend of yours, was he?"

"No. I mean, not exactly. Anyway, I told you. He wouldn't have done it."

He caught the difference in words. "You said he couldn't have done it. There's a difference between couldn't and wouldn't. Which is it?"

Leah started to turn away, and he caught her hands and drew her back to face him.

"Couldn't or wouldn't," she said. "He didn't, that's all."

"So that points to one of the cousins, since you're so sure it wasn't your boyfriend."

Her cheeks flamed. "He's not my boyfriend. And anyway, it doesn't matter how many questions you ask me."

"How old did you say the oldest cousin was?" Something flickered in his mind, an idea that was gone almost immediately.

"Fourteen, I guess. Almost fifteen. A cute girl . . . she reminded me of Judith in a way. But there's no way of knowing who did it, and nothing to be gained by talking about it."

"What do you mean, nothing? We know you didn't do it, but somebody did. Any one of them could have, it seems to me. Why did your aunt pick on you?"

"I don't know." Tears gleamed in her eyes, and she blinked as if to hold them back. "And it doesn't matter anyway. I told you, Aunt Miriam wouldn't listen to me. She'd already made up her mind, and it was forgiven and forgotten. That was the end of it."

Josiah rubbed her arms gently with his hands, wanting so much to draw her into his arms, hold her close, and comfort her. But he couldn't. He didn't have the right.

But he could wrap her hands in his, just for a moment, and feel her skin warm at his touch. He took a short breath, hardly daring to move, and tried to hold on to the moment.

Even as she pulled her hands away, he realized the truth. Leah . . . Leah had been the one. The woman for him. And he'd blown it, all for the sake of a silly flirtation with a girl who wasn't a tenth of the person Leah was.

Leah wouldn't forgive him. And not only that, he couldn't forgive himself.

LEAH TOOK A FEW STEPS AWAY FROM JOSIAH, NOT sure where she was going or why, but feeling the need to put a little space between them. His questions had been bad enough. It wasn't fair for him to . . . to what? Anyone looking on would say that she'd been upset and he'd simply tried to calm her down.

She had been upset, that was certain sure, both about having to remember a painful episode and also because Josiah seemed so determined to open everything up again when she'd just begun to think she was well on the way to forgetting it.

"Sorry, Leah." It sounded as if Josiah had trouble getting the words out.

She gave him a doubtful look, and he shook his head and smiled. "I know that look. But I really am sorry. I promised myself I wouldn't push my opinions on you, and first thing I knew I was doing it."

"That doesn't say much for your ability to keep your promises, does it?" As soon as she'd snapped out the words, she regretted them. He thought she was talking about the ending of their short romance . . . she could see that immediately. "Look, I didn't mean anything about us. Can't we forget this conversation and start over?"

"Yah, okay. I just really would like to help you."

Leah couldn't help but be moved by the genuine feeling in his voice. "There's nothing you can do. But denke. I appreciate the thought. It's over and done with."

Her thoughts flickered to her talk with her sisters the previous night. It was one thing to prepare ahead of time what you'd do in an uncomfortable situation. That could be helpful in preventing it.

Too bad that didn't work with those things that had already happened. If she were to change her way of dealing with the problems of life . . .

"You can't go back into the past," she said abruptly, caught up in her thoughts. "There's no way of fixing those mistakes that I can see."

"Maybe so." Josiah's hand, resting on top of the cabinet

he'd been working on, clenched into a fist. "But maybe there is, if you really want to."

Leah opened her mouth to say something and promptly shut it again. Anything she said would start another argument, and she'd have enough of that for one day.

"Josiah . . ." Before she could find a way of soothing the situation, she heard a car pull up in front of the cottage.

"Now who is it?" Josiah strode toward the front room. "We've had more company in the past few days—"

"Frank Conner." Leah hurried past him toward the door. "I hope it's not bad news about Jere. My mother heard that the doctors were going to have a conference today about what more to do. They said the concussion was still causing him some bad headaches and the doctors wanted more tests."

The man came to the door quickly, but Leah managed to get there first and open it to him. "Come in. I hope Jere is healing all right."

He stepped inside, his face breaking into a smile. "Good news from the doctors. They're going to let him come home tomorrow."

"Ach, that is wonderful news." She smiled back, thankful that the boy's injury proved not to be as serious as they'd feared at first. If the medical people had seen him the way they had that day . . .

"He'll have to have a bed on the first floor and lots of attention from the physical therapists, but at least he'll be home." Frank was so enthusiastic he couldn't stand still. "I'm going to turn the family room into a bedroom for him. He'll like that, and he'll have the television there to watch and be close to the kitchen."

"And you'll be wonderful glad to have him home." It was lovely to see how happy he was. "My mother is making something to bring over for your supper tomorrow, and we all want to help however we can."

"You've already done . . ." He stopped, seeming to choke

up, and then put his hand on Josiah's shoulder. "If you hadn't got him out so quickly—well, we'll never forget what we owe all of you."

Josiah flushed, embarrassed. "Ach, anyone would have done the same."

Her heart swelled, and she knew tears were not far away. "We were just glad we were there," she managed to say.

Conner wiped his eyes with the back of his hand. "He'll want to thank you all himself. He says I should tell you he's sorry, Leah."

He looked puzzled, but Leah wasn't eager to tell him about what Jere had said to her.

"Ach, it was nothing. Tell him it's all right." She smiled, thinking of how she'd pictured the small boy he'd been instead of being angry with the surly adolescent.

He glanced at his watch. "Gotta go. Lots to do." He looked as if he wanted to repeat his thanks, and Leah was relieved when he just waved and hurried out.

She was eager to hurry off home herself, wanting to avoid any more conversation about the theft and her aunt. If Josiah thought he could figure out who'd done it, he'd just have to manage it without her.

"I must go as well. I'm supposed to be taking Becky to work. I'll see you."

"Yah." He made no move to stop her, and he was smiling. "Soon. Tomorrow is the Christmas party over at Ruthie Miller's, don't forget. I'll pick you up around four."

"I . . . you don't need to do that. I told you. I don't even know if I want to go. Anyway . . ."

"Anyway, Ruthie told me I was supposed to bring you. And you're supposed to bring a gelatin salad for the supper. Your mammi said you would."

Her mother, Ruthie, Josiah . . . it seemed everyone was in on this but her. It would serve them all right if she flat out refused to go.

She couldn't do that, of course. It would just make everyone talk more than they were already.

Josiah had gotten his way over this, but he didn't need to think he could use the trip to question her about Aunt Miriam. She was ready to forget, if only he'd let her.

CHAPTER ELEVEN

WHEN LEAH AND BECKY REACHED THE COFFEE SHOP a little later, she drove the buggy around the building to the hitching rails at the side. Becky gave her a questioning look. "Do you have something to do in town?"

Leah smiled. "Something very important. I'm going to provide moral support for my little sister."

Becky's cheeks flamed. "You mean . . . but he might not even come in today. You can't look after me the whole time I'm working."

Unsure whether Becky was offended or wanted reassurance, she spoke carefully. "Maybe he won't. And I certain sure can't be with you all the time. Neither of us would like that, ain't so?"

Her lips twitching in the beginning of a smile, Becky shook her head. "I guess not."

"I just thought I'd have a cup of coffee with Dinah. And maybe get a good look at this persistent Englischer if he's there. It can't hurt."

Becky climbed down and tethered the mare. "I know we

got kind of silly last night." They walked together to the door that led to the kitchen. "But it helped. It really did."

"Good." Of course the proof would be in the pudding, as Grossmammi always said. She followed Becky inside and went to speak to her cousin.

Dinah was behind the counter, putting a fresh tray of doughnuts and crullers into the glass case.

"Leah, how nice." Dinah slid the glass panel back. "I hope today you have time to stay a bit. We can chat, yah?" She was already pouring coffee into two mugs.

"I'd love it." Leah made an effort to chase other troubles from her mind. Later. She'd worry about what to do about everything else later. Right now she wanted to let Becky know she had support.

They were soon settled at the small table tucked around the corner of the counter. "Okay, tell me." Dinah must see very well that something was wrong. "It's about Becky?"

"Yah." Leah kept her voice low. "Apparently when she was waiting for me yesterday, a man who's one of your customers pulled up and offered to take her home."

Dinah's head came up sharply. "Did you see him? Who was it?"

"I didn't get a very good look at him, because he pulled out right away. I'd seen him before, coming out of the bank. Young, dark hair, wearing a shirt and tie."

"There aren't that many men in town who wear a tie these days. Mostly people like lawyers and bankers . . ." Dinah stopped in midsentence. "It would be the new young man at the bank, I think. He comes in for coffee almost every day." She was frowning, obviously disturbed. "Becky should have told me if he's been bothering her."

"Don't feel bad. It took a lot of pushing to make her tell me." She didn't want Dinah to start feeling guilty about it. "Apparently from the first time she waited on him, she couldn't tell whether he was speaking seriously or joking. You know how shy she is." She frowned, knowing that she should have seen it sooner. After all, she'd felt the same more than once. "She probably felt it was all her fault for not understanding."

Dinah nodded. "Yah, I see that. It's harder for some girls than others to deal with, especially if someone seems to be flirting but not seriously. I'm sorry. I should have realized he was making her uncomfortable. He's new in town, and maybe he doesn't know much about the Amish. But if so, it's time he learned." She looked ready to tackle someone.

"Don't start blaming yourself. I talked to her and the younger girls last night. Told them something . . . well, that happened to me. Maybe it will help. If she is brave enough to handle it herself, that would be best."

Dinah's lips twitched. "Is that why you're here? To take over if she's not?"

"I'll try not to cause a ruckus in your shop." Leah glanced up at the sound of the bell on the door.

"Here's your chance. He's coming in now," Dinah said. "I can wait on him myself . . ."

Leah shook her head. "Let's see what Becky does."

She watched as her sister seemed to register the newcomer. For a moment Becky didn't move, but then, standing very straight, she got out her pad and headed for the table.

"Don't stare," Leah murmured when Dinah twisted in her chair. With a deliberate move, Dinah adjusted her chair so she could see.

They couldn't hear what was said, but it was very brief, and then Becky went to fill a mug with coffee.

"So far, so good," Leah murmured.

"He may have gotten the message from someone else." Dinah was frowning so hard it was a wonder the man didn't feel it.

A few minutes later, carrying a tray with coffee and a doughnut, Becky approached the table again, looking a bit more assured, Leah thought.

The man looked up at her, laughing as he put some money on the table. Becky's smile was stiff, and she shook her head.

In another instant, he had put his hand on Becky's wrist. Forgetting her intent, Leah started from her chair, only to be stopped by Dinah's hand on her sleeve.

"Wait," she whispered.

Becky stood as if frozen, and it was as if Leah stood there in her skin, feeling that embarrassment, not wanting to make a scene.

Becky's lips formed a word. The man continued talking, smiling.

"No." It was loud enough for them to hear—loud enough that several people turned at surrounding tables, and one older man started to his feet.

They saw a dull red flood the young Englischer's face as he quickly took his hand away. Becky, head high, marched back to the counter. Was it Leah's imagination, or did she look more mature than she had a moment ago?

Dinah patted Leah's hand. "Gut. She handled it. You'll maybe have to tell me that story sometime, yah?"

"I will," she said, immeasurably relieved. She watched Becky, knowing how hard that had been for her little sister. But knowing, too, that it was through the hard things that she would grow. They both would.

BY THE NEXT AFTERNOON LEAH HAD REALIZED THAT her mother was more excited about her rumspringa group party than Leah was herself.

"Of course you're going!" Her response to Leah's suggestion of missing it this year was emphatic. "All you've done since you came home is work and spend time with family."

Leah had to laugh at her mother's horrified expression. "There's nothing wrong with that, is there?" She packed the gelatin salad she was taking into a basket and covered it carefully. "I like my family."

"You should be having fun with people your own age." Mammi took a firm line. "And Ruthie has worked so hard on this get-together. She started planning early, she said, so folks wouldn't already be booked up."

"That made good sense," Grossmammi added. "December is filled up with all the groups wanting to have Christmas events. Besides, you'll have a chance to see their house and the twins. Such precious babies they are."

Leah had the feeling her grandmother was hinting. In fact, everything about this party smelled of matchmaking. When would they understand she and Josiah were not getting together again?

And as for Ruthie, she no doubt just wanted to show off her new house and her new babies. Twins. She always did have to be the best at everything.

"There's Josiah, ready to get started. At least you'll get there before dark." Mammi handed her the basket as soon as she had her wool jacket on. "Don't forget the salad."

"No chance of that, is there?" She hurriedly added her thanks, kissed her mother and grandmother, and escaped out the back door.

"Give Josiah our love," Grossmammi called after her, but she kept on going, pretending she didn't hear.

The air was brisk and cold, but the sun was still above the hills. Josiah reached down a hand to help her up and then spread the buggy blanket over her lap.

"There you go. That'll keep you warm." He took a closer look at her. "What are you so annoyed about?"

"I'm not annoyed," she snapped, and then had to laugh at his expression. "Well, all right, I am. Mammi is just so eager to put me together with the people who were in my rumspringa group. I think she feels it will encourage me to get married, seeing Ruthie's new house and twin babies."

"Ruthie wants to show them off, all right," he said. "I

ran into her at the hardware store the other day, and she told me all about them. I thought I'd never get away."

They shouldn't talk about their old classmate that way, but at least laughing together had put her in a better frame of mind.

"She always did like to show off, from the time when she was just a first grader at Orchard Hill School. Grossmammi says that people don't really change when they get older, they just get more so."

He chuckled. "Your grossmammi is always right, but I hope that doesn't mean Paul will still be playing pranks when he's sixty. I guess the right woman can cure him."

She was startled at the easy way he said that. "Do you really think so?"

"Sure. Take you. You could have cured me of flirting with pretty girls, if you hadn't run away in such a hurry."

"I didn't run anywhere." That wasn't true, and she knew it, but she certain sure wasn't going to let Josiah know that.

"Komm on now, Leah. You'd left town before I even had a chance to apologize or explain. Off to your aunt for refuge."

"Just forget about my aunt," she retorted, stung. "I don't want to hear you talking about her any longer."

They were turning into the lane at Ruthie and her husband's house, and Josiah slowed down. "Fine, but there's one thing I have to say about her first."

Someone else had pulled in behind them, and shouted at them, cheerfully wanting to know if they were lost.

"Say it in a hurry, then. You're making us conspicuous."

"Fine. Here it is. Your aunt Miriam has to hear the truth. Whether she believes it or not is up to her, but you can't leave it at the way it is. It's not right."

"Okay, you've said it." She tried to smother the little flame of anger within her. "Now get moving, or I'll jump out and walk."

With an exasperated sigh, Josiah clicked to the horse.

When they reached the back door, he let her off and went to park the buggy. Leah was able to go inside alone, which she appreciated. She could imagine the knowing smiles if she and Josiah walked in together.

Ruthie hurried to meet her, taking control of the basket. "So good to see you after all this time. I heard you're setting up a business of your own now. Do you like the kitchen? We had it all done over when we got married."

Leah complimented the kitchen and then was swept away by several other people eager to talk to her. It wasn't until she greeted everyone who was there that Anna Stoltzfus, always one of her close friends, caught her wrist and pulled her into a corner.

"It's about time you came to talk to me," Anna lectured. "You've been home two weeks and you haven't come to see me yet."

Leah smiled, hugging her. "Is that the way you talk to your scholars? How do you like being the teacher at Orchard Hill School?"

Color flooded Anna's normally pale cheeks. "Ach, I love it. I learned so much when I was assistant to Dorcas. You know she's married now?"

"Yah, Mammi keeps me up-to-date on all the weddings, that's certain sure."

"She's still trying to get you married off, ain't so?"

Leah nodded. Amish mothers were all alike in that, she figured. "The only thing that reconciled her to my going off to Aunt Miriam's was the thought that I'd find somebody to marry up there." She winced a little at the thought but kept her smile intact. "And now here I am, back again like a bad penny."

Anna grew serious. "After what happened with Josiah, maybe it was a gut thing for you. I wish my mother would stop talking babies at me. I want to teach for a few years before I even think about that."

"That's how I feel." She and Anna had a similar way of

looking at things. Probably that was what had made them such good friends. "I want to prove I can take care of my own self. I don't need Josiah or any other man."

Anna nodded, but her gaze was fixed on a group of people across the room. Leah followed her gaze. Josiah had just come in. She watched as he greeted people, slapping the men on the shoulder and smiling at each of the women. Her face tightened.

"He was wrong about that Susie Lehman," Anna said carefully. "We all know that. But as for the way he greets everyone like they're special—well, I think that's just Josiah."

Leah told herself it didn't matter a thing to her how many women Josiah flirted with. She had no interest in him at all except as a carpenter.

So why did her heart sink in her chest when she watched him talking with other women? It wasn't right that she seemed to have no control over it. Not right at all.

JOSIAH FELT LEAH'S GAZE FROM ACROSS THE ROOM . . . as if they were connected across space. Ridiculous. He had to admit that she attracted him. She always had. And he had feelings for her. But he wasn't some fourteen-year-old, imagining first love striking. And things between them were a lot more complicated.

Someone moved next to him, and he glanced over to see Amos Troyer, a distant cousin of the Stoltzes.

"Nice to see Leah back, ain't so?"

Amos had obviously noticed Josiah staring. That would teach him to start daydreaming about her.

"Yah, sure is." He felt as if something else was needed. "I'm doing a job of work for her . . . fixing up that old cottage next to the Stoltz place so she can have a business there."

"I heard. Her daad was talking to my daad. Funny."

He raised his eyebrows. "What's funny about two cousins talking?"

Amos elbowed him. "Not that. I was thinking about Leah. We all thought when she went up to Miriam's that she'd be taking over Miriam's business."

"She decided to start a business here. Nothing funny about it that I can see."

"You know what I mean." Amos gave him a sidelong look. "My mamm says it was always an accepted thing that Miriam would pass her business on to Leah, her favorite niece. Then all of a sudden everything changed. Can't keep people from talking about something like that."

"People should mind their own business." He felt like snarling. Why did people have to be so interested in everyone's business anyway. I, for one, am glad Leah decided to come back here and start her own business, instead of settling so far away. And so are her folks."

"Gives you a chance to make up for past mistakes, doesn't it?" Amos let out a bark of laughter. "Maybe you can find yourself a bride who's got a nice little business of her own, ain't so?"

Josiah unclenched his fist very slowly. He really couldn't start a fight at Ruthie's Christmas party. Or anywhere else, for that matter.

"Tactful, aren't you, Amos? You'd best be careful, or folks are going to start calling you a blabbermaul."

The expression on Amos's face was ludicrous for an instant, and then he sobered. "Hey, I was just joking. If you and Leah should make up . . . well, everybody always thought you two belonged together. You just better stop flirting with every pretty girl you see."

Was he never going to outgrow that reputation? Apparently not. Anyhow, he had to figure out how to turn this conversation to something light, or Amos would be repeating it to everyone he knew.

"I will. I promise," he said solemnly. "Now be a good

friend and don't spoil my chances by talking about it, right?"

"Sure thing. Silent as the grave, that's me." Amos, grinning, gave him a light punch on the arm. "You just tell me when to welcome you to the family, okay?"

"Right, I will."

Josiah breathed a sigh of relief. Amos wasn't the most mature guy he knew, but you could usually count on him to do what he said.

Now to talk to Leah, and this time, he had to try not to make her mad. He hadn't been doing that very well, but after what Paul said yesterday and now Amos tonight, there were rumors going around. Leah had to be prepared for that. And he had to tell her, so she wouldn't believe he was the one behind them.

Poor Leah. All that effort to keep her secret, and everyone was talking about it anyway. It didn't seem fair.

He began working his way casually across the room. They'd probably be called in to supper shortly, and he ought to warn her before then. Any minute someone else might do what Amos had done, and she wouldn't be prepared.

He finally arrived at her elbow, and before she could resist, he maneuvered her away from the others.

"What are you . . . ?"

"Listen, I have to tell you something. Pretend I'm telling you about the new shelves I'm building for the shop or something."

After a moment, Leah looked at him with a slight smile, nodding her head. "What? We don't want people to start talking about us or there'll be no end to it."

That didn't sound bad to him. In fact, it might be better than what they were likely to be talking about. He took a deep breath and plunged right in.

"It seems there's some talk going around about why you came back. And don't look at me like that. I haven't said one word to anyone about it."

"Who then?" she murmured, looking lost.

"I first heard something from Paul, yesterday," he hurried on. "He said that somebody mentioned something about problems with Aunt Miriam, and how she'd disappointed you by not leaving you the business. And wondering why."

Her lips trembled and then firmed. "I guess I shouldn't be surprised. People here have relatives in Aunt Miriam's community. I guess I thought it wouldn't be interesting enough to pass on. That wasn't very clever of me. Who else?" she asked sharply, and he suspected she would see right through him if he said there was no one.

"Your cousin Amos. Apparently the family has been talking. Not knowing anything, so far as I could tell, but saying that it was always understood you'd be taking over the nursery when your aunt retired. So they're wondering what happened."

Her face tightened, her eyes darkening. "I should have realized. Nobody knows, so everybody is talking and wondering about it. It might have been better if she'd called the police about the theft. At least then maybe the truth would come out."

He didn't bother to repeat what he'd said earlier about getting it out and fighting it. Aunt Miriam, for all her supposed wisdom about plants, wasn't very smart about people. She should have realized that folks would talk and wonder and ask questions. Maybe she thought that forgiving and forgetting would be the end of it, but it wasn't.

Leah closed her eyes, and a tear slipped out to trickle down her cheek. He took a step or two to put himself between her and the others in the room.

"I'm sorry. I know you don't want to hear it, but you ought to be prepared."

"Yah. Well, I guess I should thank you for warning me." She didn't look very thankful, but he couldn't blame her for that. "I . . . I think I'll go see if Ruthie needs any help in the kitchen."

She slipped out, and he began talking at random to the closest available classmate. But his mind was stuck on Leah and what had happened to her. People were probably going to blame either her or her aunt for the breach between them, and he didn't see a single way to stop them from talking.

Leah wasn't going to enjoy the rest of the party very much, and for that matter, neither was he.

CHAPTER TWELVE

LEAH GOT THROUGH THE REST OF THE PARTY, BUT she wasn't sure how. On the surface she talked and laughed, chattering with all her old friends and sharing memories of everything from school days to courtings and hearing news of everything from weddings to babies.

Ruthie had gone all out to decorate the supper tables with greens and candles. Despite the darkness and cold outside, inside there was warmth and laughter. It soothed her, and as the evening went on, she began to hope she'd been overreacting. These were all her friends.

Afterward, when she was alone with Josiah in the buggy, she felt relaxed. He spread the lap robe over her knees and tucked it in against the cold before he clicked to the gelding.

Neither of them said anything at first. She didn't know about him, but she was wrestling with some new insights in her mind. She hadn't wanted to come, but maybe this party had done her good. It forced her to face things.

"Well?" Josiah said at last. "How did it go?"

"I think I've been awfully foolish." She could hear the wonder in her voice, and Josiah gave a bark of laughter.

"I wouldn't argue with that, but what exactly have you been foolish about?"

She shook her head, then realized he probably didn't see the gesture in the dim glow of the buggy lanterns. "Pretty much everything as far as the situation with my aunt was concerned. I just blocked everything out and pretended it hadn't happened. And it turns out everyone has been talking anyway."

"Not so surprising, is it?" Josiah's voice was low as the silence pressed around them, almost as if he didn't want to disturb it.

"No, for sure it's not. I know as well as anybody how the Amish grapevine works. The less they know, the more people talk, ain't so?"

"Yah, for sure," he said, a little chuckle in his voice.

The buggy came out of the shelter of the tree row, and the cold wind swept across the pastures on either side of the road. Josiah moved a little closer to her, and she could feel his warmth.

"I can't think why Mamm and Daad haven't asked me about it. They just acted as if it was what they wanted all along, for me to come back here to stay."

"They probably did. Surprising as it sounds, they're kind of fond of you."

That made her smile. "Still, though, wouldn't you think they'd ask me about it?"

He seemed to consider the question seriously. "I'd guess they were waiting for you to tell them."

"And I shut them out." Leah blew out a long breath. "But what else could I do? Do you think I wanted to start a family fight over it?"

Josiah took her hand and squeezed it, then went on holding it securely in his. She could pull away if she wanted, but she didn't.

"I get it," Josiah said. "I don't blame you for that, but you can't keep trying to hide it from them. If other people are wondering what happened, think how much worse it is for them."

"Yah." All the laughter of the evening was gone now, and she'd be cold if not for the warmth of Josiah's hand. "I just don't want to hurt anyone."

"Listen, you have to get it through your head. It wasn't your doing. You didn't do anything wrong." He sounded as if it was the most important thing in the world for her to believe it. "Your aunt is the one who caused this trouble, not you." He nudged her. "Right?"

She sighed at the thought of everything that lay ahead of her. "Right. I'll have to tell them."

Josiah put his arm around her, pulling her a little closer to him on the seat. "It won't be as hard as you think it will."

"I don't know about that." She let the decision seep into her. "Maybe it's best I talk to Daad first. He can help me see how to tell Mammi and Grossmammi."

"Gut." He held her a little closer as they turned into the lane. "Promise me you'll do it."

"Yah, I'll do it. But there's something else I have to do first." It was surprising how one insight seemed to be leading to another, as if she'd turned on a light in a dark room.

"What?" His tone was wary. Maybe he feared she was reconsidering her promise.

"Write to my aunt. And tell her all the things I should have said to begin with."

He drew up under the shelter of the oak tree that marked the corner of the field, and his arm tightened around her. "Gut."

He didn't say that was what she should have done right off. He knew her better than that, maybe sometimes better than she knew herself.

"I won't back out." She looked into his face, a pale oval in the moonlight. "Don't worry about that."

"I'm not." His voice was gruff, as if he held back emotion. His face was very close . . . so close she could feel his breath, warm across her cold cheek.

Then he bent his head, and his lips found hers. She was very still for a moment, but his kiss was familiar, carrying her back to the past, back to a year ago, when she thought she was in love with him. Her arms slid around him, feeling the sturdy strength of his body within the thick wool coat. Time seemed to stop, and she wasn't sure whether they were locked together for a minute or an hour.

Josiah's lips moved to her cheek. "It's been a long time," he murmured.

"Yah." And she remembered why. She drew back slowly.

She understood herself now, and she knew she loved him. She couldn't doubt the strength of what she felt. But she couldn't let herself go, either. She'd done that before, and she'd been hurt.

She couldn't give in to the love she felt . . . not until she was sure about Josiah. Sure that the past wouldn't repeat itself. Sure she wouldn't lose him again.

LEAH COULD ONLY BE RELIEVED THAT THE FOLLOW-ing day was the off-Sunday when they didn't hold worship services in their community. She settled her kapp over her hair and slipped in the hairpins, almost ready for breakfast. It was fine to tell herself that having people wonder about her return was only natural and that she'd been silly to think she could slip back into the community without questions. In fact, she couldn't believe now that she'd been so blind.

Still, it was one thing to accept that fact and another to sit in worship aware that everyone was wondering about her. A quiet day at home would be good all around. This morning they would have family devotions, and this afternoon she'd have time to settle down and write the letter to

Aunt Miriam. Her stomach sank at the thought, but she knew now what she must do, whether she wanted to or not.

As she passed the door that linked the main house to the daadi house, Leah could hear Grossmammi's footsteps. She waited, holding the door open for her grandmother.

"Sleep well?" she asked, embracing her gently.

Her grandmother smiled, patting her cheek. "People my age don't sleep all that much, you know. Not like you young folks. You need every minute to keep up with all the things you do."

Leah fell into step with her. "Mammi is the one who needs more sleep, ain't so? Anybody's mammi."

"You're right about that. I remember nights when Judith was a baby that we had to take turns getting up with her. She always did have more energy than she needed, especially in the middle of the night."

Leah nodded, laughing a little. "That's Judith, all right."

"Now you were always a quiet baby. Peaceful, you know?" Grossmammi leaned heavily on her arm, and Leah suited her steps to her grandmother's. "What were you thinking about so seriously when you came down the stairs?"

"Just that I'm glad for the off-Sunday. I guess sooner or later, everyone in the community will stop gossiping about why I came back home, but . . ."

"Ach, now, don't think that way." Grossmammi shook her arm a little, as if to draw attention to her words. "People talk because they care, mostly. They're interested. We wouldn't be a community if we didn't pay attention to what is happening to our neighbors, ain't so?"

Leah nodded as they entered the kitchen. Grossmammi was right, but even so, she was just as glad not to be facing the whole community today.

She helped her grandmother to her chair and then circled the table to her own place. Daad already had the heavy German Bible on the table in front of him. Devotions before a late breakfast—that was their pattern for off-Sundays.

Others might do it differently, but they'd always followed the same routine.

As Daadi began to read, heads were bowed around the table. From beneath lowered eyelashes Leah looked at her family, feeling an increased contentment that she was here. Even though the process had been painful, she had ended up in the right place.

Over an hour later she pulled a chair up to the desk in her bedroom, trying to conquer the fluttering in her stomach. She knew it wasn't the aftereffects of the huge breakfast they'd served up. Fried scrapple, hash browns, bacon, eggs, pancakes, applesauce . . . her brothers and sisters had eaten some of everything, but she'd restrained herself, because the queasiness had already been there. She'd known what she had to do.

With a pen in her hand and a blank sheet of paper in front of her, she took a deep breath. If she didn't do it now, she never would. With a silent prayer for guidance, she began to write down all the things she should have said when Aunt Miriam made that shocking accusation.

It didn't actually take long. When she'd finished, she read it over once, put it in an envelope, sealed it, and stamped it. No matter what second thoughts she might have, no one in her family would dream of tearing up a stamped envelope.

Still, the sooner it was in the mailbox, the better. She hurried downstairs, envelope in hand, and took her jacket from the hook. At the sound of movement, her mother came in from the pantry.

"Leah? Are you going somewhere?"

She waved the envelope. "Just to the mailbox."

"Ah, gut." Mammi lifted a basket that sat on the counter. "I just finished putting together some things for the Conners' Sunday supper. You can take it down to them after you've mailed your letter, yah? It's practically on your way."

In fact, it was another mile and a half at least past the

mailbox, but there was no point in saying that to Mammi. Besides, a brisk walk in the cold air might sweep away the remaining shadows of the past.

"Yah, sure. Is it all ready?"

Mammi nodded and held the basket until she had her jacket fastened and her gloves on. "There, now. If you see Jere, be sure and say that we are praying for his recovery."

"I will." But she hoped she wouldn't have the opportunity. It would be embarrassing to be thanked, especially if he still thought she'd told his parents about his driving.

As she set off down the lane, a doubt crept into her mind. Was that just another example of her tendency to avoid any encounter that might be uncomfortable? If so, she guessed she still had a long way to go.

She popped the letter into the box, lifted the red flag, and set off. The walk wasn't a long way, and in fact it was just as refreshing as she'd hoped. Even though the snow was gone now, there was still a sense of Christmas in the air.

She passed two Englisch homes, already decorated with lights and wreaths. One had colored lights on a hemlock in the front, while the next had put up an outside scene of Santa and elves. It reminded her of how Judith had begged and pleaded to have elves in their yard, too. Judith had been one to push the boundaries even when she'd been three or four. She didn't envy Mammi the next few years of adolescence.

The Conners' home didn't wear any Christmas decorations yet this year, because they'd probably been too busy to bother. Still the house looked welcoming, with lamps shining in the windows even though it wasn't dark yet. The ranch-style house had a door at the side that most visitors used, so she went there and tapped, hoping she could be heard over the music she'd guess was Jere's choice.

Sheila Conner opened the door with a welcoming smile, drawing Leah inside. "Leah, I'm so glad to see you. I haven't had a minute to stop and thank you for all your help when Jere . . ." She paused, eyes glistening with sudden tears. "Well, you know." She brushed away a tear. "We're so fortunate that you were right there. I can't tell you . . ."

"It's all right," Leah hurried into speech, hoping to stem the flow. "We're all just so thankful that the accident wasn't worse. And that Jere could come home so quickly."

"He was so eager to get out of that place. He said the food was terrible, and he had some of his buddies bringing him burgers and fries at all hours."

"At least he hasn't lost his appetite," Leah said, smiling. She set the basket on the table. "This is from my mother. She knew you wouldn't have much time for cooking."

Sheila peeked inside. "Wonderful of her. Tell her how thankful we are, will you?" She clasped Leah's arm. "And now you have to come and see Jere. I know he wants to see you."

Leah wasn't so sure, but she let herself be swept through the kitchen and into the family room, where Jere was propped up with his leg elevated, a can of soda in one hand and a television remote in the other.

"Jere, look who's come to see you." Sheila's voice contained a note of warning, obviously indicating that Jere was supposed to thank her.

"I won't stay long." She had to pitch her voice above the roar of the music until Sheila reached across her son and snapped it off. "My family all sends their good wishes. Are you able to get up much yet?"

He made a face. "Doctors seem to think you've got nothing to do but lay around. I want to get moving again. How am I going to get ready for baseball season?"

Leah suspected most of that was aimed at his mother. Sheila would have her hands full trying to keep him quiet.

"Never mind that," his mother snapped as if she'd heard it all before. "Just tell Leah how thankful you are. If it hadn't been for her and Josiah and . . ." Her tears overflowed again.

"Mom, don't." He flushed, clearly uncomfortable with his mother's tears. "Thanks, Leah. I . . . I was awful glad to see your face when I was hanging upside down, I can tell you."

"We're just glad you're all right," she said again. He was so much like one of her own brothers in an awkward situation that she had to smile.

"And listen, I'm sorry I was so rude that day. That was stupid."

Sheila came alert at that. "What do you mean? What day? What were you up to?"

"It was nothing, Sheila," Leah said, her gaze meeting Jere's with understanding and sympathy. "Just a little misunderstanding, right, Jere?"

He looked relieved. "Right."

After a few more words, Leah was ready to make her escape. It was strange that she had already nearly forgotten that day when he'd stopped his car to berate her. That had been easy to forgive and forget, maybe because she didn't have a close relationship with Jere.

Was Aunt Miriam finding it as easy to forgive and forget as she'd insisted? How could she be? They were family.

Maybe, whether Aunt Miriam realized it or not, it was just as important to her to clear this up between them. She thought again of her letter, waiting now in the box for tomorrow's pickup. She might be stirring up an already-awkward situation, but she felt an increased certainty that it was the right thing to do.

WHERE HAD PAUL GOTTEN TO? JOSIAH HEADED OUT to the barn on Monday morning ready to get some work started, but his brother was nowhere to be seen. And Daad had been looking for him, as well, wanting something done.

Josiah had more important things to think about than his younger brother. He hadn't seen Leah at all the previous day, because they'd spent most of it with his uncle's family, something they often did on an off-Sunday. And he'd been relieved about it then, but now . . . well, now he could stop delaying and start thinking about that kiss on Saturday night.

He'd had no intention of doing any such thing when they'd ridden home together after the party. He'd been glad things were getting back to normal between them, and for sure he hadn't intended to complicate their relationship again.

He had to face facts. They weren't seventeen any longer. A casual kiss or three or four was fine during those early rumspringa years, when they were trying out the whole business of growing up. But at their age, a person had to think carefully before getting involved. Anything that happened between them now had to be serious.

What had Leah been thinking? She'd jumped down from the buggy as soon as he'd pulled up at the back door. With a murmured farewell, she'd darted into the house. And that was that.

Was she taking it seriously? Did he want her to?

He tried to avoid the questions as she went through the open door into the barn. "Paul? Hey, Paul, are you in here?"

No answer except for a whicker from one of the buggy horses and a couple of noisy movements as the others responded restlessly. Bessie, the oldest mare, poked her head over the stall bar and blew moistly at his neck.

"Yah, all right." He pushed her muzzle gently away, patting her. "I know you want fed. Where is that boy? Paul?"

Nothing. No answer except for Bessie nibbling at his shirt because there was no hay in the feeder.

Muttering to himself, he started up the ladder to the loft.

He'd have to throw the hay down himself—the animals always had to come first—but once he laid hands on his brother, he'd find some good chore for him to do in return.

His hat brushed the ceiling, but contrary to his expectations, the loft hatch was closed. Funny. It was normally left open. This was really Benjamin's job, but Daad had needed him for something else this morning. He gave the hatch a gentle push.

It gave a bit, but it felt heavy, as if something had been stacked on top of it. Frowning, he braced himself with his left arm and gave a powerful shove with his right. The hatch flew back. It released what felt like a dozen forks full of hay directly in his face.

Sputtering to get a breath that didn't taste like hay, Josiah stumbled back a step or two and then dropped to the floor. He spat out a mouthful of dust and bellowed.

"Paul! Get out here! If you think that's funny—"

His brother emerged from behind the last stall, his face red with the laughter he couldn't suppress. Rocking with giggles he pointed at Josiah.

"If you could see yourself. You've got hay everywhere . . . in your ears, your neck, your jacket . . ." Giggling so hard he couldn't stand straight, he bent double with laughter. "And your face when that hit!"

Josiah reached him in a few long strides. Grabbing his jacket, he pulled him upright. "I'll give you funny. What's the big idea?" He shook him.

"Hey, take it easy." He tried to wriggle his way free, but Josiah didn't let go. "It wasn't supposed to be you. What are you doing, taking over Ben's job?"

Yet another one of Paul's jokes that had gone wrong, obviously. Josiah shook him again, more lightly, trying to maintain his stern face, but Paul's laughter was contagious.

"You were supposed to be doing Ben's job. That's what I came out here to tell you." He gave him a shove toward the ladder. "Suppose you get on with it. And then you can clean up the mess you made. And grab Bessie before she tries to swallow that piece of baler twine."

He reached the mare first, though, catching the end of the twine just in time. "Foolish old mare. At your age you should know better." He pulled it gently free and tossed it at his brother. "And so should you. When are you going to grow up?"

"Hey, I've got time." He scrambled past Josiah and tossed a bale down, then hopped down himself to start filling the mangers. "Nobody takes me seriously."

Josiah set about helping him. They wouldn't be able to get to their own work until this was done. "It's not a gut thing for people not to take you seriously. You monkey around long enough, and pretty soon Daad won't treat you any more seriously than he does me."

Paul straightened up, arms full of hay, to stare at him. "Daad? What do you mean?"

His gripe burst out before he could stop it. "You ever see him putting me in charge of anything? Or trusting me to do a job of work without him standing over me every second?"

With his mouth open and his eyes wide, Paul was a caricature of astonishment. "That's crazy. You've got it all wrong."

"I know—"

"Well, I know what I hear with my own ears," Paul said. "Just yesterday Daad was bragging on you to Onkel Zeb, saying how you're doing that whole job of remodeling the cottage and how you're going to build the greenhouses. He even said he was feeling left out. And then Onkel Zeb started teasing him that pretty soon you'd be the boss and he'd just have to retire."

Now it was Josiah's turn to stand and stare. "Is this your idea of a joke?"

"No. Listen, I wouldn't joke about something like that. I just wish sometime he'd talk about me that way. When he finished talking about what a gut carpenter you are, he started on that herd of milking cows Ben wants to work with." He grimaced. "Nothing about me, that's for sure."

Josiah's head seemed to be spinning as his thoughts readjusted to this new information. Was it possible Daad's opinion of him really had changed? He couldn't quite buy that. Daad and Onkel Zeb were always trying to go one better than each other. Still, it had to mean something. It was going to take some time to get used to this idea.

In the meantime, they'd best get to work. He slapped Paul on the back. "Come on, let's get this finished. We've got to make a start on those shelves for Leah today. And if you pull anything like that on me again, I'll dunk you in the water tank and hang you up on the clothesline until your clothes turn to icicles. Okay?"

Paul grinned, undeterred by his threats. "Okay. Let's get going."

Funny thing, Josiah realized as they cleaned up. In all that time he hadn't been thinking about the issue with Leah, but now he seemed to know exactly what he wanted. He wanted her to take that kiss seriously. He wanted her to know that she was the one for him.

No sooner had he and Paul set off for the cottage than he saw Leah coming along the edge of the field toward them. His heart seemed to skip a couple of beats. He had to talk with her, had to tell her what he felt.

He glanced at Paul. "You think you could find something useful to do in the workshop?"

Shrugging, Paul looked from him to Leah and back again. "Okay, I can take a hint. I'll get lost for a bit."

With a knowing glance at Leah, he sauntered off to the workshop.

Relieved, Josiah picked up his pace toward Leah, but the closer he got, the more he wondered. What if he was assuming too much? Maybe in the months they'd been apart her feelings for him had changed? What if he was too late?

CHAPTER THIRTEEN

LEAH'S HEAD FELT AS IF SHE'D BEEN STIRRING UP
her thoughts with an eggbeater. She walked along the edge
of the field with no particular aim in mind. The day had
clouded over, and a cold wind set the sheets they'd hung out
whipping on the line.

She had taken the plunge first thing, catching up with
Daad doing the morning chores, and he'd been quick to put
down his shovel and listen. They'd sat on a couple of straw
bales, and she'd talked. It had been easier, she'd realized,
now that she'd told it once to Josiah. At least that part was
over, and Daad had been as calm and steadfast as always.
He hadn't even seemed all that surprised.

"Leah?" Josiah was standing in front of her before she
noticed him. "Are you walking in your sleep?"

"Sorry." She shook her head. "I was thinking. I'm afraid
I didn't even see you."

"Guess that tells me where I rate," he said lightly.
"Somewhere below Christmas presents and the school program props?"

"Ach, don't be silly." She pushed her concerns into the background to focus on him. "Although if you need to take some time away from the work until after Christmas . . . ?"

"Not me. Let's get in out of the cold, yah?" He lifted the bag he carried. "I've got a jug of coffee here. That'll make you feel better."

Once they were inside, he busied himself with the kerosene heater for a few minutes. Then he straightened, seeming to study her as she held out her hands to the warmth. After a moment he dragged a couple of battered chairs near the heater and handed her a cup of coffee from the thermos.

"Was ist letz? I can see something's wrong." His expression didn't show anything but friendly concern.

Relief took the place of a fraction of her stress. At least he wasn't assuming anything about their relationship after that kiss. The best resolution would be if they could both put it behind them and focus on other things.

"The letter I wrote can't have reached Aunt Miriam yet, but I feel as if it's a huge snowball rolling downhill, taking everything with it." All her frustration came out in a rush.

He eyed her cautiously, as if he were approaching a creature that might snap at him. "Writing the letter was the first step toward making things right, ain't so? You don't regret it already, do you?"

"Yes. No. I don't know." She ran her hand across her forehead, trying to calm the way her mind jumped from one problem to another. "I'm not sure."

Josiah took a gulp of his coffee, and she followed suit. It was scalding hot and sweetened as Josiah liked it, and it seemed to hearten her.

Before the silence got uncomfortable, he spoke. "What did you say in the letter to your aunt?"

Surprised, she stared at him. "Well, just what I said I would. That I was too shocked to say anything when she accused me. That I didn't do it . . . that I'd never steal from anyone, no matter what. And I was sorry she felt that way."

Josiah was frowning. "Didn't you point out that other people could have gotten at the cash box?"

That sounded accusing. "No," she said quickly. "I didn't want to point the finger at anyone else. I had enough of that myself."

He leaned toward her, his elbow on his knee, his face intent. "Think about it now. Could it have been a customer?"

"No, I'm sure not. When customers were there, the box was always locked unless we were actually putting money in it or making change. Aunt Miriam was very strict about that."

He frowned, considering that. "It'd be easy enough, probably, for someone to distract your attention long enough to get into the box, but I'll take your word that it couldn't have happened that way."

For no reason at all, Leah suddenly wanted to laugh. "Denke."

Josiah grinned. "I didn't mean that the way it sounded. But then it had to have been either one of those cousins who helped in the shop or that friend of yours." He gave her a challenging look.

"I'm sure it wasn't." She'd gone over and over it in her mind. "When he was there, he was always working on something in the greenhouse or loading the wagon. I can't remember a time when he was ever in the shop area."

"The cousins, then," he said.

She considered. "I'm sure Freddy was too young to get up to anything like that. He was usually running around getting in people's way, but nobody would have let him near the cash box. He'd be more than likely to knock it on the floor than anything else."

"I'm surprised your aunt put up with having him around, then."

She shrugged. "Well, they're her grandnieces and nephew, and she's lived near those kinder all their lives. I guess she's used to them."

Josiah leaned closer. "Leah, don't you see? What you

describe makes it seem they'd be most likely to get into the cash box. Maybe not the boy, but what about the two girls? Are you so sure about them?"

"They wouldn't steal from her, not when she's been so good to them." Her voice seemed to die out, and she could hear the lack of conviction in it.

Surprisingly, Josiah didn't jump on that. She could feel his gaze on her face, studying, probing for her feelings. "Think about it," he said finally. "You didn't do it, and it seems like those two girls are the only ones left." He paused, maybe to let that sink in, before he rose, putting his cup on the rickety table. "Did you talk to your daad?" he said finally.

She welcomed the change of subject. "I did. He . . . Daad always takes things calmly, you know? He . . ." She felt warmed, thinking of her father's reaction. "He didn't doubt me for a second."

"Of course he didn't." Josiah reached out, as if to touch her, but she stood, moving to set down her cup, too.

"I knew I could count on him. On all of them. But . . ."

"But what?" Josiah sounded impatient. "They have to know. They're your family."

He didn't understand, and she began to wonder why she'd come over here to begin with. She hadn't made any conscious decision—just walked out of the barn and headed straight here.

"I told you before what worries me, and it's not any different now. He says we must tell Mammi and Grossmammi, and when they know, how can there not be trouble between them and Aunt Miriam? I hate the idea."

Josiah took a deep breath, and she thought he was struggling for patience. "Your aunt is the one who caused it. Not you. Let them sort it out." He moved closer to her, putting his hand on her arm.

For an instant she stood still, letting his warmth comfort her. But it wasn't any good. He didn't understand. He couldn't seem to see how she dreaded the inevitable breach there would be in the family. And nothing could comfort her with that hanging over her head.

She'd just have to manage on her own. She moved away a few steps, turning to face him. "Never mind. I'll let you get on with your work."

"Not yet." Josiah hadn't moved, but he seemed closer to her. Maybe it was the softened tone in his voice that affected her. "I wanted to talk to you . . . about us."

She shook her head and went on shaking it. "Don't, Josiah. Not now."

He looked baffled. "Why not now? We've known each other for almost twenty-four years, ain't so? Isn't that enough time to know what we feel?"

Something snapped in her, and her pain spurted out. "And it's been just a year since you let me down. Am I supposed to forget that?"

"But . . . it was nothing. Just a silly flirtation. Can't you see that?"

She stared at him. "You don't understand anything about it. It wasn't silly to me."

"Look, I didn't mean it that way. If I hurt you, I'm sorry."

"If?" She could hardly find the words. "You wonder why no one will take you seriously? I can tell you why. Because you don't take yourself seriously. Loving someone isn't a game. It is serious."

Her throat seemed to close, and she couldn't have said another thing. Instead she turned and hurried out, needing to leave him behind before she burst into tears.

FORTUNATELY, BY THE TIME LEAH REACHED HOME, she had herself under control. Josiah didn't understand, and she couldn't do anything about that. To him that business with Susie had just been a silly little flirtation not worth talking about. He didn't see that, for her, it had shattered not only her dreams for the future but also her trust in him. No matter what he thought his feelings were now, how could she trust him with her heart again?

Leah paused on the back porch to wipe her damp shoes on the mat and then headed inside. The instant she entered the kitchen, Mammi darted over to sweep her into a warm embrace. Grossmammi was right behind her, and it became a three-way hug so strong it nearly knocked the breath out of her. Obviously Daad had told them, as she'd assumed.

"My poor baby," her mother crooned, her eyes overflowing with tears. "Keeping this to yourself all this time. Didn't you know that we would believe in you and trust you?"

"I'm all right, honest." She managed to smile, even though her lips trembled. "Anyway, it's all over now."

"Is it?" Grossmammi patted her cheek. "So long as it hurts you, it's not over."

"Miriam." Mamm said her sister's name and then stopped.

Leah met her eyes, knowing that they were both thinking the same thing—that they didn't want to hurt Grossmammi. Miriam was her daughter, after all.

Grossmammi kept her hand on Leah's cheek while she touched Mamm lightly with the other. "Understand this, both of you. Miriam is my daughter, and I love her. But that doesn't mean I'm blind to her faults. She's always been too quick to think she knows everything. She just sees what she wants to see."

Before Leah could reply, the sound of feet on the back porch told them someone was coming. Becky and Judith rushed through the door, laughing.

"Goodness, what's happening with the two of you?" Mammi blinked rapidly to hide any signs of tears.

"The scholars are just so funny," Becky said, unwrapping the muffler she had around her neck. "I don't know how Teacher Anna keeps from laughing at them."

Leah remembered then that the two of them had been

taking some props to the school for the Christmas program. They certain sure looked as if they'd enjoyed it.

"I wouldn't be a teacher for anything." Judith detoured around the table to stop and smell the chicken noodle soup bubbling gently on the stove. "Imagine being around little kids all day. Ugh."

"Maybe you should have stayed to help Teacher Anna get ready for tomorrow's program," Leah suggested with a smile.

"Double ugh," Judith declared.

"Anyway, we'll be busy making cookies," Becky put in. "Teacher Anna said she needs a couple more batches at least for tomorrow night. It's a gut thing I don't have to work today, so I can make them."

"And Judith can help," Mammi said firmly.

In the midst of the clamor of voices, Leah's gaze met Becky's. She was immediately reassured. Becky seemed to have gained a couple of years in maturity in the past twenty-four hours.

At least one thing she'd tried to do had worked out well. Even if other things . . .

"Leah, are you helping with cookies?" Judith evidently felt that if she had to help, everyone should.

"Yah, sure," she began, when Grossmammi took her arm.

"Give me a hand first, yah? I'll find that old set of Christmas cookie cutters that were my mother's. You can use those if you're careful."

"Always," Leah said, patting her hand. Grossmammi obviously had something else to say to her in private. She felt herself tensing, and she forced her muscles to relax as she walked, fitting her steps to her grandmother's, to the door of the daadi haus.

Whatever it was, she'd best hear it all.

The short hallway led into the living room. It wasn't much changed since Grossdaadi passed several years ago, except that Grossmammi's favorite rocker wore the new cushion set Leah and her sisters had given her last Christmas. The light green replaced a much-washed and faded dark blue one they'd persuaded her to part with.

But her grandmother didn't pause at her favorite chair. Instead, she went to the heavy old bureau that had been in the family far longer than Leah could remember. The top drawer stuck, and Leah hurried to pull it out for her.

Grossmammi muttered to herself as she looked through stacks of pillowcases and tea towels. Leah watched her, seeing again the changes in her. Her hair, thinning a little at the part in front, was nearly all white now, and her face was as crinkled as the soft petal of a rose. The lines weren't of worry or fear or temper. Each one represented love and caring and tenderness.

And she looked smaller than she had when Leah went away, shrinking with age until even Hannie was taller. She made Leah think of a flower, bending in the wind but always coming up again.

"Maybe you should take a rest," she suggested. "I can look for the cookie cutters if you want."

"They're here," Grossmammi said, holding up a bag with the metal cutters inside. She made no effort to hand them to Leah but stood looking at them.

"Is there something you want to tell me?" she asked gently, hating the thought that Grossmammi had to be troubled by this business with Miriam.

"Yah." She looked up now, her faded blue eyes still keen. "Your mammi . . . she always looked up to her older sister. Like the younger ones look up to you."

Leah wasn't so sure that Grossmammi was right about her little sisters, but what she said about Mammi was surely true.

"You mean that's why she's so hurt now."

Her grandmother nodded. "Miriam was so determined to make her own way, trusting only herself. She did a fine job with her nursery, but she didn't learn enough about other people. That's how she came to make such a mistake about you."

Leah thought about the relationship between the sisters. That must make it even harder on her mother. "I often wondered if they ever wished . . ."

"That they could change places?" Grossmammi considered. "I think they'd tell you no. Your mammi, at least, is very content. And much as she loved her sister, she didn't want to let you go to Miriam's."

"She didn't?" Leah studied her grandmother, startled. "I never knew. She never said anything."

"She wanted you to make your own decision, but she was torn. She knows Miriam is better with plants than with people." Grossmammi toyed with the cookie cutters she held. "When you have a family, you have to teach your kinder to be trustworthy. You give a child a bit of freedom to do a job, and when he does it, he earns your trust."

"And if he doesn't?" Leah didn't know where her grandmother was going with this, but it was better than talking about her mother's pain.

"Then you start over again, until he does it right. And then sooner or later, you realize that you can trust him with anything." She shook her head sadly. "Miriam never had that experience. So she made a snap decision about you, and she was wrong. We all know that."

"I didn't want Mammi to be hurt by this. That's why I tried not to tell her."

"I know, my sweet girl. But it's not your responsibility, so just let it go."

"I'll try," she said, blinking back a tear.

Her grandmother nodded, satisfied. "Now I'll sit in my chair and rest for a bit." Leah took her hands and lowered her carefully into the chair, then brought her favorite footstool for her feet.

"Here you are." Grossmammi put the bag in Leah's hand and leaned back against the cushion. "You make sure those young ones treat them right. Tell Judith I don't want to find the snowman looking like an elephant."

"I'll take care of them." Leah bent to put a kiss on Grossmammi's soft, wrinkled cheek. "Have a good rest."

"Leave the door open," Grossmammi's voice followed her. "That way I can smell the cookies baking."

Leah nodded. "I'll make sure you don't smell any burning. I promise."

With her heart lightened a little, she went back to the kitchen.

CHAPTER FOURTEEN

PAUL CAME INTO THE COTTAGE VERY QUIETLY. HE looked at Josiah, opened his mouth as if to say something, and closed it again. In another minute he'd shed his jacket and gotten back to work.

Good, Josiah thought. At least Paul was wise enough to know when to keep quiet.

He smoothed fine sandpaper down the grain of the cabinet wood, using the long, even strokes Daad had taught him. Usually he found the movements calming, but they didn't seem to be helping right now.

His jaw clenched as he thought about what Leah had said. What kind of way was that to react? He'd been trying to tell Leah he loved her. Not just that, he wanted to marry her. The man everybody said would never settle down was finally ready, and the woman he wanted said no. How was that for a joke?

What had he done that was so wrong? He'd been trying to help her, trying to understand the feelings that tormented her since her aunt had accused her of theft. He'd given her good advice, hadn't he?

Maybe his timing was bad. Still, he'd been rehearsing the things he wanted to say so much that the words had to come out.

"I'll never understand women." He didn't realize he'd spoken aloud until Paul looked up, shocked.

"You can't say that," he protested. "All the girls like you. They always have, ain't so?"

He grimaced. "That doesn't seem to matter."

"Ach, I don't buy that." Paul seemed determined to cheer him up. "Everybody knows how you can pick up girls . . ." He hesitated. "Well, not that exactly, but you can talk to any of them."

"Flirt with them you mean," Josiah said. "That doesn't seem to mean anything when it comes to understanding the one that matters."

Paul shook his head. "I get this is about Leah, but what makes it so different? I'd have said anyone can see the two of you belong together."

"Anyone but Leah." Enough, he told himself. He picked up a soft cloth and began running it along the grain in the wood, carefully removing any fragments of dust left by the sandpaper.

Sympathetic as Paul was, he shouldn't discuss Leah with him or anyone else. But he couldn't help but let his thoughts roam back over what his brother had said.

Maybe those years of being popular with other girls hadn't been as good as he'd thought. Had he been making it too easy on himself? Leah wasn't like anyone else. And he didn't want their relationship to be like anyone else's. But how was he to convince Leah of that?

He looked toward the door at the sound of someone on the porch, and a moment later Daad came in. He paused after shutting the door, looking surprisingly uncertain.

"Just thought I'd stop in and see how you're getting along. Okay?"

With the memory of what Paul had said fresh in his mind, Josiah was tongue-tied for a moment. Then he shook his mind free.

"Sure thing." He gestured. "We're working on the pieces that will go on the wall where the sink is. What do you think?"

Daad looked at the wall where they'd go and then looked at each of the shelf units. He stood back a little, looking at them from every angle.

Josiah had to suppress a smile. He'd seen Daad do that a hundred times. He never approached any project until he'd looked it over carefully. "Use your eyes first, before you jump in with tools." Josiah had heard it since he could walk.

Daad squatted in front of the cabinet he'd been working on, touching the grain of the wood, opening and closing the doors, looking at every inch.

He nodded gravely. "Gut work."

That was all, but from Daad, it was high praise. He was far more likely to point out the one tiny flaw you'd thought no one would ever notice.

Daad moved on to the piece Paul was working on. "No doors for this one?" he asked.

"No. Leah wanted some open shelves just there for pots and supplies to repot seedlings." He pointed to the spot to the right of the sink where it would go.

Daad nodded and turned back to Paul. He reached out to put one finger on the back of the top shelf. "The part you don't see should be finished as well as what you do," he commented distantly.

"Yah, Daad." For once, Paul didn't argue. He didn't even try to say that if no one saw it, it didn't matter. Well, he should know that wouldn't work with their father.

Daad stepped back again. "You'll make a fine job of the

renovation for Leah. Then she can get her business off to a gut start."

An expression of concern crossed his father's face as he spoke, making Josiah wonder if he, like so many other people, questioned why Leah had returned.

But if that was in his mind, he didn't speak. Instead he moved toward the door. "Denke. I'm glad to see your work."

He looked lingeringly at the place where the finished cabinet would go and took another step toward the door.

Josiah thought again of what Paul had said. He wasn't sure he accepted the conclusions Paul had drawn, still . . .

He spoke on impulse.

"If you have a few minutes, how about helping us fit this in where it belongs? I want to be sure it's right."

The pleased expression on his daad's face made his answer unnecessary. "For sure." He shed his jacket in an instant. "Let's give it a try."

As they grasped either side of the cabinet, Josiah tried to straighten out his thoughts. Maybe he had been wrong about his father's feelings.

If so, what else had he been wrong about?

THE DAY OF THE CHRISTMAS PROGRAM AT SCHOOL was a busy one, so Leah was relieved to find herself alone in the sewing room. She needed more time than she had to work on Christmas gifts. That seemed to happen every year.

After today school would be out, and with Hannie around all the time and Christmas approaching at full speed, there would be no extra time and certainly little privacy or quiet.

It would be fun, that was certain sure. The cheerful chaos was what she'd longed for when she was away, and she had it in abundance now. But somehow she had to finish these gifts.

In addition, keeping busy kept her from thinking about Josiah. She did a fairly good job of that during the day. It was a shame she had no control over her dreams . . . dreams in which those moments in the cottage were relived over and over.

Josiah had said he wanted to talk about "us." She'd known what he meant without asking. His tone had been warm and intimate, just as he'd spoken to her when they were courting.

Now he seemed to think they could just start all over again and go on as if the last year hadn't happened. She was supposed to understand that Susie Lehman had been nothing but a flirtation.

She understood, all right. He was the one who didn't understand—when you were practically promised to someone, you didn't go around flirting with other girls.

Jerking herself back to the present, Leah discovered she had sewn the seams of the pillow she was making with the fabric wrong way round. Muttering to herself, she grasped the seam ripper and began picking the stitches back out again.

She might just as well have gone over to the schoolhouse to help set up for all the work she was accomplishing at home. Becky and Judith were already there, helping Teacher Anna. The kitchen still smelled of baking, and she could hear Mammi's and Grossmammi's voices as they worked.

If she'd thought they'd finished yesterday, she'd been wrong. It took a lot of cookies to feed all the people who'd come to the program tonight, and the leftover cookies would be packaged and sold to make money for the school.

"Leah? Can you come out here?" Mammi called from the kitchen, her words accompanied by clattering pans.

"Right there." She folded up the pillow cover and put it in her basket before hurrying to the kitchen.

"Do you need some help?"

"Not with this." Mammi reached into the oven to test for doneness by poking a cookie with her forefinger, then closed the oven door. "Needs a few more minutes. We'll handle this, but will you run next door and pick up the cookies Josiah's mother made?"

"Aren't they going tonight themselves?" It wasn't that she was unwilling. She just didn't want to run into Josiah if she could help it.

"They won't be there early, since they don't have anyone in the program. I said we'd take them with ours." She waved a tea towel at Leah. "Hurry along now."

"Yah, I will." She tried to ignore the look that Mammi exchanged with Grossmammi. Those two would do anything to throw her together with Josiah, but it wasn't going to work.

She'd have to speak to him again about the shop, of course, but a few more days might get the taste of their last exchange out of her mouth. She'd given away her feelings too clearly.

A few minutes later, with her scarf snuggled around her neck over her jacket, she started off across the field. It was a dark day, with lowering clouds. By the look of the sky, they might have more snow before Christmas. She didn't care for herself, but the children would enjoy it.

The wind caught her scarf and flapped it in her face, as if chiding her for her thoughts. All right, she would enjoy a white Christmas for herself. The thought of being snowed in with only her own close family was very appealing just now.

Meaning without Aunt Miriam. She forced herself to admit it. Mammi had asked her sister to come for Second Christmas some time ago, but it seemed she hadn't had a response. Either that, or she was keeping it quiet.

As for Leah's own letter . . . There was time enough now for Aunt Miriam to have received it and answered it, but she hadn't heard anything, either. Of course, the mail was always slow over Christmas. Besides, what could Aunt Miriam say? She'd already made up her mind about the theft. Leah couldn't imagine that her letter would change her aunt's mind. She'd written that for her own satisfaction, to prove that she could stand up for herself.

Leah was walking along the edge of the field, intending to bypass the cottage altogether and head straight for the kitchen. She told herself she wouldn't even glance in that direction, but a flicker of movement caught the corner of her gaze. And once she looked, there was no going back.

Josiah was standing outside the cottage, talking to a man who stood next to a shiny new van. The man slid into the driver's seat almost before her gaze registered, but she recognized him anyway.

Why was Bart Lester back here? Hadn't he given up on trying to buy the cottage yet, after all they'd said to him?

Her errand slipping away from her thoughts, she turned and headed straight for the cottage, her speed quickening as she went. What was Josiah doing talking to him? Whether or not they sold the property was no concern of his.

She was going so fast that she was nearly out of breath by the time she reached him. Nearly, but she still had enough to say what was on her mind.

"What was that man doing here again? And why were you talking to him?"

Josiah put up both hands, as if to shield himself from her anger. "Take it easy, Leah. It wasn't anything to do with you."

His easy smile annoyed her no less than his words.

"If it's happening on my property, it certainly is to do with me. Why was he here?"

"Okay, okay. Next time I have to talk business with someone, I'll make sure I'm not on your property. Satisfied?" He seemed torn between amusement and annoyance.

"Business?" She caught her breath with a sinking feeling that she was making a fool of herself. "What business . . . ," she began, and then stopped herself. If it really wasn't anything to do with her, she didn't have a right to ask.

"Never mind," she snapped, and started on toward the farmhouse.

She heard Josiah's footsteps crunching on the frozen ground, and then he caught her arm.

"Hey, take it easy. I'll tell you. Where are you going in such a hurry, anyway?"

"I'm picking up some cookies your mamm made for the program tonight." She pulled her arm free and headed for the house.

He didn't attempt to take her arm but walked beside her, fitting his steps to hers. "Lester stopped by to talk to Daad about doing some of the interior work on the new restaurant he's going to build. On the other side of town, by the way."

She felt as small as could be. "I see. I'm sorry I jumped to conclusions." She deliberately didn't look at him.

Josiah didn't seem affected by that. He just continued walking with her. "Daad wanted him to see some of the cabinet work we've done," he said as if there'd been no interruption. "That's why he was on your property. If it happens again, we'll be sure to ask first."

She'd been foolish, behaving that way. Why couldn't she behave like the calm, responsible adult she knew she was when it came to Josiah? She didn't think she wanted to hear the answer to that question.

JOSIAH COULD SEE THAT LEAH WAS EMBARRASSED. IF he could think of something to say to ease the situation . . .

"Is your daad going to take on the job?" Her gaze was on the house, not on him.

"He's being cautious about it."

At least this was a neutral subject. He'd gotten over being angry at the things she'd said. At least he thought he had, but he suspected it wouldn't take much to make him flare up again.

"Daad's working up an estimate, and we talked about spelling out exactly what materials we'd be using. Neither of us want to throw something together with cheap materials."

"We?" She looked at him, questioning. "My project . . ."

"No, don't worry about that. Daad knows it comes first, and he'll help so we can finish faster. Anyway, nothing on the restaurant interior can be started until the building is finished, and with winter setting in that won't be anytime soon. But like I said, we may not come to an agreement with Lester anyway."

He stood back to let her go into the house and then followed her in. Mammi had several boxes of cookies ready to go, so he stacked them and picked them up while Leah was greeting his mother.

When she saw what he was doing, Leah shook her head. "No need for you to carry those. I can easily manage them."

"Ach, don't be silly." Mammi made his argument for him. "Josiah is happy to carry them, ain't so, Josiah?"

"Right. Now if someone will get the door . . ."

His mother turned to Leah. "But you'll stay and have some tea . . ."

"Another day," Leah said quickly. "There's so much to do before we leave for the school, my mother will be wondering where I've gotten to."

"We'll see you there, then." Hannah smiled, taking it for granted that Josiah would carry things for her.

Shooting an irritated glance at Josiah, Leah held the door open while he went through with the boxes. They both knew she didn't want to spend any more time in his company, but she couldn't do anything about it.

They walked back side by side. After a few moments of silence, she seemed to force herself to speak. "I thought you wanted to do the remodeling yourself to show your daad what you could do. Did you change your mind?"

He comforted himself that she wasn't watching him closely enough to see that he was embarrassed. "Yah, well . . . I think maybe I was wrong about Daad. Paul heard him bragging to my onkel about what a gut carpenter I am. He wouldn't do that without meaning it."

"That must make you feel better."

Josiah shrugged. "He still tells me how to do things that I can do perfectly easily by myself." He had to smile. "But I heard him telling Mamm how to put a sandwich together, so maybe it's just his way."

"Habit," she suggested, smiling a little. "And maybe he wants to be sure he's passed on all the things he knows."

"Maybe so. I thought he didn't have any confidence in me, and it seems like he thought I was leaving him out. Guess we were both wrong."

"It can be hard to know what other people are thinking about you," she murmured, stepping carefully over an icy patch in the path.

"You mean your aunt?" He looked at her when he spoke, stepped on the icy spot himself, and nearly lost his grip on the boxes.

"Watch out!" Leah grabbed for the boxes, and between them they managed to rescue them before they hit the ground.

"If any of those cookies are broken, my mother will have something to say about it. I'm supposed to be helping you, not the other way around."

Smiling a little, she steadied them until he was clear of the ice. "I won't tell her."

"Denke." He hesitated, afraid to anger her but feeling he needed to know. "About your aunt . . . you didn't have any idea something was wrong between you?"

"Nothing. Not until she told me." Her lips closed firmly. He knew she didn't want to talk about it. In fact, she probably regretted telling him anything about it to begin with.

Truth was, he'd like to say a few of the things he thought about her aunt, but that would start another quarrel, so he didn't. "Have you heard anything from her yet? She'd have gotten your letter by now, I'd think."

"No. Maybe it's better that way." She was looking down the lane, and he turned to see what attracted her interest.

Hannie was coming along from school, trailed by her two sisters. Judging by the way she danced along, she was excited, probably about the program tonight. Or maybe because she'd be on vacation from school.

"Josiah, I . . ." Leah seemed to be forcing herself to speak. "I shouldn't have said what I did. About people not taking you seriously." She rushed the words as if to get them out before they reached the others.

He shrugged. "Forget it."

"I can't." Her face was serious and intent. "No one knows better than me how thorough and careful you are with your work. I'm sorry I implied you weren't."

He hadn't been that careful with her. That seemed to be written in large letters across his mind. Now he'd reaped the fruit of that. She didn't want to hear what he had to say about them.

He was still trying to find the words when Hannie darted up to them. She was going so fast that he had to lift the cookies out of the way in case she barreled into him.

Leah caught her, laughing, and spun her around. "If you make Josiah drop those boxes, you'll be sorry. His mammi made some of those nut cookies that you like."

"Oh, yum. Can't I have just one now?" She reached for the boxes.

"Not now." Leah caught the reaching hand just in time. "Maybe after we get them into the house. Walk along with us and tell us what you'll be doing in the program tonight."

He thought that would work as a distraction, but Hannie shook her head solemnly.

"It's a surprise. We're not supposed to tell. Teacher Anna has a brand-new program this year."

"I hope that doesn't mean we won't be hearing some of

our favorite things," he said, smiling at her intensity. It was a long time since he'd been that excited about a Christmas program.

If he ever had kinder of his own, he'd probably regain all those feelings. If. The way it stood now, he finally knew who he wanted to have those children with, and she didn't want to hear it.

Somehow, one way or another, he had to make Leah listen to him. And more, believe in him.

CHAPTER FIFTEEN

JOSIAH HAD FOUND IT IMPOSSIBLE TO SAY ANYTHING more privately to Leah that afternoon. Their house had been a whirl of activity as they prepared supper and got ready for the program. All he could do was say he'd see them at the school and tell Hannie he was sure she'd do fine. She'd been too distracted to reply, her lips moving silently as if she was saying her part of the program to herself.

Now, as they found seats in the already-crowded school-house, he could see that this wouldn't give a minute for a private word with Leah, either. About all he could do to-night was look at her from afar.

If only they could talk, he felt sure he could break down this wall that had sprung up between them. Once she realized how serious he was, how much he loved her, everything would be all right.

Paul elbowed him. "Push over, will you? I'm falling off this seat."

"Well, I'm practically sitting on Mamm's lap. Maybe you'd better lean on the chalkboard." Josiah nodded toward the wall, where several of the men had propped themselves against the chalk rack. And close to the door, probably in case they felt the urge to slip out.

"No way. Not for the whole program." Paul squeezed over a bit more and seemed to settle. "It's too crowded to breathe deeply."

"It always is," Josiah pointed out.

The school's Christmas program was the only time during the year that the children did anything that could be called entertaining their elders. Even the end of the school year was mostly a picnic combined with goodbyes to the eighth graders who'd be leaving.

"I remember the program my last year." Paul sounded like someone settling down for a conversation. "Seems like no time at all ago."

"It wasn't," Josiah muttered. "Shut up or talk to someone else. I'm thinking."

Paul followed the direction of his gaze. "No, you're not. You're looking at Leah. Why don't you just tell her how you feel and stop mooning around?"

"Shut up," he hissed. "Someone will hear you."

Paul desisted, leaving him to watch Leah helping Teacher Anna line up the scholars . . . a little hard because they kept popping out of line.

Paul's question repeated itself in his mind. *Why don't you just tell her how you feel?* The answer to that question came clear in his mind . . . so clear he could hear it over the noise and chatter and laughter of the crowded schoolhouse.

He didn't tell her because she didn't want to hear it. Not now. She'd made that abundantly clear. It was wishful thinking that he could just talk to her and it would be all right.

Was he that conceited? He clenched his hands between his knees and prepared himself to pay attention as the program began to a spurt of applause.

It took a lot to make himself focus, and when he did, the

program didn't improve his feelings. The first reading was about giving at Christmas . . . not thinking of yourself proudly as the giver but humbly, remembering your own failings.

He seemed to have a few too many of those to count.

The program moved on, with every child having a part. He watched Hannie, her cheeks pink, standing with four or five others to recite the proper gifts of Christmas: selflessness, helping, caring for others. He began to feel as if every word of the program was aimed at him.

He spotted Leah in brief fragments, helping Anna by directing traffic to get the right class on at the right time. Of course she'd offered to help. He'd nearly forgotten how close she and Anna had been back when they were in school.

The program ended with carol singing. The scholars led, and everyone joined in on the old familiar words. He guessed they didn't sound as fine as a trained choir, but they surely were making a joyful noise to the Lord. So many happy faces, singing with pleasure and shining with happiness at being together to celebrate.

For a second he found he was picturing the schoolhouse from outside, as if he could see the yellow light glowing from the windows and hear the voices ringing through the cold night and rising up toward the stars. His eyes were wet, he realized suddenly, and he blinked rapidly.

Then it was over, and there was a fresh burst of activity and noise as kinder rushed to their parents and other people hurried to pull forth the table containing the food and get cold drinks out of jugs.

Leah was struggling with the improvised curtain that had shielded the food table while the program was going on. Acting on impulse, he scrambled out of the row of chairs and hurried to help.

The sheets that had done duty as curtains had gotten stuck along the wire from which they hung. He reached over Leah's head to try to untangle them.

"Denke," she began, and then she saw who it was. Her expression grew wary.

Suddenly he knew what he had to do, and it was something that wouldn't take more than a couple of minutes, if that. Now if only he could get it out.

"Don't worry," he said softly below the clamor of voices. "I'm not going to embarrass you by saying anything you don't want to hear."

"Please, Josiah . . . ," she murmured, not looking at him. "Just leave it." She jerked at the curtain. He grabbed it before it could tear and lifted it free.

"There. Now rest easy. I get it. I won't say a word about my feelings."

She began folding the first sheet, and the way she avoided his eyes said she wasn't sure he meant it.

"Nothing, I promise," he said. "That's my Christmas present to you."

She glanced up, her eyes widening, and he felt like laughing at her surprise.

"Not just tonight," he said. "Ever. Until you get around to asking me. Merry Christmas."

The sheet started to slip from her arms, and he caught it and bundled it together.

The promise was made, and he just hoped it was the right thing to do. For both of them. It was up to Leah now.

"LEAH! I'M STUCK AGAIN." HANNIE'S PLAINTIVE CRY had been coming regularly the next day as they sat around the sewing room table working on Christmas gifts. At least, the girls were. Leah couldn't guess what the boys were doing about gifts.

Pushing the chair back, she rounded the table to where Hannie was waving her crochet hook and yarn in the air. It was beginning to seem doubtful that the scarf she was crocheting for Daad would ever near completion.

"Told you it was too hard for you," Judith said, smoothing out the calendar she was making. "It's going to be more Leah's work than yours."

Hannie clouded up, and Leah put a comforting hand on her shoulder.

"That's not so, Judith. I'm just finding the missed stitches for her so she can fix them." The look she gave Judith seemed to work almost as well as Mammi's did. At least, Judith subsided.

"Besides," Becky added. "Daadi will know you put a lot of work into making it just right for him."

Hannie sniffled a little. "If I get it finished in time."

"You will. It's getting longer every day." Judith, apparently repenting, managed a comforting word for her little sister. "I made lots of mistakes on my first scarf, too."

Leah frowned over the scarf. The dark navy blue made it hard to see exactly where Hannie had gone wrong. She held it up toward the window so that she could find the row where Hannie had unintentionally decreased a row.

"It's not too bad," she said, pulling the stitches out. "Only two rows went wrong." It was tedious, catching poor Hannie's mistakes every few minutes, but at least it kept her from brooding about what Josiah had said the previous night.

And now she was thinking about it again, after just promising herself she wouldn't. Focusing, she caught up the errant row and added the stitch to keep it even. With a glance at her little sister, she quickly started the new row for her.

"There now. I've put three stitches in, so you can start counting from there." Hannie hadn't yet learned to tell by looking where she was, so she had to count. And naturally, she kept losing track.

With an elaborate sigh, Hannie took her crocheting back, winding the yarn on her left hand to hold it in place. Laughing a little, Leah reached over her head to loosen it.

"Careful. You don't want to cut off the feeling in your fingers."

Hannie looked up, grinning. "Maybe it would be better that way."

Laughter ran around the table at that, and Becky looked up from the sewing in her lap. "I think you're just still too excited after the program last night."

Leah relaxed as she looked around at the faces of her sisters. This was what she needed . . . familiar work with familiar faces. It had the power to push her worries to the back of her mind.

"The program was wonderful gut. It made everyone feel in the spirit of Christmas, I'm certain sure."

It must have affected Josiah, in any event. She replayed the words of his promise in her mind. Now she could finish getting ready for Christmas without worrying about what he might say next.

That was what she wanted, wasn't it? A nice, quiet Christmas with the people she loved. She wouldn't mind being around Josiah as long as she knew he wouldn't suddenly bring up a painful subject. They could safely go back to working together.

Only not too much togetherness, she warned herself.

Leah came back to the present to find that Judith had set about teasing Becky because the rumspringa group was going Christmas caroling.

"You won't do much singing if you're too shy to open your mouth," Judith said. "I could sing nice and loud if they let me come."

"There won't be anything wrong with my singing," Becky said confidently. She glanced at Leah, her smile sure. "You'll just have to wait your turn, Judith."

Judith made a face at that, but the look Becky gave to Leah lingered for a moment. Her lips formed the words. *Thank you.*

"Leah, will you come help me?" Mamm's voice came

from the kitchen. Leaving Hannie's crocheting to its fate, Leah brushed fragments of yarn from her skirt as she scurried to the kitchen.

"What can I . . ." Leah's words drifted away as she came into the kitchen and found her mother standing next to the table, what seemed to be an open letter in her hand.

The sight gave Leah a momentary qualm. "Is something wrong?"

Mammi shook her head, but her smile was forced. "Not wrong, exactly." She glanced down at the paper in her hand. "It's a note from your aunt Miriam."

She had expected that her aunt might reply to her letter, but she hadn't dreamed she'd write to Mammi instead. Leah straightened herself to take whatever was coming next.

"What does she say about my letter?"

"She doesn't say much at all." Her mother looked at the letter again and then held it out to Leah. "That's what's so funny. I don't know what to make of it."

Feeling as if it might explode in her hand like one of Paul's practical jokes, Leah spread it open. The firm, precise handwriting was familiar. It was also brief.

"Leah's letter received," she read softly, not wanting her voice to carry beyond the room. "I would like to come for Christmas, but I leave it up to you. I will understand if you'd rather not have me."

Leah looked at her mother, to find her face as puzzled as her own must be. "I don't know, Mammi. I would think . . ." She let that trail off, not sure what to think.

Mammi should know her own sister well enough to make some guess at the feelings behind the writing, but she didn't seem to. Almost as if she understood Leah's thoughts, Mammi shook her head.

"I used to think I understood Miriam, but maybe it's not possible when we've been apart so long." Her face was troubled. "She was always so sure of herself, even when she was a girl. I'd have said she's even more so now. But it sounds . . . well, unlike her."

She looked so troubled that Leah moved close to put her arm around her mother's waist. Together they looked down at the words and then at each other.

Mammi's face lost its worried expression, and she smiled gently. "I leave it up to you, Leah. If you would rather not have her here just now, that's how it will be."

"But what about Grossmammi? I don't want to keep her from having Christmas with her child."

"I already spoke to your grandmother. She wants you to decide."

Leah had a brief moment of wishing that someone would take the decision out of her hands. But that was foolish . . . that would be saying that she wanted to be a child again, who couldn't take care of herself.

She stood a little straighter. "Then I think she should come."

There, it was done. Awkward or not, she'd always known there'd be a point when she had to confront Aunt Miriam face-to-face. It was just going to be sooner than she'd hoped.

LEAH CAREFULLY PASTED ON THE LABEL SHE'D CRE-ated for her teas. She'd been working on pint jars of tea as Christmas gifts for family and friends. Now all that remained was to tie a bow around the top, and they were ready to go.

She hesitated for a moment as she did the first of the jars destined for Josiah's mother and glanced at the clock. It should be all right to take these over this afternoon. Josiah should be at the lumberyard with his dad for a time yet.

Not that she was hiding from Josiah. No, of course not.

But she still wasn't comfortable with his promise. If he meant it, if he really would refrain from saying anything about their relationship . . . well, that was what she wanted, wasn't it? A chance to return to friendship, the time she needed to settle with Aunt Miriam . . .

There wasn't any reason to doubt him, except that he'd seemed so lighthearted when he'd said the words that she'd automatically doubted them.

She finished the bow and went on quickly to the next. If she could avoid seeing him for a few days, so much the better. But if she did see him, and if he broke his promise, then she'd know. She could be sure he wasn't for her. It would be painful, but it would be final.

The jars and several of her herbal sachets tucked in a basket, Leah headed across the field toward the Burkhalter place. She felt sure Hannah would be home, even if the boys were out.

And Hannah would welcome a visitor, she knew. She often teased Mammi that she should lend her a daughter from time to time. With their little Hannie, named for her, there was a special relationship. It was very like the one Leah had had with her aunt Miriam at one time, and Leah winced a little at the thought. But Hannah would never do anything to hurt Hannie. That she was sure of.

"Leah!" Hannah looked up from the quilt patch she was working on, and then she set it aside to come and greet her. "It is so gut to see you. Komm, sit down, and we'll visit."

"I'd best not stay too long." She'd said that too often lately, but she couldn't seem to help it. "You know how busy Mammi is." And she'd rather not risk running into Josiah. "Is that a gift you were hurrying to finish?"

Hannah's eyes twinkled. "Don't tell, but it's a doll crib quilt for little Hannah. I'll finish it by Second Christmas, at least."

"Not much time left, but somehow it always gets done." Leah began lifting things out of the basket and setting them on the table. "Here are some teas for you, and the other things have tags with the names on."

"That is so sweet of you, Leah." Hannah gave her a

warm hug. "I'm sorry you've missed Josiah, though. Is there anything you want me to tell him?"

"No, nothing." Now that his name had been mentioned, she was foolishly eager to be gone. "I'll be off." With a quick wave, she was out of the kitchen and on her way.

The wind caught her as she moved toward the field between the houses. Dark clouds were moving in from the west. Snow, maybe? If so, it could change Aunt Miriam's mind about making the trip.

She was immediately ashamed of herself, but she couldn't get the idea out of her thoughts until the sound of a wagon chased it. Glancing back over her shoulder, she saw the wagon drawing up to the barn, with Josiah and Paul on the wagon seat.

Josiah hopped down, waving in her direction, and called something she didn't hear. Or didn't want to hear. She kept on walking.

It was no use, and she should have realized it wouldn't be. Josiah's footsteps made little sound, but she sensed him behind her. Then he was next to her, taking the basket from her arm.

"In a hurry?"

She shrugged. "Lots to do. What about you?"

"I picked up some hardware for the cabinets, so I want to see if it's going to look right."

That explained the paper bag in his hand. Leah was suddenly exasperated with herself. She looked at him and saw the familiar sparkle in his eyes.

She began to laugh. "What are we doing?"

"Ferhoodled, that's what we are." He hesitated. "I made a promise, Leah. And I'll keep it. Now can we get back to normal?"

She nodded. "Yah. That's gut."

He studied her face, his eyes intent. "Was ist letz?"

"Nothing's wrong," she said, knowing he wouldn't believe her.

"You heard from your aunt, yah?"

He knew too much, at least about her. That's how friends were.

"Mammi got a note from her. She says she wants to come at Christmas, if we want her to. So Mammi left it up to me, and I told her okay. So I guess she'll be here."

"That's it? She didn't say anything about what you told her?"

"Nothing." That was strange, however you looked at it. "So I still don't know what she's thinking. But she doesn't usually change her mind."

"I'd like to tell her a few things that might do it," he muttered.

"Don't you dare." She grabbed his arm. "Promise me you won't."

He hesitated, his face serious. "I can't do that, Leah. I'll try not to say anything, if that's what you want, but I won't make a promise I can't be sure I'll keep."

He handed the basket to her and loped off toward the cottage, leaving her speechless.

CHAPTER SIXTEEN

"LEAH! LEAH, WAKE UP!" SOMETHING THUMPED ONTO the bed, jolting it, and Leah's eyes flew open. She was looking right into the big blue eyes of her littlest sister.

"Didn't you hear me? Wake up!"

Leah struggled onto her elbow. "What are you doing awake so early?"

"Look." She bounced again, as if to make sure Leah was awake, and pointed to the window.

Even before her eyes had focused, Leah became aware of a difference in the light that filtered through the plain blue curtains at her window. It had that soft, glowing look that combined with the absolute stillness outside to mean snow.

Scrambling out of bed, she let little Hannie tow her to the window, the floorboards cold under her feet. She snatched up a shawl and wrapped it around both of them as they stood at the window.

"Snow." Hannie whispered the word. "It's the day before Christmas, and we have snow. It's perfect, ain't so?"

Leah hugged her, a jumble of emotions whirling through her. A perfect Christmas? Most folks found a lot of joy in it. Except, maybe, those people who had to get out and clean the roads. She was ashamed of herself that her first thought was once again that Aunt Miriam probably wouldn't come.

She shouldn't think that way, but she couldn't seem to stop feeling that it would be a much happier Christmas without Aunt Miriam.

". . . set up the putz, and light the candles, and tomorrow will be Christmas Day." Hannie had gone on talking without her, rehearsing all the things that would happen. "Look, the boys are clearing the path to the barn."

Through the thickly falling snow, she spied Daad in the barn doorway, milk pail in his hand, while Micah and James shoveled the few inches of snow off the grass to make a path. Daad always said it was much easier in the long run to shovel as the snow fell, while the boys maintained they'd wait until it stopped. Needless to say, Daad won that argument.

"When you have your own home, you'll do as you please." That was always Daad's refrain, and the boys' arguments had become more of a joke than a serious protest.

Thoroughly chilled, she stepped back from the window and jumped onto the rag rug next to the bed. "We'd best get moving, Hannie. There are plenty of chores to be done, Christmas Eve or not."

Hannie nodded. She hopped and skipped to the door, probably trying to keep her feet warm. "But you'll go out with us later, won't you?"

"For sure. Get along now, do, and wake up somebody else."

Grinning, her sister went out and shut the door. Leah hurried to dress. Mammi and Grossmammi would be busy already, determined to have everything just right on this day and the next. They'd need her to help. Breakfast first, and she could already smell the fresh sausage cooking.

By the time they gathered around the table, everyone had worked up a hearty appetite and the table was laden with everything from sausage and scrapple to eggs and porridge to fried potatoes and potato cakes . . . another big breakfast for Christmas Eve.

Leah spotted her grandmother about to get up and fetch something, and hurried over to press her gently back into the chair. "Tell me, and I'll get it," she said softly.

"You're a gut girl." She patted Leah's cheek. "The coffee needs to go round again, yah?"

Leah hurried to bring the pot. Daad had finished his first mug already and was more than ready for his second. He drained it. "If it keeps snowing this way, we'll need everyone to help with digging us out. Who would think we'd get this much?" He shook his head.

"I think we should call this the first snow," Hannie announced, having eaten her way through a full plate already.

"First?" Judith stared at her. "Did you forget the snow when Jere crashed his car already?"

"I didn't forget," she said. "But that was a sad snow, because it made him have a wreck, but this will be a happy snow, because it's Christmas, so we can call it the first one." She was obviously satisfied with her reasoning, even if no one else was.

Judith opened her mouth to argue, but Mammi frowned her down. "You heard what Daadi said. If you're finished, girls, you can start clearing."

Leah could almost hear what was going through the younger ones' minds. They were imagining this special day just filled with pleasures. Was it a sign of maturity that she could so easily see all the work that went into making it one? Or just a negative attitude?

Getting up, she hustled the girls into clearing the table, while Daad and the boys tramped out to get more outside work done.

Grossmammi smiled at her as they began to wash up.

"You're thinking about all the things to be done to make a happy Christmas, ain't so?"

Leah had to chuckle. "I was wondering if being away made me able to see things differently. Or if it was just growing up that did it."

"Maybe a little of each," Grossmammi said.

Just as the last dish was dried, Hannie popped her head back in. "Leah, can't you come yet? After we shovel, we're going to put fresh greens and candles in all the windows to light tonight. Won't it be pretty?"

"Pretty, yah," Grossmammi answered. "But we do it to remind ourselves of the birth of the Lord, ain't so?"

Hannie nodded vigorously. "I'll find some special greens for the daadi house windows. Komm schnell."

Leah looked at her grandmother questioningly, but Grossmammi waved her out. Smiling at Hannie's impatience, she took her jacket from the hook. "Yah, I'm coming, I'm coming."

Her sister obviously thought her too slow, but finally she and Leah were hurrying outside, holding hands.

It was just about a perfect snow, Leah had to admit. The snowflakes were drifting down lazily now, looking like bits of lace floating in the cold air. The bright wool scarves the children wore made spots of color against the snow. Even as she watched, smiling, Judith stopped shoveling toward the chicken coop long enough to throw a snowball at Micah. It smacked him right in the back, and by the time he turned around and looked, she'd managed to be shoveling busily.

Across the expanse of white covering the pasture, they could see more people out shoveling. As she looked and waved, she spotted Josiah. He had started shoveling a path toward them along the back edge of the pasture.

Hannie jumped and began waving wildly toward him. "Josiah's making a path to us. Let's shovel out to meet him."

Daad hesitated a moment and then waved in that direction. "Yah, okay. Mammi wants to take some eggs over anyway."

Naturally, it became a race to see who could reach the middle of the field first. By the time they were close enough to speak, Leah knew her cheeks were as bright a red as Hannie's were.

Josiah and Hannie finally met, and Josiah clicked shovels with her solemnly and smiled at Leah, his brown eyes warm. "We're getting the sleigh down from the loft once we finish here. We could use some help. What about it?"

"Me, me!" Hannie waved her arms, nearing hitting him with the shovel. "I'll help."

"What about you, Leah?" Lines crinkled around his eyes as he gave her a hopeful look.

He could probably see how much she wanted to say yes, but she managed to restrain herself.

"I'd love to, but I think I'd better remember I'm a grown-up and help Mammi with the food. Sorry." She hoped he could see that she really meant it.

He nodded, his face unchanged. "We'll drive over to give you a ride later, then. All right?"

"Yah, all right." She hesitated. "I . . . we'll love it."

With a sense that she'd given away more than she'd intended, she turned back toward the house.

JOSIAH TURNED TO LEAH'S LITTLE SISTER, WHO clearly intended to join him. "Come on, little Hannie. Let's get the sleigh ready." He tucked in her woolen scarf, unwrapping itself in the wind, and they headed toward the barn.

Patience, he reminded himself. Leah's attitude toward him seemed easier. That was gut, unless it was only because she trusted him not to push her toward a relationship.

In a way, he could congratulate himself that she trusted him now. But that didn't mean Leah loved him, he reminded himself. He'd been acting as if he could be sure of her feelings. Maybe that was too optimistic.

If his thoughts kept going around and around like that, he'd soon be too ferhoodled to do a thing.

"Boost me up, and I'll help Paul." Hannie tugged at his hand, and he came abruptly back to the barn.

Paul was up in the side loft where they'd put the sleigh after the last time they used it. It didn't take Paul's horrified expression to make him sure little Hannah wasn't going up there to get knocked off the ledge or squashed under a runner.

He took her firmly by the shoulders. "You stand right here and keep your eyes on the runners. We need you to tell us when they've cleared the edge, so look sharp."

Pride at her important job had Hannie standing straight with her gaze fixed on the edge of the loft. Satisfied she'd stay there, Josiah scrambled up the six feet or so. This side area had been planned so that equipment could be parked underneath and lighter pieces lifted on top, doubling the available space.

"It must be four or five years since we had enough of a snow to be worth getting it out," he said, pulling at the tarp that covered the sleigh.

"Five, anyway," Paul said, catching the other end of the tarp and pulling it back. "But it doesn't look bad. Just a little dusty is all."

He nodded. Daad had taught them to care for their equipment whether it was for farming or for carpentry. The sleigh had been carefully cleaned and recovered each year, even if it hadn't been used.

"Okay, you have your end?"

Paul nodded. "You ready, Hannie?"

"I'm ready," she called up, still safely out of accident range.

Josiah gave a tug at the rope at his end, and the pulley squeaked and began to turn. Holding each end, they lifted the sleigh up and out. At Hannie's call, they lowered it smoothly to the barn floor.

"Yah!" Judith had come in by then to join her little sister, and the two of them clapped excitedly.

"Okay, now, let's get her ready to go."

With eager hands helping, the harness was readied, and they slid the sleigh out the barn ramp. The girls climbed on, grinning.

"Stay put while we get the horse, mind." They nodded, so he and Paul headed back inside. "Best take Daisy," Josiah said. "She's had more experience with snow."

Together they brought out the black-and-white mare. She stepped forward sedately enough, but when her hooves sank into the snow and she felt the flakes, she flung her head up and sniffed.

Paul laughed. "Even old Daisy feels like a young one at the snow."

"Gut. Maybe that'll give her energy for the sleigh rides I can see we'll be giving."

In a few minutes they were ready. Judith eyed the seats. "How many can go at a time?" She probably wanted to be sure she wouldn't be left out.

"Five or six, so long as you're skinny enough. Looks like you are," Paul told them. "Climb in the back seat."

"We know how to drive," Judith muttered, but then hopped in without argument.

Paul took the reins, and Josiah turned to speak to the girls. "We're going to stop at the kitchen to pick up some presents for the neighbors. We'll stop at your place first and see if Leah wants to go. And to make sure it's all right with your parents for you to go."

"They won't care," Judith said quickly.

"We'll see."

He nodded to Paul, who clucked to the mare. They moved toward the house, the runners sliding smoothly and silently, the snowflakes whirling around them. With everyone helping, it took no time to load Mammi's boxes and tins of cookies and candy under the seat, and then they were off.

As soon as they reached the road, the girls changed from giggles to singing a Christmas carol, and Paul said, soft voiced, "Is everything okay with Leah?"

Josiah hesitated for a moment, but Paul had figured out his feelings with no difficulty. And he'd discovered that Paul, despite his love of laughter and jokes, had a serious, sympathetic side that was unusual at his age.

"I wish I knew," he muttered. In response to another questioning glance, he went on. "A year ago she was ready to marry me. And I was so young and foolish I shouldn't have been courting at all. So I messed things up."

"Sorry." Paul stared over the horse's head at the road. "What are you going to do now?"

"Wait," he said with finality. "She knows how I feel, and right now she doesn't want to hear it. I told her I wouldn't push, and it's up to her. There's nothing else I can do."

They turned in at the Stoltzes' lane, and he spotted Leah's face at the kitchen window. As soon as they stopped, she was at the door.

"Well, don't you four look fine, dashing through the snow like that."

"We have space for you, right up here," he said. He turned back to hand a couple of tins to the girls. "Take those in to your mother and ask if you can go on down the road with us. We won't be gone long."

Judith and Hannie scrambled down, carrying the tins of candy, and Leah stood aside to let them go in.

"Better get your jacket and scarf," he told her. "It's a little nippy sailing along in the snow."

Leah hesitated just a moment. Then she smiled and darted inside. He let out a sigh of relief.

In a few minutes all three were back again. Paul handed him the reins, hopped down, and in a moment had handed Leah into the front seat. He then quelled a revolt from Judith, who thought she should go in front, and climbed in with the girls.

Before anyone else could start an argument, Josiah clicked to the mare and made a wide turn to go back out the lane.

Leah bent to tuck the candy tins under the seat. "Wise man, not putting those in the back with the kids. No one can resist your mammi's candies."

"I just hope she saved enough for us." He smiled, jerking his head toward his brother. "I think Paul was counting every separate candy."

"Why not?" Paul said from the back. "I have to have my share."

Leah laughed. "I'm afraid I'd do the same."

Josiah took the turn onto the road. The sleigh struck a small icy patch, and the runners slid to the side. Leah gasped, clutching his arm.

"Don't worry." He patted her hand. "I won't tip you over. Daisy is an old hand at this."

"And what about you—have you had a lot of practice?"

"If this is a foretaste of the winter we're going to have, I'll get quite a bit," he said. "We haven't had snow like this before Christmas in years."

He stole a glance at her. She'd lifted her face to the oncoming snow, and the flakes landed on her cheeks and dusted her hair. She looked carefree in a way she hadn't since her return.

"It's so quiet. I almost wish the plow wouldn't come through."

"I don't think you have to wish too hard. As fast as it's piling up, and with tomorrow Christmas Day, I don't think they'll get to these back roads very quick."

A smile lit up Leah's face. "We'd be cut off."

He saw then what she was thinking. They'd be cut off, and she wouldn't have to face a visit from her aunt.

Leah wouldn't like it if she could see his thoughts right

now. Because no matter what she thought she wanted, he felt sure Leah wasn't going to be free of the damage her aunt had done, or ready to move on, until she'd faced her.

Until then, she wouldn't be ready to hear anything from him about the future . . . especially words of love.

SOMETIME LATER LEAH REALIZED THAT SHE WAS still hugging to herself the hope that the snowy roads might keep Aunt Miriam away. Guilt swept through her. How could she think that, when she could see that her grandmother was watching the snow with the opposite hope? Grossmammi would be hoping to have this Christmas with her eldest daughter, knowing she might not have many more chances to do so.

"Leah."

She turned away from the window at the sound of her grandmother's voice. "Yah, Grossmammi? Can I help?"

Her grandmother smiled. "No sense in worrying about the snow. It's one thing we can do nothing about, ain't so?"

"You're so right." She put her arm around Grossmammi's waist. "What shall we do next?"

Christmas Eve was a time for traditions, and in Mammi's family they had always done special things in a special way on this night. Grossmammi was the authority when it came to Christmas Eve.

"The putz next, and I think I can use a little help getting it."

That was unusual, Leah realized as she walked with her grandmother over to the daadi haus. The putz, or Christmas creche, or manger scene as different groups called it, was a very old Pennsylvania Dutch tradition, brought with the first Amish settlers to America. Grossmammi had a very old set that had been hand-carved by her grandfather.

Already the wooden stable had been brought out and set up on a small table in the living room. The younger ones had surrounded it with bits of evergreen, while Mammi added the candles behind it.

"Are you getting it?" Hannie rushed along behind them, breathless in her excitement. "Can I watch?"

Grossmammi nodded, patting her cheek. "No touching, though. Not yet."

Hannie grasped her hands together, as if to keep them from wrong. "I promise."

"Gut." Grossmammi pointed to the bottom of the jelly cupboard that stood in her kitchen. "Down there, Leah. Will you bring it?"

Nodding, she bent to do as her grandmother asked. Grossmammi made each step in getting ready for Christmas considered and serious, while still being joyful. Her ways had impressed each of her grandchildren with the importance of what they were doing.

Leah caught a quick glimpse of Hannie's eyes, widened with awe, as she straightened with the square box in her hands. She smiled and knew that the same quiver of expectation moved in her.

"Ah, there." When Leah made a move to hand it to her, Grossmammi shook her head. "You take it."

Conscious once again that Grossmammi finally recognized her for an adult, Leah held the box carefully between her hands as they walked back through to the living room. Hannie hurried around them, skipping in her excitement.

"Come quick, everybody," she called. "It's the putz."

By the time Leah reached the table and set the box down carefully, everyone had gathered around. Mammi was last, her thoughts clearly still on the venison sausage that was cooking for the traditional supper.

As Grossmammi opened the box, Hannie came close to jumping out of her shoes. "Please, Grossmammi. Please may I take the first one?"

Leah gave Judith a warning look, but she wasn't paying attention. Instead she was actually smiling at her little sister. It seemed the Christmas spirit could even subdue Judith's sassiness, Leah thought, smiling to herself.

Grossmammi took the figures out, handing each to a different member of the family, who put it in place. With each one contributing, the scene took shape until it was complete with everything except for the baby. Grossmammi, Leah knew, would put the baby on the fresh straw early in the morning.

When she and Micah were very small, they had tiptoed down the stairs at first light, eager to watch. They'd sat on the cold steps, looking through the railings, and she'd had to shush him at least three times before Grossmammi appeared. She'd put the baby carefully in the manger, then looked up, clearly knowing they were there. "Christmas is come," she'd said.

Leah's heart swelled at the memory. She glanced at Micah and saw from his answering smile that he was thinking the same thing.

Mammi finished lighting the candles. With a glance that collected all her daughters, she sped off to the kitchen. Supper came next, and it wouldn't do for it to be late. Mammi was a person who liked everything to be done at the proper time.

And in the proper way, Leah added to the thought as Mammi removed a metal spoon from Judith's hand and substituted a wooden one to stir the beans.

"Komm, girls. Let's get everything on the table, schnell."

A minute later the boys came in, followed by Daadi. Daadi was teasing James about how many pieces of venison sausage he planned to eat, while James insisted that he'd never eaten as many as Daadi.

"Come now," Mammi said. "You each got a deer during hunting season, so there's plenty enough to feed everyone."

"There always is," Leah added.

"Think of our fathers and mothers in the old country going hungry and in hiding for their faith and be thankful." Grossmammi, as she often did, had the last word.

They gathered around the table, falling quiet as Daadi led the silent prayer, and then the sound of clattering serving dishes was so loud that Leah wondered if the neighbors could hear it.

She glanced out the window, seeing the snowflakes still landing on the windowpanes. The Burkhalters would have gone to Matthew's brother's house for supper, their usual Christmas Eve. A slight glow of light was all that she could see from their house.

They'd be here on Second Christmas for a meal, and tomorrow would be with whichever of Mammi's relatives could get through. And if no one could make it . . . well, it would still be Christmas.

An hour or so later, they had just finished the dishes when Leah thought she saw a light flicker somewhere out in the field. Leaning over the sink, she peered out, focusing past the window's reflection of the kitchen to see what it was.

Mammi beat her to it, looking out the other side of the window. "Why, it's Hannah and her family! They must not have gone anywhere after all. Quick, put the coffeepot on."

Leah grabbed the pot while Becky pulled out the coffee. A little flutter in Leah's stomach had to be suppressed. All right, she was going to see Josiah sooner than she'd expected. But they had an agreement, and they were back to being just friends. That was nothing to be excited about.

A few minutes later the kitchen was filled with laughter and chatter. Hannah had brought trays of cookies, and Mammi was protesting that they had plenty, and the boys were helping find someplace to put jackets damp with snow.

Leah brushed off Josiah's jacket as she hung it up. "We thought you were going to your aunt and uncle's. Something happen to the sleigh?"

Josiah shook his head, laughing a little. "Sleigh and horse both okay after our ride this afternoon. But we heard a tree had come down across the road out that way. So it seemed better to go someplace we could walk."

"Glad to know we came in second place," she said, laughter in her voice.

"For sure. It's always gut to know your family is only a short walk away." He glanced around the busy kitchen, smiling a little. It must be as familiar to him as his own home, after all these years.

Once everyone had been supplied with cookies and coffee or tea or hot chocolate, they drifted into the living room, admiring the creche and finding seats, the younger ones on the floor.

Daad caught Leah as she started for a seat. "Light the rest of the candles, Daughter. Matthew agrees they'll join us for devotions."

She'd guessed as much, but of course Daad would consult with Matthew. Climbing across a couple of pairs of long legs stretched out on the floor, she made her way to the nearest window. As each candle was lit, the room began to fill with a soft golden glow.

When she'd finished, Hannie tugged her to a seat next to her on the end of the sofa. Belatedly she realized that Josiah sat on Hannie's other side.

But what did it matter? She and Josiah were friends and neighbors. She couldn't go on being wary each time he came near. Smiling, she put her arm around her little sister, and Hannie leaned back between them.

Daad, in his favorite chair, opened the heavy Bible on his lap. He adjusted his glasses, found the right page, and began to read. "'And it came to pass that in those days a decree went out that all the world should be taxed. And each went . . .'"

His voice was full and sonorous, echoing through the quiet room in the High German that was right for scripture reading. Leah relaxed, listening. She leaned back, feeling Josiah's strong shoulder against hers. Candlelight flickered on faces . . . attentive and listening, young and old, smiling or sparkling with eagerness.

And loving. She felt a sudden impatience with herself. What did it matter whether Aunt Miriam talked or was silent, believed in her or not? What mattered was that Leah was back here, among people who loved her and believed in her.

Josiah moved slightly, and his hand touched hers. She looked at it. She could draw away, but she didn't. She was at peace.

Still, he didn't speak. She could hardly blame him for that, because she'd been the one to agree so quickly to his promise. Deciding that this subject would disturb her peace if anything would, she brought herself back to the moment.

By the time they'd sung a couple of Christmas carols, Hannie was asleep, cradled in the circle of Josiah's arm. Leah wasn't quite sure how that had happened. Together they looked at her, and Leah expected Josiah was as reluctant to disturb her as Leah was.

Hannie's cheeks were rosy, and her eyelashes made crescents against her fair skin. She slept with the abandonment of a baby. Mamm's last baby, probably, and Leah wondered if she sometimes slipped into the girls' room to see her baby this way.

"What do we do?" Josiah said softly. "Do you want me to carry her someplace?"

Leah shook her head. "Just hand her to me . . . ," she began, but at that instant Hannie's forehead puckered in a frown. Her eyelashes quivered, and then she woke. She smiled up at them.

"I'm awake. Honest."

Leah tried to suppress a laugh. "You won't be much longer. Come and see Josiah to the door, okay?"

Together they walked through the kitchen to where Josiah's family was putting on jackets and wrapping up in scarves and mittens. As they stepped out onto the porch Josiah paused.

"Look." He pointed up at the sky.

Leah gasped. The snow had stopped, and the night had become as clear as crystal. Stars twinkled, seeming brighter than ever after the snow.

"Beautiful," she murmured.

Josiah squeezed her hand, and then he was on his way.

She stood there another moment, and Hannie seemed content to wait, leaning against her heavily.

"It's like the stars the shepherds saw, ain't so?" Her words were punctuated by a large yawn.

"Yah, it is. And it's time for bed." Leah led her reluctantly back into the house.

CHAPTER SEVENTEEN

LEAH WENT THROUGH HER EARLY-MORNING chores still with that profound sense of peace. She didn't doubt that it would be tested, especially if and when the relatives began arriving, but for the moment she could hold to it.

Some would be coming, she felt sure. At least the nearby ones. The plow had gone up the road about half an hour ago. There was no Christmas Day vacation for the people who worked on the roads.

After chores and breakfast, the younger girls persuaded Mammi to leave the kitchen long enough to open gifts, but they barely had time to exclaim over them before everyone was swept into getting ready for the relatives. There were tables to set up in the dining room, the sewing room, and even the basement in case there were more than expected.

Several dozen trips up and down the steps later, Becky caught Leah's arm long enough to whisper to her. "The next holiday meal is at Aunt Esther's house, ain't so?"

Leah's laughter bubbled over. "Then you can have pity for your poor cousins."

Neither of them needed to say more. Aunt Esther was the fussiest of Mammi's married sisters, and her daughters and daughters-in-law would be worked off their feet when it was her turn to entertain.

The sound of buggy wheels sent an alert through the house, and everyone rushed to finish what they were doing. The boys, who'd gotten off easy so far, scrambled into jackets and out of the house to tend to buggies and horses, and a moment later the first of a stream of relatives began to pour in the back door, and the house filled with talk and laughter.

A few hours later Leah found a moment to lean against the kitchen counter and take a breath. Everyone had reached the dessert-and-coffee stage, the turkeys had been moist and the gravy amazingly smooth, and Mammi was happy. The old house seemed to bulge at the seams with talk and laughter from Grossmammi down to the youngest of the cousins playing on the living room floor.

The sound of a buggy approaching startled Leah out of her trance, and she looked through the window to see the Burkhalters' buggy pulling up. She hurried to the back door. They'd be on their way to Matthew's sister's, no doubt, who always had their big meal in the evening.

Josiah was on the porch by the time she got there, and his father was turning the buggy.

"Happy Christmas." His smile was wide, but there was a question in his eyes. "My parents have something for you, but first"—he glanced past her to the house—"did your aunt Miriam show up?"

"No. Or at least, not yet." She couldn't help being relieved. "Apparently she called Aunt Esther to say her driver said the roads were too bad to try it."

He raised an eyebrow. "Make you feel better?"

"Maybe a little." Before she could say anything else, the buggy was back at the door, and Hannah beckoned to her.

"We wanted you to have this on Christmas Day, dear Leah." She held out a large wrapped bundle. "For you."

"Ach, you've already given us the candies and cookies and . . ."

"This is just for you," she said firmly. "Open it."

Paul leaned perilously far out to add his voice. "Yah, open it now, Leah."

Blushing at all the attention, Leah pulled the paper off. Her breath caught, and for an instant she was speechless.

"It's . . . it's wonderful. How did you . . . who . . . ?"

Hannah was laughing. "Matthew's idea. He said you must have a sign for your new business. He and the boys will put it up for you whenever you're ready."

"Denke." She was caught between laughter and tears as she held up the wooden sign. *Leah's Herb Garden*, it announced in bright painted letters. "Denke. I don't know what else to say. It's wonderful gut of you."

Matthew shook his head, his eyes twinkling. "We are in at the beginning of your business, ain't so? We'll be there to put your sign up at the grand opening." He clasped her hand for a moment. "Now we must go, or my sister will be sure we've had an accident."

Josiah climbed aboard. Waving and smiling, they drove out to the road. Leah stood there for a moment longer. Everyone inside would be wondering, and she'd have to go in and share this. But for now, she just wanted to stand here and savor this concrete sign that her business would be a reality.

AS FAR AS JOSIAH COULD TELL, SECOND CHRISTMAS was one of the holidays most folks couldn't explain very well, but they certain sure wouldn't be willing to give it up.

Everyone in the community agreed that three Christmases . . .
Christmas Day, Second Christmas on the twenty-sixth,
and Old Christmas on January sixth, were far better than
just one.

They had their own tradition for celebrating Second
Christmas. While Christmas Day was for family, today
they would get together with the Stoltz family as they always did.

No elaborate cooking today . . . their custom was to
share the huge amount of leftovers in a big relaxed meal.
For sure, no one would go hungry.

Josiah had shrugged into his jacket and was standing
next to Daad to pick up whatever Mammi wanted them to
carry over.

"There you are." She handed Daad a container holding
two pies and then gave him a basket heavy with a casserole
dish. Moving out of the way so his brothers could be loaded
up, he followed Daad out of the house.

In a few minutes he'd see Leah again. He kept hoping
for the moment when she'd let him speak, and there had
been moments when he'd wondered if it would ever happen.
If not, then what would he do?

The sun was out, glittering in blinding fashion on the
crust of the snow. He narrowed his eyes and tilted his hat
forward.

"We'll have a lot of shoveling to do tomorrow if we're
back to work," he observed. "With this cold, the snow won't
melt very fast."

"Yah, we'd best get the cottage done first, and then the
workshop." He frowned against the light. "Reminds me. I
want you to go over the proposal for that work on the restaurant. I'm still not sure we ought to take it on."

Josiah had to clear his throat to be sure his voice was
calm. He couldn't remember a time when Daad had actually asked for his opinion on a project. "I'd be glad to go
over it. But even without seeing it, I'd say that if you have

doubts, it might be best to forget about it. You won't want to work for someone you don't trust. There'll be plenty of other work."

"Yah, that's so." Daad nodded, satisfied.

Josiah shifted the basket to his other arm. "If Leah's mother has as much left over as we do, we'll be able to feed half the township."

"I wouldn't doubt it," Daad said, chuckling. He went up onto the porch, and Hannie was there waiting to open the door and take their bundles into the kitchen.

"Wilkom." Leah took the basket and set it on the counter. She moved to help Daad off with his jacket. Then, to his obvious astonishment, she went on tiptoe to give him a light kiss on the cheek. "Thank you again so much for my beautiful sign."

Daad flushed, obviously pleased. "Hannah wrapped it."

"But it was your idea," Josiah's mother said, giving Leah a hug. "Josiah should show you his present."

"No." She glanced at him, a question in her eyes. "Did you get something special?"

"You might say that." He grinned, sure he was showing his foolish excitement over what Daad had given him. "We have a new sign for our business, too. It says *Burkhalter and Son, Carpentry.*"

"Daad says he'll probably add another *s* to it one day," Paul said.

Josiah elbowed him. "Don't make Micah feel bad."

"I'll have a sign of my own one day soon," Micah said. "Once I have the herd of cows I want."

"Everyone's happy, yah?" Leah was shepherding them out of the kitchen. "Keep moving now, unless you're helping set out the food."

He obeyed, having learned long ago when his help wasn't welcomed. Setting up for dinner was definitely one of those times, especially right now, with all those girls to help.

But he did find a spot from which he could study Leah's face for a few minutes. She looked relaxed and at ease, laughing at something Hannie said. It seemed clear that she didn't regret not seeing her aunt Miriam for Christmas. He was glad to see her happy, but he couldn't help wondering how long it would last. Sooner or later, she'd have to face her aunt in person.

Sooner or later came even quicker than he'd expected. They were finishing their dessert when a car drove into the farm lane. Hannie, already finished eating, darted to the closest window.

"It's Aunt Miriam," she announced, her eyes wide.

He looked at Leah, of course. For a moment her face was frozen. Then, pressing her hands on the table as if she needed a push, she went with her mother and grandmother to greet her.

Sitting there stiffly, he fought back the urge to go and stand beside her. He didn't have the right to do it. Not now. Not yet.

They came in with her aunt to a flood of greetings from everyone. Miriam didn't need introduction to them. She'd seen them on many occasions when she'd come to visit.

"Komm, sit." Leah's mother ushered her to a chair that was quickly vacated by Hannie. "Are you hungry? There's plenty of food left."

"No, no." She glanced around the table. "I'll just have dessert and coffee with you."

The interrupted conversation was renewed, but in a more subdued manner. They didn't all know the whole story, but everyone here surely knew that Leah's job with her aunt had ended in an unhappy way. Everyone seemed to be pretending to talk while taking covert glances at Miriam, at Leah, even at their grandmother, who must know everything.

Miriam seemed to become aware of the tension she'd

created. At the same time, Leah's mother cleared her throat. "You young ones may be excused. If you're going out in the snow, be sure you bundle up. It's even colder today than yesterday."

They seemed glad enough to depart, even Micah, who didn't usually consider himself a young one. After a noisy discussion in the kitchen, they all decided to go sled riding, and with a great deal of clatter, they finally all got out. Silence descended.

Miriam set her coffee cup down firmly. "This is as gut a time as any, I guess." She looked around, her gaze hesitating on him for an instant. "I'm sure you all know that Leah's time working with me ended . . . well, unhappily."

Leah flushed, clamping her lips together and staring down at her hands, clasped in her lap. As for him . . . well, if his anger grew any greater it would most likely blow the top off his head.

"I thought I should say this in front of all of you." Miriam stopped, as if for breath. Or perhaps the will to go on. "I was wrong. I accused Leah of wrongdoing, and I was mistaken. I am so very sorry." She turned so that she faced Leah. "Leah, will you forgive me?"

Leah's eyes filled with tears, but the embarrassed color faded, leaving just her natural flush. "Ach, Aunt Miriam, of course I do. I'm just wonderful glad to have it cleared up."

It seemed to Josiah that everyone at the table let out a relieved sigh at the same time.

"Gut." Miriam had resumed her commanding air. "I want to make it up to Leah. I had intended to turn my business over to her, but—"

"That's not necessary," Leah said quickly. "I don't want anything . . . only to know that it's over, and I can forget about it. I appreciate all I learned from you, and I want to go on and build a business of my own."

"That's very good of you, Leah."

Miriam seemed ready to let it go at that. Josiah knew quite suddenly that he couldn't. He rose before he knew what he was doing.

"It's not enough," he said, and everyone looked at him . . . some aghast, and some approving. "You owe it to Leah to tell her just what you found out, and who really is guilty, and why you picked on her to begin with. The rest of us don't need to know. But Leah does."

Leah gave him a look that, had it been a shove, would have pushed him into the next room. "That's not necessary. You—"

"No, Josiah is right. It's only fair." Miriam walked around the table. "Komm, Leah. Let's go into the sewing room, where we won't be interrupted."

With another burning look at him, Leah followed her aunt out of the room. In a moment everyone else heard the door shut.

They all sat in embarrassed silence. Then Leah's grandmother spoke. "Denke, Josiah. That was the right thing to do."

LEAH STOOD BESIDE THE PLANTS IN FRONT OF THE south window, absently touching an aromatic leaf or two as she waited for her aunt to speak.

"That's a determined young man you have there." Aunt Miriam sounded a little disapproving. "But I guess he's right. You have a right to know." She stopped. Maybe she was finding it hard to put into words.

The confusion in Leah's mind slowly cleared. She thought about her time at her aunt's, and she seemed to know the truth.

"It was Alice, wasn't it?" Alice, the cousin, teetering on the verge between girl and young woman. Alice, who never seemed to open up to anyone.

"How did you know?" Aunt Miriam's voice was as sharp as a whip. "Did you see her do it? Why didn't you tell me?"

"I didn't," Leah protested. "Just . . . thinking about it, it seemed she was the only one who might."

Aunt Miriam's face tightened. "I wouldn't have thought it. I never dreamed there was anything wrong. How could I know?"

Leah watched her face, seeing the struggle her aunt was going through. No, Aunt Miriam hadn't seen. She'd known Alice all her life, but she never really saw her.

"Well, I'm sorry if I . . . if I made a mistake."

Aunt Miriam couldn't manage to say that she'd been wrong again. Whatever hurt lingered in Leah's thoughts slipped away. That was her aunt. She was as apologetic as she was ever likely to be. She wasn't one who could see herself as being in the wrong. She didn't have that ability, any more than she'd been able to see anyone else clearly.

But that didn't matter. Leah was content in herself, and content, as well, that she would be staying here. She couldn't very well say it to her, but Leah didn't want the life Aunt Miriam had built, no matter how successful. She would stay here, and she'd build her own life.

"It's all right," she said, and meant it. "It's over now, and I'm glad we're straight with each other."

There was a long, awkward pause. Finally Aunt Miriam nodded. "That's all right, then. I'll just . . ." She let the sentence trail off, and she moved toward the door.

Leah stood where she was, brushing the tops of the oregano with her fingers to release the pungent aroma. Poor Aunt Miriam. Leah could actually feel sorry for her. She wasn't the perfect person Leah had once thought her, but that didn't seem to matter any longer. Leah was content to see her as a real person, fallible and struggling.

There was a step behind her. Had Aunt Miriam come back? She couldn't imagine that anyone else would come . . .

Josiah. For a moment she couldn't say anything, and then she glared at him. "You should be ashamed of yourself. Telling my aunt what to do was uncalled for. You had no right to interfere."

He took a long step toward her, his eyes blazing. "Right? I love you, Leah Ann Stoltz. That gives me the right."

Leah froze, staring at him, her mind numb.

"There," he said. "I broke my promise by saying it, but I had to. You have to know the truth." The anger, if that's what it was, drained from his face. "If you don't love me, tell me so and I'll go. But if you do—"

As if something tight and strained had broken in her, she knew what to do. She stepped forward into his arms and felt them close around her, holding her tight, keeping her safe and cherished. Then his lips found hers, and she was enveloped in what seemed a great shell of love and caring and tenderness, and the rest of the world faded away.

"Josiah," she murmured his name against his cheek. "I thought . . . I was afraid . . ."

That was it, she knew. She'd been afraid, but not for the reason she'd told herself.

"Afraid of trusting me?" He drew back enough to see her face, but he didn't let go.

She shook her head, seeing clearly at last. "Not you. Myself. After everything that happened, I couldn't trust myself to be sure of anyone. But it was me I doubted, not you. Never you."

He was so close she could see every tiny line of the face she'd known since she was hardly more than a baby . . . a face that was so incredibly dear to her.

"You had reason not to trust me," he said, his voice somber. "A year ago I was so immature I didn't know what I had until you were gone. And even then I kept on denying that it was my fault. I tried to blame everyone else. But then when I saw you were in trouble, I knew. I had to face it if I was going to help you."

He kissed her again, a long, slow kiss that stirred her heart and set the room spinning around them. "Forgive me," he murmured finally, his breath against her cheek.

"We'll forgive each other," she said. That was what love was—the ability to look at each other and see the flaws and the temper and the foolishness, and still feel exactly the same. She and Josiah would always be able to see through each other and still go on loving.

"We're all right now. That's all that matters."

Over Josiah's shoulder, she caught a glimpse of movement. Hannie stood in the doorway, staring at them openmouthed, about to speak. Then Judith clamped her hand across Hannie's mouth and pulled her away, closing the door.

Leah smiled. Judith was growing up.

"What is it?" Josiah seemed aware of her every thought.

"Nothing," she said firmly, and wrapped her arms around his neck.

WHEN THEY FINALLY EMERGED FROM THE SEWING room, it was to smiles and slightly stilted conversation as everyone pretended not to know what was going on. Josiah looked questioningly at Leah, and she nodded, blushing.

"You can all stop being so careful," he said. "Leah has agreed to marry me. With her father's approval, I hope." He looked at Isaiah, who smiled and nodded.

"We've been waiting for you two to see what was plain to everyone else." Isaiah came to hug them both. "Du Herr bei mit zu."

And then everyone was hugging everyone else, even Leah's aunt.

Paul's cheeks were rosy and cold as he hugged him. "Congratulations," he muttered. "It worked, yah?"

He wasn't sure whether his brother was talking about his resolve to keep silent or his obvious breaking of it, but it didn't really matter. He and Leah were together, as they were meant to be, forever.

EPILOGUE

IT WASN'T UNTIL THE NEXT DAY THAT JOSIAH REALized there were still some unanswered questions. He went looking for Leah and found her in the daadi haus with her grandmother.

"Here you are at last." Grossmammi was the first to greet him, but Leah was there a moment later with a kiss. "It is time to tie up some loose ends, ain't so?"

He clasped Leah's hand, grinning. "Does your grandmother always know what everyone is thinking?"

"Pretty much," she admitted. "What do you want to know?"

He glanced around, half-afraid that Miriam would pop out from another room.

"Don't worry," she said. "Aunt Miriam's driver has picked her up already."

He couldn't help his relief but realized that Leah's grandmother might not feel the same way.

"Sorry she had to leave so soon," he told her.

Leah's grandmother smiled. "It's kind of you to say, but

there's no denying it was best for Miriam to get back home. There were things to deal with there."

He nodded and turned to Leah. "It was the young cousin, then?"

"Yah. Poor Aunt Miriam. Of all the possibilities, I think that hurt her the most. She's lived next to those cousins all this time, saw them every day." Leah looked shaken at the revelation.

"Alice was very dear to her," her grandmother said, and then shook her head. "But Miriam never did know people very well. She should have seen how troubled the child was."

Alice, he thought, was the oldest one of the cousins Miriam lived with. Only fourteen or so . . . young to be stealing.

"It wasn't so simple," Leah said. "I wish she'd come to me, but I was never able to get close to the girl."

"She probably saw you as the enemy," Grossmammi said. "Miriam was so foolish, playing favorites and saying that Leah would have her business. Like I said, she doesn't understand people. Just plants."

"Ach, Grossmammi, don't say that. She was wonderful gut to those kinder, and Alice loved her, I know. That's how she got into such trouble, not wanting Aunt Miriam to know she'd done something wrong."

Josiah shook his head. "Slow down. I don't understand."

"It seems like Alice sneaked out and went to a party one night. An Englisch party. And one of those kids knew who she was and got money out of her by saying he'd tell Miriam if she didn't pay him."

He shook his head. "So she robbed her aunt to keep him from telling her about a party. That's ferhoodled."

"Not when you're a young girl," Leah said, her voice filled with pity. "And she did confess to Aunt Miriam, once she realized that Aunt Miriam was questioning who had done it."

He squeezed her hand. "You're quick to forgive," he said.

She seemed to wince. "I know what it is to feel the way she did, poor child."

"It's settled now, and we must pray for her. And for Miriam. I hope she's learned not to make snap decisions and think she knows it all." Grossmammi sounded as if she weren't so sure of what Miriam might learn. "But enough of that now. Where are you two going to live once you're married?"

Josiah smiled at Leah. "We haven't had time to talk about it yet. But I was thinking that since we're remodeling the cottage anyway, we might fix those upstairs rooms for us. Then when we need more space, we could easily add on. And we'd be right here where we want to be."

Leah's cheeks were flushed again, and she was smiling. "That sounds wonderful gut to me."

Her grandmother chuckled. "A doghouse would sound wonderful gut to you right now." She pointed to the massive old dower chest that stood against the wall. "Open that bottom drawer, and you'll find something for the two of you."

He and Leah moved together, opening the drawer. Leah took out a tissue-wrapped bundle.

"That's it," her grandmother said, and Leah carried it to her.

With a quick pull, the tissue was torn away, revealing a double wedding ring quilt in so many shades of green that it looked like the valley on a spring day.

"For us?" Leah said softly, unfolding it.

Her grandmother nodded. "I started it last year when you two were courting." She gave them a knowing look. "I just kept working on it. I knew that one day you two would be back together, where you belonged."

Josiah had such a lump in his throat that he couldn't speak. He bent and kissed the soft withered cheek. Then he turned to Leah, clasping her hands around the quilt so that they both held it.

"We belong, all right," he said quietly. "Forever."

The soft glow in Leah's eyes told him that she agreed. Forever.

GLOSSARY OF
PENNSYLVANIA DUTCH
WORDS AND PHRASES

ach. oh; used as an exclamation

agasinish. stubborn; self-willed

ain't so? A phrase commonly used at the end of a sentence to invite agreement.

alter. old man

anymore. Used as a substitute for "nowadays."

Ausbund. Amish hymnal. Used in the worship services, it contains traditional hymns, words only, to be sung without accompaniment. Many of the hymns date from the sixteenth century.

befuddled. mixed up

blabbermaul. talkative one

blaid. bashful

boppli. baby

bruder. brother

bu. boy

buwe. boys

daadi. daddy

Da Herr sei mit du. The Lord be with you.

denke (*or* danki). thanks

Englischer. one who is not Plain

ferhoodled. upset; distracted

ferleicht. perhaps

frau. wife

fress. eat

gross. big

grossdaadi. grandfather

grossdaadi haus. An addition to the farmhouse, built for the grandparents to live in once they've "retired" from actively running the farm.

grossmammi. grandmother

gut. good

hatt. hard; difficult

haus. house

hinnersich. backward

ich. I

kapp. Prayer covering, worn in obedience to the biblical injunction that women should pray with their heads covered. Kapps are made of Swiss organdy and are white. (In some Amish communities, unmarried girls thirteen and older wear black kapps during worship service.)

kinder (*or* kinner). kids

komm. come

komm schnell. come quick

Leit. the people; the Amish

lippy. sassy

maidal. old maid; spinster

mamm. mother

middaagesse. lunch

mind. remember

onkel. uncle

Ordnung. The agreed-upon rules by which the Amish community lives. When new practices become an issue, they are discussed at length among the leadership. The decision for or against innovation is generally made on the basis of maintaining the home and family as separate from the world. For instance, a telephone might be necessary in a shop in order to conduct business but would be banned from the home because it would intrude on family time.

Pennsylvania Dutch. The language is actually German in origin and is primarily a spoken language. Most Amish write in English, which results in many variations in spelling when the dialect is put into writing! The language probably originated in the south of Germany but is common also among the Swiss Mennonite and French Huguenot immigrants to Pennsylvania. The language was brought to America prior to the Revolution and is still in use today. High German is used for Scripture and church documents, while English is the language of commerce.

rumspringa. running-around time; the late teen years when Amish youth taste some aspects of the outside world before deciding to be baptized into the church.

schnickelfritz. mischievous child

ser gut. very good

tastes like more. delicious

Was ist letz? What's the matter?

Wie bist du heit? How are you?; said in greeting

wilkom. welcome

Wo bist du? Where are you?

yah. yes

Festive Snickerdoodles

2 ¾ cups flour
2 teaspoons cream of tartar
1 teaspoon baking soda
Dash of salt
1 ½ cups sugar
1 cup shortening
2 eggs
2 Tablespoons milk
2 teaspoons vanilla
Decorative sugar—green and red

Heat oven to 400°F. Mix flour, cream of tartar, baking soda, and salt together. In a large bowl, beat sugar and shortening until it is light and fluffy. Add the eggs, milk, and vanilla and mix. Gradually add the flour mixture and beat until well mixed.

Sprinkle the decorative sugar on sheets of waxed paper. Shape the dough into 1-inch balls and roll in decorative sugar as desired. Place on ungreased cookie sheets, allowing space for them to spread. Bake for 7 to 8 minutes until lightly browned. Cool completely.

Candy Jar Cookies

1 cup brown sugar
2 sticks of butter or margarine
3 cups flour
2 Tablespoons orange juice
1 ⅓ cups chopped dates
1 cup chopped walnuts
Powdered sugar, for dusting

Heat oven to 300°F. Cream the sugar and butter or margarine together. Add the rest of the ingredients and mix well.

Shape the dough into approximately 1.5-inch balls. Bake on ungreased cookie sheet for 15 to 18 minutes. Cool slightly and sprinkle with powdered sugar. Cool completely. This makes about 4 dozen small cookies.

Dear Reader,

I hope you'll let me know if you enjoyed my book. You can reach me at marta@martaperry.com, and I'd be happy to send you a bookmark and my brochure of Pennsylvania Dutch recipes. You'll also find me at martaperry.com and on Facebook at Marta Perry Books.

Happy reading,
Marta

Don't miss

A CHRISTMAS HOME

A Promise Glen Novel

by Marta Perry

Available now
from Jove!

THE BUGGY DREW TO A STOP NEAR THE FARMHOUSE porch, and Sarah Yoder climbed down slowly, her eyes on the scene before her. Here it was—the fulfillment of the dream she'd had for the past ten years. Home.

Her cousin, Eli Miller, paused in lifting her cases down from the buggy. "Everything all right?"

"Fine." *Wonderful*.

Sarah sucked in a breath and felt the tension that had ridden her for weeks ease. It hadn't been easy to break away from the life her father had mapped out for her, but she'd done it. The old frame farmhouse spread itself in the spot where it had stood since the first Amish settlers came over the mountains from Lancaster County and saw the place they considered their promised land. Promise Glen, that was what folks called it, this green valley tucked between sheltering ridges in central Pennsylvania. And that's what she hoped it would be for her.

The porch door thudded, and Grossmammi rushed out. Her hair was a little whiter than the last time Sarah had seen her, but her blue eyes were still bright and her skin as soft as a girl's. For an instant the thought of her mother pierced Sarah's heart. Mammi had looked like her own mother. If she'd lived . . . but she'd been gone ten years now. Sarah had been just eighteen when she'd taken charge of the family.

Before she could lose herself in regret, Grossmammi had reached her, and her grandmother's strong arms encircled her. The warmth of her hug chased every other thought away, and Sarah clung to her the way she had as a child, when Grossmammi had represented everything that was firm and secure in her life.

Her grandmother drew back finally, her blue eyes bright with tears. She took refuge in scolding, as she did when emotions threatened to overcome her.

"Ach, we've been waiting and waiting. I told Eli he should leave earlier. Did he keep you waiting there at the bus stop?"

Eli grinned, winking at Sarah. "Ask Cousin Sarah. I was there when she stepped off the bus."

And she'd seen him pull up just in time, but she wouldn't give him away. "That's right. I was wonderful surprised to see my little cousin—he grew, ain't so?"

"Taller than you now, Sarah, though that's not saying much." He indicated her five feet and a bit with a line in the air, his expression as impudent as it had been when he was a child.

"And you've not changed much, except in inches," she retorted, long since used to holding her own with younger siblings and cousins. "Same freckles, same smile, same sassiness."

"Ach, help!" He threw up his hands as if to protect himself. "Here's my sweet Ruthie coming. She'll save me from my cousin."

Ruthie, his wife of three years, came heavily down the back porch stairs, looking younger than her twenty-three years. She looked from him to Sarah, as if to make sure Sarah wasn't offended. "You are talking nonsense." She swatted at him playfully. "Komm, carry those things to the grossdaadi haus for Sarah. Supper is almost ready."

"Sarah, this is Ruthie, you'll have figured out," Grossmammi said. "And here is their little Mary." The child who slipped out onto the porch looked about two, with huge blue eyes and soft wispy brown hair that curled, unruly, around her face.

And Ruthie couldn't have more than a month to go before the arrival of the new baby, Sarah could see, assessing her with a shrewd eye. When even the shapeless Amish dress didn't conceal the bump, a woman knew it wasn't far off.

Eli loaded himself up with Sarah's boxes, obviously intent on getting everything in one trip. "Surrounded by women, that's what I am," he said cheerfully. "And now there's another one."

He stopped long enough to give Sarah a one-armed hug, poking her in the side with one of her boxes as he did. "We're wonderful glad you're here at last, Cousin Sarah."

Sarah blinked back an errant tear. Eli hadn't lost his tender heart, that was certain sure. And Grossmammi looked as if she'd just been given the gift of a lifetime. As for Ruthie . . . well, she had a sense that Ruthie was withholding judgment for the moment. That was hardly surprising. She'd want to know what changes this strange cousin was going to make in their lives.

As little as possible, Sarah mentally assured her. All she wanted was a place to call home while she figured out what her new life was going to be.

Eli, finally laden with all her belongings, headed toward the grossdaadi haus, a wing built onto the main house and connected by a short hallway. Grossmammi had lived there since Grossdaadi's death, and when Sarah walked into the living room and saw the familiar rocking chairs and the framed family tree on the wall, she felt instantly at home.

"You're up here, Sarah." Eli bumped his way up the stairs until Sarah retrieved one of the boxes and carried it herself.

He flashed her that familiar grin. "What do you have in there? Rocks?"

"Books. I couldn't leave those behind. I just hope there's a bookcase I can use."

"If there isn't, we can pick one up at a sale. The auction house is still busy, even this late in the year. Almost December already."

"Grossdaadi used to say that any farmer worth the name had all his work done by the first of December."

"Ach, don't go comparing me to Grossdaadi," he said with mock fear. "Here we are. I hope you like it." He stacked everything at the foot of the old-fashioned sleigh bed. "Ruthie says supper is about ready, so komm eat. You can unpack later."

She'd rather have a few minutes to catch her breath and explore her new home, but Ruthie was her hostess. It wouldn't do to be late for their first supper together. With a pause in the hall bathroom to wash her hands, she hurried downstairs and joined Grossmammi to step the few feet across the hallway—the line that marked off their home from Eli and Ruthie's.

The hall led into the kitchen of the old farmhouse. Ruthie hurried them to their places at the table and began to dish up the food. Sarah glanced at her, opened her mouth to offer help, and caught Grossmammi's eye. Her grandmother shook her head, ever so slightly.

So something else lay behind the welcome she'd received. Best if she were quiet until she knew what it was.

This was a little disconcerting. She'd dreamed for so long of being here, but those dreams hadn't included the possibility that someone might not want her.

Nonsense. Ruthie seemed shy, and probably she was anxious about this first meal she'd cooked for Sarah. The best course for Sarah was to keep quiet and blend in.

But once the silent prayer was over and everyone had been served pot roast with all the trimmings, it wasn't so easy to stay silent, since Eli seemed determined to hear everything about everything.

"So what was it like out in Idaho? I didn't even know there were any Amish there." Eli helped himself to a mound of mashed potatoes.

"Not many," she admitted. "It was a new settlement." She didn't bother to add that anything new was appealing to Daad—either they understood her father already, or they didn't need to know. "Ruthie, this pot roast is delicious. Denke." The beef was melt-in-your-mouth tender, the gravy rich and brown.

Ruthie's face relaxed in a smile, and she nodded in acknowledgment of the praise. "And your brothers and sister?" she modestly moved on. "How are they?"

"All married and settled now." They'd wisely given up finding a home with Daad and created homes of their own. "Nancy's husband is a farrier in Indiana, and the two boys are farming—Thomas in Ohio and David in Iowa."

"Far apart," Grossmammi murmured, and Sarah wondered what she was thinking. To say it was unusual to have an Amish family so widespread was putting it mildly.

"They all invited me to come to them," Sarah said quickly, lest anyone think that the siblings she had raised were not grateful. "But I thought it was best for me to make a life of my own. I'm going to get a job."

Eli dropped his fork in surprise. "A job? You don't want to be working for strangers."

She had to smile at his offended expression. "Yah, a job. Some work I can do in order to pay my own way."

That wasn't all of it, of course. Her desire went deeper than that. She'd spent the past ten years raising her brothers and sister, and it had been a labor of love. What would have happened to all of them after Mammi died if she hadn't?

But that time had convinced her of what she didn't want. She didn't want to become the old maid that most large families had—the unmarried sister who hadn't anything of her own and spent her life helping to raise other people's children, tending to the elderly, and doing any other tasks that came along. She wanted a life of her own. That wasn't selfish, was it?

Even as she thought it, Eli was arguing. "You're family. You'll do lots of things to pay your own way. You can help Ruthie with looking after the kinder, and there's the garden, and the canning . . ."

He went on talking, but Sarah had stopped listening, because she'd caught an apprehensive expression on Ruthie's face. This, then, was what Ruthie was afraid of. She feared Sarah had come to take over—to run her house, to raise her babies . . .

Ruthie actually did have cause to be concerned, she supposed. Sarah had been in complete charge of the home for the past ten years, through almost as many moves and fresh starts. It wouldn't be easy to keep herself from jumping in—with the best will in the world, she might not be able to restrain herself unless she had something else to occupy her.

"I'll be happy to help Ruthie anytime she wants me," she said, using the firm voice that always made her younger siblings take notice. "But I need something else to keep me busy."

"And I know what," Grossmammi said, in a tone that suggested the discussion was over. "Noah Raber needs someone to keep the books and take care of the billing for his furniture business. I've already spoken to him about it." She turned to Sarah. "You can go over there tomorrow and set it up."

Sarah managed to keep her jaw from dropping, but

barely. She'd intended to look for a job, but she hadn't expected to find herself being pushed into one as soon as she arrived.

"But . . . bookkeeping? I don't know if I can . . ."

"Nonsense," Grossmammi said briskly. "You took those bookkeeping classes a couple of years ago, didn't you?"

She nodded. She had done that, with the hope of finding something outside the home to do. But then Daad had gotten the idea of moving on again, and she had given it up. Did she really remember enough to take this on?

"Mostly Noah needs someone to handle the business side," Grossmammi went on. "The man loves to work with wood, but he has no idea how to send a bill. That's where you come in."

"But Noah Raber." Eli looked troubled. "Are you sure that's a gut idea? Noah's situation . . ."

"Noah's situation is that he needs to hire someone. Why shouldn't it be Sarah?" She got up quickly. "Now, I think we should do the supper cleanup so Sarah can go and unpack."

Grossmammi, as usual, had the last word. None of her children or grandchildren would dare to argue when she used that tone.

Carrying her dishes to the sink, Sarah tried to figure out how she felt about this turn of events. She certain sure didn't want to continue being in a place where she was only valued because she could take care of children.

But this job . . . what if she tried it and failed? What if she'd forgotten everything she'd once known? Noah Raber might feel she'd been foisted on him.

And what was it about his situation that so troubled Eli? She tried to remember Noah, but her school years memories had slipped away with all the changes in her life since then. He was a couple of years older than she was, and she had a vague picture of someone reserved, someone who had pursued his own interests instead of joining with the usual rumspringa foolishness. Was he interested in offering her the job, or had Grossmammi pushed him into it?

But Sarah had already made her decision in coming here—coming home. She shivered a little as a cold breeze snaked its way around the window over the sink and touched her face. There was no turning back now.

"WHY DIDN'T YOU PUT YOUR SHOES TOGETHER UN-der the bed like you're supposed to?" Noah Raber looked in exasperation at six-year-old Mark, dressed for school except for one important thing—his right shoe.

"I did, Daadi." Mark looked on the verge of tears, and Noah was instantly sorry for his sharp tone. Mark was the sensitive one of the twins, unlike Matthew. Scoldings rolled off Matty like water off a duck's back.

"It's all right." He brushed a hand lightly over his son's hair, pale as corn silk in the winter sunlight pouring in the window. "You look in the bathroom while I check in here."

There weren't that many places where a small shoe could hide, but the neighbor kids were already coming down the drive, ready to walk to school with the twins. With a quick gesture he pulled the chest of drawers away from the wall. One sock, but no shoes.

From the kitchen below he heard Matty's voice, proba-bly commenting on the fact that the King children were coming. But a woman's voice, speaking in answer, startled him out of that assumption. Who . . . ? Well, he had to find the shoe before anything.

When his mother had been here, this early-morning time had run smoothly—he hadn't realized how smoothly until he'd had to do it himself. Still, it had been high time Mamm had had a break from looking after his twins, and her long-ing to visit his sister Anna and her new baby was obvious. Naturally he'd encouraged her to go, insisting he and the boys would get along fine. If he'd known then . . .

"I found it!" Mark came running in, waving the shoe. "It was in the hamper."

Noah started to ask how it had gotten there and decided he didn't really need to know. The important thing was to get them out the door.

"Let's get it on." He picked up his son and plopped him on the bed, shoving the shoe on his foot and fastening it with quick movements. "There. Now scoot."

Mark darted out the door and clattered down the stairs, running for the kitchen. Noah followed in time to see Mark come to an abrupt halt in the kitchen doorway. He stopped, too, at the sight of a strange woman in his kitchen.

"Who—" He didn't get the question out before Matty broke in.

"This is Sarah. She's come to work for you, Daadi."

The woman put a hand lightly on Matthew's shoulder. "Only if your daadi hires me." She smiled. "Matthew and I were getting acquainted. This must be Mark." Her eyes focused on Mark, hanging on to Noah's pant leg, but she didn't venture to approach him.

"I'm sorry. I don't . . ." His mind was empty of everything but the need to get the boys off to school. "Just a minute." He turned to his sons. "Coats on, right this minute. And hats and mittens. It's cold out. Hurry."

Apparently realizing this was not the time to delay, they both scrambled into their outer garments, and he shooed them toward the small mudroom that led to the back door. "Out you go."

"I think—" the woman began, following him.

"Just wait," he snapped. Couldn't she see he was busy? "Have a gut day, you two. Mind you listen to Teacher Dorcas."

He opened the door, letting in a brisk wind. A hand appeared in front of him, holding two small lunch boxes. The woman was standing right behind him.

"Aren't these meant to go?"

Instantly he felt like a fool. Or at least an inept father, chasing his sons out without their lunches. He grabbed them, handing them off to the boys, and saw to his relief that, by running, they reached the lane to the schoolhouse at the same time as the other children.

He gave one last wave, and then it was time to turn and apologize for his rudeness. The turn brought him within inches of the woman.

"Sorry," he muttered. "You must be Sarah, Etta's grand-daughter. I didn't expect you so soon."

"No, I apologize. I shouldn't have come so early. My grandmother assumed you started work at eight, and I didn't want to interrupt."

Looking at her, Noah realized she wasn't quite so strange after all. Etta Miller had talked about her granddaughter coming, of course. He had said that he didn't remember her, but now it was coming back to him.

"You were a couple of years behind me in school, weren't you?"

She nodded, face crinkling in a quick smile. "That's right. By the time I was big enough to be noticed, you'd left school and started your apprenticeship, I guess."

"Sarah Yoder," he said, the last name coming to him.

Her mother had been Etta Miller's middle girl, her father a newcomer from down in Chester County. If he didn't remember anything else, he should have remembered hair the color of honey and eyes of a deep, clear green. She was short and slight, but something about the way she stood and the assurance when she spoke made her hard to over-look.

He realized he was staring and took an awkward step back. It seemed suddenly intimate to be standing here in the narrow mudroom with a woman he hardly knew.

"You're here about the job." He reached past her to grab his wool jacket from the hook. "Let's go to the shop and talk. No need to be hanging out in here."

She nodded, buttoning her black coat as she stepped outside, then waiting for him to lead the way to the shop.

"Didn't your great-onkel used to live here?" He heard her voice behind him as they crossed the yard through frost-whitened grass.

"Yah, that's so. We moved in about eight years ago." When he and Janie had married. When he'd still believed marriage meant forever. "My great-onkel used this building as a workshop, so I started my business here."

He found himself looking at the building he called the shop, seeing it through a stranger's eyes. It wouldn't look like much to her—hardly more than a shed with a small addition on one end.

But when he looked at it, he saw the future—the future that was left to him after what Janie had done. He saw a thriving furniture business where his handcrafted furniture was made and sold. He saw his sons growing, working alongside him in the business they'd build together.

"I understand from my grandmother that you need someone to handle the paperwork so you're free to spend your time on creating the furniture."

He nodded, liking the way she put that—*creating*. Each piece of furniture he made was his own creation, with his hard work and whatever gift he had pressed into the very grain of the wood.

"I'd best show you the paperwork, since that's what would concern you." *If I hire you,* he added mentally. But who was he kidding? He hadn't exactly been swamped with people longing to work for him, especially ones who knew anything at all about running a business.

He held the door open and ushered her into the shop, stopping to put up the shade on the window so that the winter sun poured in. Fortunately he'd started the stove earlier, so the shop was warming already, and the sunlight would help. He'd added windows all along one side of the shed, because he needed all the light he could get for working.

"Over here, in the far corner." He gestured toward the office area—a corner of the workroom with a desk, some shelves, and a chair. At the moment the desk was piled high with papers. "I haven't had time to get at it lately."

He wasn't sure why he was explaining to her. It was his business. But he guessed it was obvious he needed help. "You can take a look at it. See what you think."

Instead of commenting, Sarah walked, unhurried, to the desk. He followed her, not sure how to conduct this interview, if that's what it was. She began leafing through the papers, seeming to sort them as she went. After a moment she looked up.

"Where do you keep the receipted bills?"

"Um, there should be a box . . . yah, that. The shoebox."

Sarah looked at it, still not commenting. Her very silence began to make him nervous. "It's not always such a mess." Just most of the time. "My mother has been away on a trip for several weeks, so I've had the boys to manage as well as the business."

"I see. Sorry. That must be difficult. If you'd like me to see what I can do with this . . ." She hesitated. "I take it your wife doesn't help with the business?"

He froze, his stomach clenching. Didn't she know? Didn't she realize that was the worst thing she could possibly say to him?

SHE'D SAID SOMETHING WRONG—VERY WRONG. NOAH looked as if she had hit him with a hammer. His strong-boned face was rigid, the firm jaw like a rock. His dark blue eyes had turned to ice. Remorse flooded her. If the poor man had lost his wife, why hadn't Grossmammi thought to tell her?

Standing here silent wasn't helping matters any. "Noah, I'm so sorry. I didn't know. I'd never have said that if . . . I suppose the family thought I knew your wife had passed away—"

"No." The word was a harsh bark. He swallowed, the strong muscles in his neck moving visibly. "Janie didn't die. She left us a few months after the twins were born. We haven't heard from her from that day to this."

Sarah struggled for words. "I . . ."

"There's no need for expressions of sympathy." His mouth clamped shut like a trap.

Whatever she did, she mustn't show pity. It wasn't easy, but she schooled her face to calm. "You are the fortunate one, then."

Noah gave a short nod, as if he understood her instantly. "Yah. I have the boys. They are worth anything."

He spun, turning away from her, and looked yearningly at his workbench. Clearly he didn't want to talk anymore. Did that mean he didn't want her around at all?

"What do you think?" he said, not looking at her. He gestured toward the desk with the papers on it.

Sarah touched the stack of papers in front of her, mentally measuring it. If Noah wanted to carry on as if nothing had happened, surely she could manage to go along with him.

"It might be best if I look through these and sort them. Then we'll have a better idea of where we are. If that's all right with you." She trod as carefully as if she were walking barefoot on broken glass.

"Yah, gut. Denke." He still didn't look her way. They were both being cautious and polite, trying to pretend nothing had happened. "However long it takes. I'll pay for the time it takes to decide if you want to do this or not."

"You don't need to—"

"The laborer is worthy of his hire." He flashed a smile. It was a feeble effort, but it was the first she'd seen from him. "That's what my daad always says."

She nodded, sitting down at the desk while Noah moved

quickly to his workbench. Her family might have been better off if Daad had adopted that saying. His, unfortunately, had been more in the nature of *The grass is always greener on the other side of the fence.*

Somehow, no matter how often he had been proved wrong, Daad had clung to that belief. Still did, she supposed. But at least she wasn't going with him now, the way she'd had to for the sake of her brothers and sister.

They worked without talking, and the workshop was silent except for the gentle swish of fine sandpaper against wood. Sarah glanced around the room. It was well designed, she supposed, with that row of windows bringing in a lot of light so Noah didn't have to depend on gas lighting.

But there wasn't much space. The small addition, which she'd assumed was a showroom for his finished pieces, was instead filled with all the equipment he didn't have room for in here. She began mentally rearranging it, putting her desk and chair in the addition with a few display pieces and moving all the work into the larger space. It would still be crowded, but it would be a better use of the space.

Noah glanced up and caught her looking at him. "Did you want to ask me something? You can interrupt, you know. Unless I've got my fingers near a saw blade."

The attempt at humor encouraged her. He wouldn't bother, she thought, unless he wanted to make this work.

"I haven't run across any tax papers." Sarah said the first thing that popped in her head. "I suppose you do keep tax records."

"If you can call it that." He rubbed the back of his hand across his forehead. "If you can figure out the taxes, you're better than I am. The file is in the house. I'll get it when we stop for lunch."

Sarah nodded, but before she could go back to sorting, he spoke.

"So what do you think? You've probably never met such a mess in any of your other jobs."

The expectation revealed in the comment startled her. Clearly he thought she'd been working as a bookkeeper. What exactly had Grossmammi told him?

"It . . . it's just what I would expect if you haven't had time to do anything with it in the past month or so."

Noah grimaced. "Make that three. Or four." He looked a little shamefaced. "Even when my mother was here, I didn't spend enough time on that side of the business."

She nodded, unsurprised. "So I see." She hesitated. "Just so we're clear—I don't know exactly what my grandmother told you, but I haven't actually had a job in bookkeeping." Before he could react, she hurried on. "I took all the classes, and I'd accepted a job, but then we moved before I could start work."

"You moved a lot, did you?" His voice had grown cool quite suddenly.

So it did make a difference to him. Disappointment swept over her. She could do this job, she thought, but not if he didn't give her a chance.

"I kept house for my daad and took care of my brothers and sister. When Daad decided to move on, we went with him."

It wasn't as if she'd had a choice. So she ought to be used to disappointment by this time.

But she wasn't giving up on getting this job before she'd shown what she could do, so she continued.

"It looks as if it will take a week or so of full-time work just to get everything organized. Once a system is set up, you may only need to spend a few hours a day on it."

Sarah waited, giving him the opportunity to say that in that case, he wouldn't need her. Or to agree that he'd hire her. But he didn't say anything. He just nodded and turned back to his own work.

Well, she'd have to take silence as his permission to go on with the sorting, at least. Perhaps he was thinking that would buy him time to see how well it worked out, having her here.

Did her presence upset his work? She studied him covertly over a stack of receipts. His eyebrows, thick and straight, were drawn down a bit as if he were frowning at the curve he was sanding . . . the arm of a delicately turned rocking chair. The curves of the legs and the back were what many Amish would consider fancy, but the whole piece was so appealing that it seemed to urge one to sit and rock for a bit.

Maybe he wasn't disappointed in the work—that look might be one of deep concentration. His strong features could easily look stern, she supposed, even if that wasn't his feeling. The twins hadn't inherited that rock-solid jaw, or at least, it didn't show yet. Their faces were round and dimpled.

Did they look like their mother? She didn't even know if the woman was someone local or not. Obviously, Grossmammi had some explaining to do.

Thinking of the twins caused a pang in the area of her heart. She shouldn't let herself start feeling anything for those two motherless boys. She knew herself too well—she'd fall into mothering them too easily, and that wouldn't do.

Presumably Noah's mother would take over again when she returned from her trip. Noah had been fortunate to have her available when his world had fallen apart.

Grossmammi had offered to take Sarah and her siblings when her mamm died, but Daadi hadn't wanted it. And Sarah, at eighteen, had been fully capable of looking after the younger ones—not only that, but she'd felt it her duty. She couldn't regret the years she'd spent raising them, but she didn't want to do it again, not unless it was with her own babies.

She stole another glance at Noah, his closed face giving nothing away, his dark brown hair curling rebelliously as he worked. He hadn't offered her the care of his children. He hadn't even offered her the bookkeeping job yet.

And if he did . . . well, given how difficult his situation was, she wasn't sure she should take it.

Ready to find
your next great read?

Let us help.

Visit prh.com/nextread

Penguin
Random
House

pushed through her as he commandeered her mentor's chair.

Alex was a very handsome man, with just enough flecks of gray in his black hair to make him looked distinguished. He possessed glacier-blue eyes and a dimpled chin. His shoulders were presidential, his waist lean. He nodded at a chair across from the desk. "Sit down."

"I'd rather stand."

"Suit yourself."

She crossed her arms. His smirk irked the hell out of her. "What do you want?"

"Aren't you going to congratulate me on my new position?"

"No."

He leaned forward, rested his elbows on the desk, and pressed the tips of his fingers together. "You know, things don't have to be this way between us."

She glared.

This was the scumbag who'd bruised her ego and usurped her mentor's place. It wasn't so much that he'd lied to her about his wife. If she was honest with herself, she'd admit she wasn't even that upset over losing him. What really hurt was his betrayal. Just when she'd decided to finally trust a man and put her heart on the line. She'd taken a chance and it had blown up in her face. Plus, he'd made her an unwitting partner in his adultery. She couldn't forgive him for that.

The bastard.

Shame. That's what she felt when she looked at Alex Fredericks. Shame and remorse and self-loathing.

"I'd like to give you the benefit of the doubt, Jillian.

We can start over fresh, you and I." Alex raked his gaze over her, his eyes lingering on her breasts.

Her fingers twitched to reach across that desk and smack his smug face. "Give *me* the benefit of the doubt?"

"I'm merely saying there are ways we can repair our tattered relationship." Alex got up and came around the corner of the desk toward her. Surely he was not suggesting what she feared he was suggesting. Was he hinting about resuming their affair?

Jillian held her ground. She was not about to let him make her back up, but she hated being this close to him. Hated the familiar smell of his cologne in her nostrils. Hated that she'd ever thought he was worthy of her caring.

He stood right in front of her, his eyes predatory.

"I've missed you, Jillian," he said.

She snorted.

"It's true."

"Does your wife know how much you've missed me?"

Alex shifted his weight. "My wife and I . . . we have an understanding."

"What? You screw around and she doesn't understand?"

"I've especially missed that sarcastic wit." He reached out and stroked the back of his hand across her cheek.

"Don't." Jillian grabbed his wrist and flung his hand away from her. "Don't you ever touch me again."

"I *am* your boss."

"And this is sexual harassment. I can file charges."

Alex's expression was hooded, inscrutable. He was too good of a politician to acknowledge her accusation. He didn't move.

Jillian sank her hands on her hips and stepped forward

until their noses almost touched. She'd seen this man naked, done intimate things with him that she now sorely regretted. She couldn't believe she'd slept with him and even stupidly imagined having a future with him. She felt like a complete idiot. She'd been right all along—love was for suckers and fools.

He blinked and she saw a flicker of contrition in his eyes, but the whisper of humanity was gone as quickly as it appeared. "Ms. Samuels," he said coldly.

"Yes?"

"I wouldn't recommend that course of action. It would be my word against yours, and I could make your life here quite miserable, indeed."

He was right and she knew it. Blake was gone, and even before that she'd been feeling a strong sense of unease. Now with Fredericks in charge, it was too much to bear.

She experienced that end-of-the-tunnel sensation again she'd been feeling ever since that day in court with Randal Petry. The same day Blake died.

"I don't have to put up with this," Jillian said, injecting her voice with steel as cold as his.

"What do you intend on doing about it?" He drew up his shoulders, puffed out his chest.

"You're a real ass, and I can't believe I slept with you."

"As I recall, we didn't do much sleeping. I miss you, Jillian. Your fire and your guts and your passion. Seriously, I'd really hate to demote you."

That did it. She wasn't going to put up with his threats. She'd had enough. "You know what, Alex? Shove this job up your ass. I quit."